WYATT AND THE MORESBY LEGACY

In this second breath-catching espionage thriller by David Gethin, Wyatt, the head of a multi-national conglomerate, is again pitted against British moles and KGB killers, who are planning a royal assassination, a coup d'état in an oil-rich Gulf state and the transfer to the enemy of a British missile system manufactured, ironically enough, by Wyatt's own firm. Once again Wyatt out-smarts and out-shoots all comers. And once again he becomes involved with a bevy of women— fiery, radical Jo; icy, double-dealing Vennaway; overtrusting Christine; deadly Camilla; and, not least, Annabel, the unfaithful wife with her lover's murder to avenge.

WYATT AND THE MORESBY LEGACY

David Gethin

ATLANTIC LARGE PRINT
Chivers Press, Bath, England.
John Curley & Associates Inc.,
South Yarmouth, Mass., USA.

Library of Congress Cataloging in Publication Data

Gethin, David.
   Wyatt and the Moresby legacy.

   (Atlantic large print)
   1. Large type books.   I. Title.
[PR6057.E76W95 1985]   823'.914   84–20043
   ISBN 0–89340–855–7

British Library Cataloguing in Publication Data

Gethin, David
   Wyatt and the Moresby legacy.—Large print ed.
   —Atlantic large print)
   I. Title
   823'.914[F]   PR6057.E76

   ISBN 0–7451–9046–4

This Large Print edition is published by Chivers Press, England, and
John Curley & Associates, Inc, U.S.A. 1985

Published in the British Commonwealth by arrangement with
Victor Gollancz Ltd and in the U.S.A. with St Martin's Press, Inc

U.K. Hardback ISBN 0 7451 9046 4
U.S.A. Softback ISBN 0 89340 855 7

WYATT AND THE MORESBY LEGACY

CHAPTER ONE

They buried Sir Philip Moresby on Wednesday 8th September. He had died of a heart attack the previous Friday at an Embassy reception in Paris. On the Monday his obituary appeared in *The Times*. Like the eulogy spoken over his grave by a rambling Anglican clergyman, it was mainly fiction. But no relative had attended the funeral and only two men present knew the real truth. They stood apart from the customary clutch of bowler-hatted civil servants congregated at the graveside. In death, as for the last forty years of his life, Moresby had somehow contrived to hide the truth from public scrutiny. Par for the course from a true professional, and Moresby had been a particularly gifted professional—Head of the Special Services Department of British Intelligence, the last Court of Security Appeal, and the Prime Minister's personal adviser on all security and Intelligence matters—the eyes and ears of government.

Moresby's successor did not attend, nor did any member of the government. The Cabinet Office had gone so far as to send an anonymous wreath. The funeral, a final charade, had been acted out as the final chapter of Moresby's cover. The statutory mourners departed, uttering the usual insincere banalities and climbed into chauffeur-driven cars to be whisked back to Whitehall. The unwarranted intrusion of the funeral meant that sherry would have to be taken half an hour late.

The two men who had stood apart from the graveside did not leave. The first, a sad, forty-year-old private man watched the last car disappear from view and lit a cigarette. Dark glasses hid witch-hazel eyes and accentuated a scar on his left cheek. A small, square, lean-featured man, he was known only as Alpha.

His companion, Richard Lansbury, was a direct contrast to the somewhat sinister-looking Alpha. Fifty-three, tall, broad-shouldered, Lansbury's lined, long face reminded those who met him of a bereaved spaniel. He lit an old briar pipe and broke the spent match between heavy fingers. Lansbury was Director of Operations, M.I.5. As such he had known Moresby's real function and on several occasions had worked closely with him.

'End of an era, Alpha,' Lansbury observed.

Alpha nodded. A shadowy character who had watched Moresby's back for almost twenty years, Alpha had come out into the

2

open to pay his last respects to the Master.

'Radical changes will be made, D.Ops. I expect to be one of them.'

Lansbury was not sure whether Alpha was thinking aloud or giving an oblique warning. Moresby's successor was not an Intelligence man, but a bureaucrat, a cunning political Welshman, Gareth Llewellyn Jones. Often referred to as 'that counterfeit Lloyd George', or even 'that unspeakable Welsh Richelieu', Llewellyn Jones was customarily identified in Whitehall as 'L.J.'.

'He scares the hell out of me,' Lansbury observed: 'I have only met him once and have no wish to renew the acquaintance.'

'Politician,' Alpha replied, as if he had found something unpleasant crawling out from under a stone: 'That power-monger has had Downing Street's ear for some time. Centralization is the watchword. His management consultants have already started on Special Services. They're castrating it. You boys in Five will be next on the list. I dread to think what will happen to S.I.S. Their budget will probably have lower priority than the Arts Council.'

Lansbury did not reply. The gravediggers were approaching. Alpha walked quietly away and Lansbury followed. Both men conversed in low voices until the fresh earth had been piled on Moresby's grave and the wreaths and flowers were arranged in a blaze of colour. The gravediggers stood back for a few seconds, consulted their watches and decided it was time for a cup of tea.

Alpha then walked to the graveside and stood in what Lansbury took to be silent homage. After almost five minutes, Alpha crouched down to read the inscription on a large crucifix of red roses. The message was a single word, in gold lettering: VALHALLA.

Alpha spoke aloud:

'Valhalla.'

'Viking place, wasn't it?' Lansbury asked. He was not considered one of Five's intellectuals.

'Afterlife for those Norse warriors killed in battle. The Valkyries descended on winged horses and carried the fallen off to Valhalla,' Alpha replied. 'As in Ride of the Valkyries, Wagner.'

'Mate of Adolf Hitler's, wasn't he?' Lansbury joked.

Hitler, he thought. A lifetime away. Moresby had first worked for the old Special Operations Executive in 1942. Among the old hands he had been considered immortal. His death had come not only as a surprise, but as a mind-numbing shock. Sixty-three was not old, and Moresby had been actively healthy.

4

'I suppose it really was a heart attack,' Lansbury wondered aloud.

'D.Ops, you are being maudlin and sentimental. Moresby was a one-off, a genius and in time he will be a legend. We think a legend can't die. Wrong. Moresby suffered a heart attack. Fact. It's even in Five's report. You have read it?'

Lansbury nodded. Alpha continued:

'I have checked the circumstances of his death very thoroughly. We had a post-mortem carried out, just in case.'

Any incident affecting senior Intelligence personnel, whether S.I.S. or Special Services, was investigated by M.I.5, the Security Service. They were the department with police liaison via Special Branch—something the other two services avoided at all times. The report had reached the same conclusion as others: Moresby's heart attack had been a tragic misfortune.

The other reports were from a wide spectrum of agencies. Service Two of the French S.D.E.C.E., France's parallel police, had been extra thorough: Moresby had died in Paris and they had received political instructions to ensure no blame existed to be laid at the door of the Elysée. The C.I.A. had dissected the incident. Not only had Moresby died in the American Embassy, but the

5

Secretary for Defense had been present. The U.S. Secret Service, not an espionage agency but a section of the U.S. Treasury, had insisted on a 'brass tacks job'. They were responsible for protecting not only the President, but also key members of the Administration and were almost paranoid about assassination attempts in the proximity of their charges.

Lansbury knew Alpha was right. He watched the small, square, lean-featured man walk away, muttering to himself: 'Valhalla, I wonder who sent that?'

★　　★　　★

The kingdom of Bakar occupies a peninsula that points like a fat, raised thumb towards Iran. Surrounded on three sides by the Persian Gulf, Bakar has its only land border with Saudi Arabia. Referred to by the Foreign Office as a 'Gulf State', Bakar lies to the north-west of the United Arab Emirates, has a population of 158,000 and a booming economy based on vast oil reserves and massive mineral deposits.

Bakar's deep-water port and bulk tanker terminal is Ad Said, on the north-east coast. Two hours after Sir Philip Moresby had been buried, and at 15.30 hours local time, Simon

Ablett-Green waited in the town's dock area. After watching the shipping in the deep blue of the Gulf for some minutes, he consulted his watch and recalled the telephoned instructions; he was in the right place at the correct time; but no contact had been made. The futility of it irritated him, as did everything about Bakar—the heat, the sand, and now the smell of the dockyards, the noise of cranes, fork-lift trucks, and the incessant babbling of Bakari dockers.

'Somewhere inconspicuous,' the contact had said. Ablett-Green reckoned it was bloody nonsense to drive the sixty kilometres to Ad Said when the visa section of the Raza Embassy would have been inconspicuous enough. He lit a cigarette and looked forward to the only bright spot on his immediate personal horizon: a month's leave due to start on September 21st. The twenty-five-year-old Wykehamist would use some of that time to call in person on Uncle, a mandarin in the Diplomatic Service, and apply for a transfer. No harm in oiling the wheels-within-wheels, as he had done before, on coming down from Oxford.

Ablett-Green looked at his watch again. This was not his job—picking up gossip and going to clandestine meetings. The Embassy kept Barrett for such purposes. He was the

7

eyes-and-ears-open man in Bakar. But Barrett just happened to be on leave. Never there when he was wanted, Ablett-Green decided. Worse, Barrett had left him to take all calls.

'Good afternoon, Mr Green.'

The voice startled him. He had heard no-one approach. He turned to see a tall, blond European, wearing dark glasses and a safari-style suit. Ablett-Green stiffened slightly. The contact should have been an Arab, from the Chief Minister's Office. This man sounded German, about his own age, but taller, bigger built and very relaxed.

'Good afternoon,' Ablett-Green replied, waiting for the man to introduce himself.

But no introduction was forthcoming. The German took out a gold cigarette case and offered it. His hands were heavy, strong and very steady.

'Thanks.' Ablett-Green took a cigarette.

The German was holding a tubular cigarette lighter that appeared slightly larger than usual.

'The Second Secretary was unable to come,' he explained smiling. 'So the Chief Minister's people suggested I meet you.'

As he spoke, the German's lighter clicked twice but no flame ignited. Ablett-Green had tensed at the words 'Chief Minister'. Something had gone very wrong. He inhaled

8

deeply, partly out of fear and partly in expectation of a light. Suddenly, he was gasping for air as the breath was driven from his lungs. An invisible heavy hand seemed to squash him in an unyielding grip. Shock waves of pain lanced through his chest and his entire body pressed inwards, crushing the life from itself. Circles of darkness enveloped his brain, swirling any coherent thought into dizzy oblivion. His eyeballs bulged, trying to tear themselves from their sockets, and he collapsed to the concrete.

Simon Ablett-Green was dead before his twice-twitching body hit the ground.

The cause of death would later be diagnosed as massive cardiac arrest. The German walked away. There had been no witnesses to the meeting.

CHAPTER TWO

Unit Alpha was known in the security apparatus as a section within the Special Services Department whose official function was oversight. It had been Moresby's creation. The unit would probe, question, receive information and, on very rare occasions, initiate top-level action with the deadly speed and effect of a spitting cobra.

But only Moresby had known that Unit Alpha consisted of one man—and a highly sophisticated computer.

That one man had adopted the name of Alpha. His own identity was buried in time and so many personality switches that he himself would have been able to hide it from even a lie-detector. The truth regarding Alpha had died with Moresby.

Since the funeral Alpha had not used his usual office, the Monk's Cell, in the basement of the Ministry of Defence. Moresby no longer resided in the fourth-floor inner sanctum and Alpha had no wish to be noticed by the new management before he was ready for them. Instead, he had remained in the safe house off the Bayswater Road, location known only to himself and Moresby. Purchased through the estate of a supposedly deceased, in fact fictitious, Dutchman, the house was owned by a charity registered in Liechtenstein whose affairs were in turn administered by a retired French lawyer in Lucerne. Any penetration of this triple-screened defence, if only partial, would alert Alpha in time for him to avoid discovery.

The computer was located in the basement, within a self-contained and secure bunker. Moresby used to joke that Alpha and the

Kremlin would probably be the only survivors of any nuclear war—and that his money would be firmly on Alpha. The isolated secrecy in which the base had been prepared indicated how vital Alpha had been to Moresby. All service directives and circulatory information was fed to the computer link in the Monk's Cell by the various security, Intelligence and police departments.

Alpha sat at his desk console on Wednesday 15th September, coffee mug to hand, lighted cigarette between his lips. He keyed in the codes which would enable him to find all relevant instructions and changes made since Moresby's death.

The sweeping changes he had predicted to Lansbury had taken place. The new men were faceless men, mediocre men, who could be relied upon never to rock the boat, take any risks, or even step a centimetre outside the new strict, procedural guidelines. It was common knowledge on the top floor of the Ministry that Llewellyn Jones considered Moresby to have been a virtuoso soloist whose brilliance had almost been his undoing.

None of Moresby's men figured prominently in the new order. Structured political control of the clandestine services had been firmly imposed. The Prime Minister favoured centralization. As the new broom,

11

Llewellyn Jones had gone even further. He took full advantage of a flurry of Press reports concerning a well-placed traitor in Signals Intelligence. He had fed his political masters statements regarding regular operational control of all the clandestine services by one authority, his own. The politicians liked that. They could make confident announcements in Parliament that stable doors had finally been closed.

Alpha did not like the new ideas. Centralized operational control meant only one organization for the other side to penetrate. The dangers of the new centralization were apparent when Llewellyn Jones set up this 'filtration unit'.

In Moresby's day, Special Services Department (S.S.D.) concerned itself operationally on a random basis in the affairs of both the Security Service (M.I.5) and the Intelligence-gathering Secret Intelligence Service (S.I.S.). Special Services took ultimate command should the need arise. Now, Llewellyn's Jones's 'filtration unit', already named 'Directorate', would sanction all operations by M.I.5 and S.I.S. only on receipt of operational objectives and continual progress reports.

Alpha lit another cigarette and fleetingly wondered what would become of Unit Alpha under the new regime. His own position could well be a precarious one. Llewellyn Jones would not want any ghosts from the past. Twenty years of watching Moresby's back, being Joker to the Master, would mean nothing to the new chief. As yet no directives had been issued with regard to Unit Alpha. He still had work to do. The King is dead. Long live the King. Meanwhile, someone had to arrange the Changing of the Guard.

Every fourth Wednesday for as long as he could remember, Alpha had checked the S.I.S. Station reports. Moresby had always kept a watchful eye on those far-flung corners of what was left of the British sphere of influence. Station Residents transmitted coded reports to S.I.S. who programmed the details into the Unit Alpha computer. Alpha pressed the keyboard instruction key to begin his task. No Station reports were forthcoming. Instead, a flashing directive appeared on the screen: KEY MONITOR EMERGENCY CODE.

Alpha caught his breath involuntarily. He felt as though a ghost had laid a chilled hand on his heart. MONITOR EMERGENCY was Moresby's most secret channel of communication, a fail-safe procedure known only to both men to enable contact to be made under the direst circumstances. The device

13

had never been used. Now Moresby was dead and his ghost had a message.

Alpha was uneasy. A logical, practical, level-headed man who could offer rational explanations for biblical miracles, he could have sworn, on oath, that there was someone else in the room with him. He ignored his feelings and keyed in the code, given verbally to him by Moresby years ago: the last line of Houseman's 'Epitaph on an Army of Mercenaries'. Alpha's fingers drummed a frenzied tattoo on the keyboard: 'And saved the sum of things for pay.'

The computer answered: ENTRY DATED 1100 HRS. 3 SEPTEMBER. KEY PASSWORD:

Alpha keyed in 'Reynard', Moresby's former Resistance Codename. The old hands of S.O.E. had a sense of humour about their identifications: witty, stylish, and not like the binary mathematicians who were today's encoders.

The computer responded. Alpha sensed a whiff of Moresby's Havana Corona. No, foolishness. It was his own cigarette. The message read:

ALPHA, UNLESS YOU ARE BEHIND ON S.I.S. REPORTS YOU WILL READ THIS BY THE 15TH. YOU MUST CANCEL PROGRAMME DESIGNED TO REPEAT THIS MESSAGE EVERY SEVEN DAYS. KEY BACK-UP CODE.

'Crazy old ghost,' Alpha spoke out loud. 'You and your literary allusions.'

Then he keyed in: 'The time has come, the Walrus said.'

The computer replied:

REPEAT PROGRAMME NOW CANCELLED. ALPHA, THIS NEXT INSTRUCTION VITAL: P.M. AND SELF AGREED ON 2ND, LLEWELLYN JONES MY SUCCESSOR. I WILL RETIRE EARLY NEXT YEAR. MY HEALTH IS NOT GOOD. CARDIAC CONDITION. TODAY I DISCOVER GRAVE ERROR. L.J. UNDER SUSPICION. FACTS NOT PROVEN. WATCH HIM. TIME SHORT. MY HEART NOT STRONG TODAY. IF L.J. APPOINTED, CONTACT BEAUCHAMP CABINET OFFICE. CODEWORD JANUS-REPLY MYTILENE. TRUST ONLY JANUS OR WYATT WHO CAN BE RELIED UPON TO SUPPORT YOU. CODEWORD FRIDAY-REPLY VALHALLA. WATCH DEVELOPMENTS BAKAR. REYNARD.

Alpha stared at the message, reading and re-reading it. He lit another cigarette and before he was aware of it, another. His initial reaction was one of disbelief. Yet there could be no possible doubt. The message was from Moresby.

The Master had left a will. Alpha was his executor.

*　　*　　*

15

Moresby's legacy had instructed Alpha to watch events in Bakar. So he read the S.I.S. Cairo Station report first. Bakar came under Cairo Station for administrative purposes. After four thousand words on matters Middle Eastern, a four-line paragraph regarding Simon Ablett-Green had been tacked on to the report, almost as an afterthought. His death from a heart attack received an almost casual mention, as if good weather or a lively Embassy party might have been reported in its place.

Alpha requested Ablett-Green's medical record from F.C.O. Personnel. No history of cardiac problems there. Via G.C.H.Q.'s anonymous station in Kent, Alpha's Most Immediate signal was transmitted to Bakar. The reply, decoded by his computer, was prefaced by a curt: 'Do you dull buggers know what time it is out here?' Alpha had no idea but could picture the blunt, pipe-smoking Barrett cursing in his best Lancashire.

Alpha was not impressed with the story. Ablett-Green had been discovered in Ad Said's dock area at 6.15pm after leaving the British Embassy in Raza at 11.35am. He had given no reason for his visit. Barrett had surmised he had gone to see a girl who worked for one of the oil companies. Ablett-Green had been certified dead from the heart failure by a

16

British doctor at an Ad Said hospital at 6.45pm. The body had been flown home and cremated on the 7th September. Barrett did admit verbally that the young man might have been on official business and ignored procedures. This was unlikely, though. Nothing ever happened in Bakar. Ablett-Green had not even done the basic security course yet had stood in for Barrett.

'Lambs to the slaughter,' Alpha muttered. 'If you are right, Moresby, and something is going on down there, the poor bastard never knew what hit him.'

There was no hard evidence to suggest anything untoward, so he typed up his report for the new Head of S.S.D.

*   *   *

Alpha paid off his taxi at Victoria Station. He took another to Dolphin Square. From there he made his way on foot through Claverton St, along Lupus St, before doubling back along Charlwood St. Elaborate measures were needed to counter any surveillance. A proper tail job could take as many as twenty cars and double that number of pedestrians. Alpha knew, he had planned many in his time.

He turned into Cambridge St, his final destination. Witch-hazel eyes searched the

17

shadows and scanned the Georgian windows for any signs of movement—a curtain ruffled in a darkened room, doors that clicked open and shut for no reason. Only when doubly sure he was unobserved did he knock at the black door of the terraced house. Parked outside was a Porsche Turbo sports car. The safe signal.

The door opened without the hallway light being switched on. Alpha emerged from the shadows and stepped inside. He had broken cover again and offered a silent prayer that Moresby was right to trust Janus. A young woman in the hallway asked:

'Shall I take your coat, Mr Caldicot?'

The voice was soft yet confident, the confidence of a practised society hostess.

'No thank you.'

A light went on upstairs, the landing light. Alpha tightened his grip on the comforting butt of his Browning G.P.35 automatic pistol concealed in the right hand coat pocket. Thirteen rounds of 9mm Parabellum aggravation if any of the house's inhabitants even looked like making any wrong move.

'You can put the safety catch back on that gun of yours,' a man's voice announced. Not a threat, a reassurance.

A lean man had walked down the stairs with the landing light still switched on behind him.

He presented a perfect target. Alpha thought fleetingly how easy it would be to kill the man without even drawing the gun. The man knew it.

'Moresby told me if I ever had to make contact with you, I was to be careful. I am Janus.'

'Mytilene,' Alpha replied.

'Camilla,' the man waved a hand to indicate the girl.

She walked past Alpha leaving a smile and a hint of Rive Gauche.

'Do go up, Mr Caldicot.'

The added reassurance of his cover name relaxed Alpha's grip on the Browning. He had only given it to Beauchamp's secretary.

Alpha followed the man up the stairs to a small but expensively furnished lounge. Sir Russell Beauchamp of the Cabinet Office was a tall, studious-looking man, shoulders slightly rounded, who wore a benevolent expression, Arran sweater and corduroy jeans. He handed Alpha a brandy. There was a glint in the light grey eyes and Alpha always watched a man's eyes. Everything else about him might fool you, but rarely the eyes.

Beauchamp lapsed into an armchair and filled a meerschaum pipe which soon belched smoke furiously as he lit up. Camilla came in carrying a tray of coffee. Alpha took it from

19

her. She thanked him with smiling eyes. Twenty-three, twenty-four, Alpha thought. Secretary? Mistress? No, probably daughter. There was a faint resemblance. She had ignored Alpha's signal to leave him and Beauchamp alone.

'Do sit down, Mr Caldicot,' she invited. 'I always remain with father during discussions.'

From a black leather handbag she took a Security pass. Inside the bag, Alpha could see the outline of an automatic Colt .45. Since when did M.I.5 Records wander around tooled up, he thought. Swiftly, he grabbed the handbag, seized the pistol, and emptied the contents of the magazine on to the Axminster.

She made no attempt to stop him. She walked across the room to another armchair and sat, long legs crossed, while Alpha scooped up the fallen ammunition.

'Nasty little things, hollow points,' Alpha observed, examining the bullets: 'Make very big holes in people.'

'Very impressive, Mr Caldicot,' she smiled. 'Now why the crash meeting?'

Beauchamp listened as Alpha told them of Moresby's legacy and the death of Ablett-Green in Bakar. He handed Beauchamp copies of his report to Llewellyn Jones and of Moresby's instructions. As Beauchamp read, the benign air of the harmless academic evaporated, and he passed each sheet to Camilla. She read faster than he did because they both finished almost simultaneously. They exchanged glances and Beauchamp spoke. This time a Baron of the Establishment confronted Alpha. The voice was crisp and clear:

'If these documents are genuine I would put them down to an old man's suspicions. The boy in Bakar was probably going to see his girlfriend. In the absence of any supportive evidence, I would say coincidence.'

Alpha was watching the girl. An attractive girl, short dark hair, blue eyes and a small mouth. She in turn watched Alpha and spoke as if to reinforce her father's scepticism:

'Mr Caldicot, we are tired of being bothered by every feuding faction in the security sphere. They all tittle-tattle about reorganizations that are weakening their respective fiefdoms. Your position is somewhat delicate. We have only a dead man's word for your bona fides. There is considerable feeling that Moresby rather played to the gallery over the Minrod business. Something of an old man's swansong.'

Attractive but hard, Alpha thought. If it had not been for the likes of Moresby you'd be blonde, blue-eyed and on the production line

21

in a Herrenvolk baby factory. He was angry at the way both Beauchamps had dismissed Moresby.

'For the last twenty years I have worked with Moresby to ensure the security of this country. He was a brave, cunning, devious old man who was probably one of the best Intelligence men in the world. In that time I met only three men fit to stand in the same street with him and two of them were outsiders. Making both your acquaintances has not changed my view.'

Beauchamp re-lit his meerschaum. Alpha did not like the half-smile.

'Mr Caldicot, your survival is your problem. Don't expect any help from this quarter. For God's sake man, Llewellyn Jones has been positively vetted. I suggest you go and talk to him with a view to obtaining a decent pension. He has spent thirty years in the service of his country and thirty very valuable years they have been.'

Alpha finished his brandy.

'I won't take up any more of your valuable time,' he replied. 'Thank you for seeing me.'

'Camilla will see you out.'

'I can see why Moresby code-named you Janus,' Alpha parted with the best insult he could think of.

Beauchamp said nothing.

Minutes later the girl walked back into the room. She asked her father:

'Was it wise to leave him thinking no-one believes him?'

'Certainly. Camilla, that man was Moresby's joker. He will go to the ends of the earth to prove L.J. has been a naughty boy. Which keeps our noses very clean when the political flak starts flying.'

'And if he is killed in the process?'

'Then we'll know exactly where we all stand, won't we.'

Camilla Beauchamp wondered fleetingly what her father really meant.

CHAPTER THREE

Alpha was back in the Bayswater safe house by midnight. No-one had followed him from the meet with Beauchamp. He sat at the computer again and studied the printout of Moresby's legacy.

'Any more bright ideas, old ghost?' he asked.

Beauchamp was no help. Wyatt could have been, but two days after Moresby's death, Wyatt's executive jet had disappeared over the North Atlantic. No wreckage and no survivors had been found despite an intensive search by the U.S. Coastguard.

Alpha thought about Operation Nimrod which Wyatt had helped to thwart. A Moscow Centre operation, conducted in person by the late Alexei Svetkin, Head of the First Chief Directorate, K.G.B.—a brilliant concept to replace Moresby with a high-ranking sleeper. Had it been successful, the K.G.B. would have in effect commanded Special Services, been able to subvert the very basis of decisions in Whitehall, and the Politburo would have influenced the mind of Downing St.

But Nimrod had failed. Department Five, First Chief Directorate, K.G.B., specialized in 'wet' or 'bloody' affairs and in the final stages of Nimrod had been on the receiving end of one. They had killed the beautiful Vicky Keane, a British agent, which was against house rules. Contrary to popular belief, agents did not continually kill each other: bystanders, yes; civilians, frequently, but not each other. Wyatt was not an agent, but a close friend of Moresby's. He had once been a soldier, and after finding Keane beaten and tortured to death, he had become pure bloody angry. There had been no chance for anyone to call house rules. Wyatt had picked his ground and visited murderous retribution on the girl's killers. Six top-flight K.G.B.

operatives had died as well as Svetkin.

Alpha remembered thinking that the K.G.B. might have arranged Moresby's death out of pure spite. The reports proved otherwise. Now Alpha sat reading Moresby's legacy again. Beauchamp had been no help. Wyatt had disappeared and his own time was fast running out. Sooner or later, Llewellyn Jones would order the disbandment of Unit Alpha, and if Beauchamp had mentioned the visit from Alpha, the consequences could prove terminally fatal.

Alpha poured himself a vodka. He was alone and a little afraid. Moresby, you old fox, why no hint of your reasons for suspecting L.J.? Your brief is deficient. Somewhere he could hear Moresby's voice. Was it echoing in his subconscious, or was he in the presence of the ghost again?

'Think it out, Alpha. Think it out. Use that tricky box of yours, your networks and your devious mind. We guard these poor, benighted complacent fools against desperate forces, mirror images of inverted minds, men that are not men but ghoulish undead things, drooling to enslave the human spirit. Think it out, Alpha, before the Gulag comes to the Alps, the ravenous hordes overrun Hampstead and we have no refuge left.'

'Moresby, you old guerrilla, you'd have

liked that. A last stand outside the M.O.D. with a tin hat and a Sten gun.'

The joke was not funny. He knew Moresby was right. Unless he thought it out, the price of failure was one he was likely to pay only once.

Contact Wyatt. Codeword Friday. Reply Valhalla. Alpha, you idiot, remember the wreath, the crucifix of red roses with the inscription Valhalla. No coincidence, it was Wyatt who sent that. And he sent a message—Valhalla.

Alpha lit another cigarette and put himself in Wyatt's position. Moresby had died of a heart attack on the 3rd September. Wyatt's plane had disappeared on the 5th or early 6th. There was no time to send a wreath to the funeral. Yes, there was. But the message. Valhalla. The Vikings lived on in immortality.

Proposition. Put yourself in Wyatt's place. Moresby died only days after Nimrod is foiled. Wyatt is suspicious. If Moresby is dead, it might be a K.G.B. revenge job. No-one to trust now, so disappear. Yes, Wyatt, you're capable of it, faking an aircraft disappearance. Then you put the codeword on the wreath so Moresby's joker will know he is not alone.

Alpha knew it was not perfect. It could be his own emotional response to the problem.

26

He had ribbed Lansbury about such feelings at the funeral. But it was a chance.

★   ★   ★

At 10.15am on Thursday 16th September Alpha was walking through a Paris quartier. He smiled at a young mother hand in hand with a toddling child. He remembered that his own mother had been crushed under the wheels of a T.52 tank on 4th November 1956 in Budapest. She had died instantly.

Alpha found the café, tired and jaded, bereft of customers. He took a corner seat, ordered *café au lait* and watched the street. Today the whole world seemed tired. Passers-by hurried going nowhere. The coffee arrived, dirty beige in a pale white cup. He had the feeling that his life was going nowhere. For want of anything better to do he lit a cigarette and drew the faded tin ashtray towards him. Moresby's death was a personal loss, and in a wider sense he was losing the fight, the contest against Moresby's 'desperate forces', a contest that had started almost thirty years before in Budapest.

At sixteen he had drifted into the Underground which became a focus for his hatred of the invaders who had killed his mother and imprisoned his father. He never saw the old man again. At nineteen he was running a string of agents and came to Moresby's notice when the Master was S.I.S. Controller (Eastern Europe). Two years after his marriage, Alpha's wife and daughter had been rounded up by the Security police. Moresby brought him out just in time but failed to bring his wife and child. They died in a Gulag two years later. It had taken Alpha a long time to bury the hatred. With Moresby's help he became the perfect Intelligence man, a man whose emotions were concealed deep in the past and deeper within himself. Seeing the mother and young child had reminded him of the past. Yet the past had to remain under deep cover if he was to survive.

The old woman did not look directly at him. She sat at a far table and unpacked items from a wrinkled brown leather bag that matched her nicotine-stained fingers. Purse, lighter, cigarettes. Her spidery grey hair was pulled tight into a bun, her pale grey, creased face concentrated intently on the tired waiter as she ordered. Twenty years ago she had been handsome, attractive even. But the years of bereavement, of wasting exile, of the struggle to live in a strange country had etched every waking hour of sorrow for ever in the lines and folds of her skin. Alpha was so intent upon reading her engraved life story that he almost failed to notice the signal—the pack of Winston standing on and next to the coffee cup. But he did not hurry. The signal meant his quarry was going nowhere in a hurry.

Ten minutes later he was with Pavel. The studio was desolate—flaking white walls, a chipped easel, the dull brown floorboards worn bare of polish long ago. The smell of oil paint mingled with stale tobacco. Thin stained curtains did their best to prevent the sunlight gaining access to what was really a dismal garret. Alpha was sitting in a severe upright chair. He accepted *vin ordinaire* and a Gitane. Exiled despair trembled through Pavel's shaking fingers as he held a cigarette for Alpha to light. The garret was cold. Alpha hunched into his overcoat. Pavel stretched a thin arm to the wine and poured himself another glass.

Pavel was a gaunt, philosophical man, of uncertain age, but never young. Dark hair shot through with grey, unkempt and uncared for, the curious gaze settled on Alpha.

'Fifteen years,' Pavel whispered: 'You are an unwelcome ghost, a spectre of hopelessness.'

Alpha looked at the emaciated remains of a man who had once personified the spirit of freedom.

'So you paint,' he spoke quietly.

'What else is there? Twenty years, forty, a

hundred—Does it make any difference? I am alive, if you can call this living. I paint, I talk, I get drunk and I think what I damned well please. There is no Gulag here, no psychiatric hospital to scramble my brains. And I want to stay here alone.'

'They leave you alone?'

'Why would the K.G.B. bother with me, a broken, hopeless, dying man?'

Only Pavel's eyes were sapphire bright. Eyes of fear, yet strangely eyes of courage.

'Your freedom may not last as long as you think,' Alpha warned, heading for the door. Pavel leaped from his chair. Fast as a pouncing cat he seized Alpha's left arm and twisted. The grip was ferocious. Pavel looked incapable of such strength. But Alpha had turned into the hold and jammed the muzzle of the Browning into Pavel's bony ribs. Pavel smiled.

'So you would sell me out.'

'No, but others would. I am in danger. Damn you, Pavel, I need you. The streets may no longer be safe for any of us. If they take me, then you and many others are dead.'

'So use that gun now.'

'You want that?'

'I have been a hunted animal for too long.'

'But you could still hunt.'

Pavel walked back to the rickety table and

30

swallowed the last of the wine. A gesture of defiance; he had taken his decision.

'What do I do?'

Alpha handed him a large Manila envelope. Pavel's deft fingers examined the contents: a passport, ten thousand pounds in cash and a photograph of Gareth Llewellyn Jones. A foolscap sheet of typed instructions was attached to the photograph.

'Destroy when memorized. Observe your target carefully. Very senior man. He has the best babysitters.'

'Your S.A.S. in plainclothes.'

Alpha nodded, then:

'Who else will you use?'

'Gador is in London.'

'If you are taken, you are on your own.'

Pavel smiled. He no longer seemed emaciated. The thin fingers no longer trembled.

'When was I not?'

       ★   ★   ★

Alpha knew he was followed from Gatwick Airport, which was why he had taken a taxi. The flight to Paris has been booked in the name of Caldicot. To ensure a legitimate reason for his visit to Paris, he had called in at the Embassy to see the S.I.S. Station officer.

He had casually mentioned he was returning to London that night. But he omitted to mention the visit he was about to make to Pavel. Someone had put out on all stations alert regarding Unit Alpha and the name Caldicot was registered in Personnel as belonging to a member of Unit Alpha. He knew by the look in the Station officer's eyes. The girl who followed him near Charles de Gaulle Airport confirmed his suspicions.

He had half-expected to be detained at Gatwick so he used his Security pass to skirt Customs. He still carried the Browning and one or two other illegal surprises. He did not need any nosey official asking stupid questions. The French D.S.T. were always understanding about such matters in Paris. Mr Caldicot could always be relied upon to extend similar courtesies in London. S.I.S. had not requested the French to detain him, so he knew it must be a personal matter between himself and another department. S.I.S. had obviously been instructed to be discreet.

The taxi driver at Gatwick accepted two twenty pound notes and glanced at the Metropolitan Police warrant card. Tradecraft. Alpha collected identities. The driver kept watching his rear view mirror. Twenty minutes and two detours later he confirmed:

'Blue Sierra.'

'Correct,' Alpha replied.

The cabby was a big man. Fat, friendly and a little nervous. He asked:

'They 'aven't got shooters, 'ave they?'

Alpha shook his head. His followers' instructions must have been to do just that. Otherwise, they would have tried for him at the airport. Olympia now and Alpha was prepared to take them on a scenic tour of greater London if necessary. The blue Sierra was still in position, two men in the front. Still there passing Wormwood Scrubs. Very unusual. A proper tail job needed far more vehicles. So it had to be an interception or a hit. Yes, revised thinking coincided with the numbing fear that lay in the pit of his stomach. He was scared now. The fear was like an elastic wall, making the taxi, the nervously garrulous cabby and the London night almost surreal. Alpha took the decision to stand. There was no point in delaying any longer. He handed the driver a further twenty pounds:

'You have not seen me if you want to keep your licence.'

The cabby seemed offended:

'No need to come on strong, guv. I might want to do this again some time.'

Alpha was used to frightened people

33

cracking bad jokes. Self-defence mechanism, part of the 'Please leave me out of it. I'm a harmless fool' syndrome. Fool, all right. When the going got rough, even the harmless were wiped out as a precaution.

'Forgive me,' Alpha apologized. 'I'm not used to dealing with reliable people. Take a left turn, then first right and stop outside that disused warehouse just long enough for me to get out. Don't hang around.'

As the taxi slowed, Alpha was out and running. The adrenalin pumped through his system. In the darkness behind, the Sierra stopped. The entrance gates to the waste land of a warehouse yard were off the hinges. Alpha ran towards the side door of the building.

Somewhere, far away, he could hear children playing. The years fell away. He was back on those deadly streets in a grey country where the border watchtowers were built to keep the people in.

Inside the dusty, littered, gantried barn of a warehouse that even the rats had deserted, a stack of oil drums stood like a modern sculpture, severe and stark in the middle of the floor. Perfect, Alpha thought: and only two entrances—the small side door through which he had come, and the main sliding doors, already bolted and barred from the inside.

He took his briefcase and opened it, placing it at eye level on top of two oil drums. Then he moved against the wall in which the small side door was set. Agent training had taken over now. Never wait behind a door. Incomers can squash you flat against the wall and kill you while you are still tasting the wood. Always face the opening crack. A diversion is necessary: the suitcase on the oildrums would attract attentions for a split second. Escape route: well, nothing was perfect, but there were only two of the opposition; worse than one, better than three.

The footsteps were a long time arriving, but not long enough for them to have waited for back-up. One man went around the outside of the building. The second pushed open the side door. Although a young man, hard-faced, tense-eyed and quick, he failed to look to his right. The open briefcase had attracted his attention. Alpha squeezed the trigger of the Crossman Medallist pump action air pistol. Its dart buried itself in the man's cheek. Before a speed-reflexed right hand could touch the burning pain, the intruder had sunk to the floor, unconscious.

Alpha moved fast. He dragged the man from view behind the oil drums. The inert weight and concern regarding the whereabouts of the second man caused him to breathe heavily. Steady, Alpha. Take your time. The rattling sound as the second man tried to open the main doors unnerved him. His right hand was shaking. Steady, Alpha. One down, one to go. Come on you bastard, come and find your friend.

'Tony,' a voice called, a neutral London voice with no urgency and no humour.

'In here,' Alpha replied, and moved back to his original position.

Footsteps. Alpha swallowed. He pocketed the Crossman. This time it was the Browning he held in the right hand, steady now. The door creaked. A short, heavy man walked through, casually. He wore leather jacket, denim trousers and looked almost hurt as Alpha said:

'Stay very still. Your friend is asleep.'

The newcomer did not panic at the sight of the gun. He obeyed Alpha's order to put both hands on his head. The Browning did not waver by a millimetre and the heavy man knew it. Young he might be, but not impetuous. Five fatal yards separated him from the gun.

A small, square card landed at the heavy man's feet.

'Take a very good look,' Alpha ordered.

Recognition dawned in the heavy man's

eyes as he saw the top clearance Blue security pass. No name, but a photograph. He was clearly embarrassed and apologized: 'We were told to follow and intercept you, sir. Someone has obviously got a crossed wire.'

'And take me?'

'Local nick, sir.'

'Who said?'

'Detective Superintendent Colclough.'

'Tell him Caldicot will come in when he's ready. Now I'll help you with your colleague.'

The heavy young man had turned. The blue pass and Alpha's obvious authority had lulled him into a very false sense of security. He did not feel the blow that tumbled him into oblivion. Alpha dragged another insensible weight behind the oil drums. A search revealed two Metropolitan Police warrant cards, a set of car keys—for the Sierra, Alpha presumed—and a regulation issue Smith & Wesson .38 Special.

Alpha pocketed the items, collected his briefcase and walked nonchalantly from the warehouse. He drove the Sierra towards Kensington, alert to the possibility of other followers. There were none. After parking the car off the High St, he walked briskly away. Some minutes later he called from a payphone and spoke very precisely to Detective Superintendent Colclough of Special Branch liaison:

'This is Caldicot. I will report in when I am ready. Meanwhile, tell the monkey who instructed you to lay off.'

Colclough did not have the chance to reply. He was too busy taking down directions as to the whereabouts of his two men and their car. Nor did he have time to trace the call.

Minutes later, Colclough lifted another telephone and spoke angrily about not being properly briefed. An icy female voice concisely suggested his operatives were incompetent.

CHAPTER FOUR

Gareth Llewellyn Jones walked briskly up the steps of the Georgian house in Lancaster Gate. The black entrance door opened automatically to admit him and he crossed the marble-floored entrance hallway where a sergeant in Royal Marine dress uniform saluted him.

His progress through a door to his left was continuously monitored by closed-circuit television. A thin, severe-looking woman in her late fifties looked up from behind a typewriter and smiled at him. Llewellyn Jones did not smile back. A wall partition slid open and he entered a soundproofed, windowless room containing a single desk, chair and armchair. Electronic maps and diagrams covered the walls. A bank of computer screens, visual display units and a control console ran the entire length of one wall.

'Beast in its lair,' the Marine Sergeant reported by phone to a security room as soon as Llewellyn Jones was out of earshot.

8.05am, Friday 17th September. The Head of the Special Services Department had arrived for work.

A portly, bespectacled Welshman whose immaculately pin-striped exterior concealed a soul of pure selfishness, Llewellyn Jones would have turned the most partisan Cardiff Arms Park crowd anti-Welsh. Referred to as 'that unspeakable Welsh Richelieu', or more usually 'that bastard Llewellyn Jones', he probably did not have a friend in the world. A prime-ministerial adviser in his own right even before his recent appointment, he had spent thirty years in the pursuit of power. He was feared in the decision-making processes of Whitehall yet his undoubted brilliance was also admired.

He had come a long way from his parents' drapers shop in what had once been a small Welsh steel town. His journey had been a conscious effort to eradicate his beginnings

39

and his accent. Hard work, single-mindedness and an ability to kick an opponent comatose had put him where he was. He intended to stay there.

The dark bushy hair showed no signs of greying or loss despite his fifty-five years. Piercing blue eyes checked each visual display unit for some figure he had carried in his head on the journey to the office. He smiled to himself. He had calculated the correct figure.

His brief on appointment to head S.S.D. had been on the face of it a simple one. Centralize. Stop the political embarrassment of espionage disclosures and centralize. So he had gone one step further and established centralized control. His method had been simple but devastatingly effective. First he had called a series of consultative meetings at which he had listened and put forward nothing. This enabled him to identify opposition and potential troublemakers at a very early stage. His reorganization then brushed aside this opposition, either removing it or promoting its exponents sideways and on to quangos where they could do no harm. He had then set up the Directorate.

All policy was decided by the Directorate which wielded the power of absolute operational and policy control. The private armies and independent republics of the security apparatus no longer existed. Llewellyn Jones chaired the Directorate while his old assistant from the Foreign Office was brought over to take up a second seat. The third, as yet vacant, he intended to give to Vennaway, depending on Vennaway's ability to carry out his instructions to the letter.

Llewellyn Jones lit his second cigarette of the day, opened the blue file that lay on his desk and then summoned Vennaway who arrived immediately and sat in the armchair to be ignored for a full five minutes. Eventually, Llewellyn Jones spoke:

'So, Unit Alpha is playing games. Made fools out of Mr Colclough's boys.'

'So it would seem, L.J.'

Vennaway was one of a select handful of personnel allowed to address Llewellyn Jones by his initials. Vennaway was also a very unusual Intelligence officer, although not popular with some of the former incumbents at S.I.S. Llewellyn Jones put this down to two reasons. One: Vennaway was efficient to the point of nausea. Two: an attractive, thirty-three-year-old woman had never before been promoted as far as quickly as Vennaway had been.

But then Naomi Vennaway was no lady. She twisted the departmental knife with the best of them, took unpleasant operational decisions coldly and impersonally, and always argued her case analytically. Quite simply she was deadlier than the male.

She lit a thin cigar. Llewellyn Jones thought the cigar went well with the leather trousers, the boots and the polo-neck sweater. She never dressed conventionally, wore little make-up, and always wore her blonde hair cropped close. Her mouth was a little too wide and her jawline a little too heavy for anyone to describe her as exceptionally beautiful, but the eyes, a brilliant green, were magnetically attractive. Everyone noticed Vennaway's eyes.

'Your analysis?' Llewellyn Jones asked.

'Unit Alpha was Moresby's creation, a unit to watch his back. I managed to sneak a look at some of the Nimrod files before they were shredded. The only registered personnel is one Caldicot who does not officially exist. No trace at Somerset House, D.H.S.S., Passport Office and no dummy bank accounts for salaries. Obviously the monthly payments identified in Schedule 3 in front of you took care of Unit budget and salaries. The basement office in M.O.D. has remained empty since the funeral of our late chief. All stations alert missed him in Paris, although I am inclined to believe they funked picking him up.'

'Why?'

'He could have killed both Colclough's men. Useful character whoever he is.'

Llewellyn Jones handed Vennaway the report Alpha had compiled on the death of Simon Ablett-Green in Bakar.

'What do you make of that?'

'The Gulf is not my field.'

'He marked it for my personal attention.'

'Maybe he is trying to justify his position.'

'Or conspiring with some cabal of the Old Guard. Or someone else.' Llewellyn Jones let the sinister possibility sound matter-of-fact.

Vennaway's brilliant green eyes flashed:

'So what are your instructions?'

'We want rid of him. When you can catch up with him, he's fired.'

As soon as Caldicot, or Unit Alpha, could be found, then executive action would be taken. Llewellyn Jones was perhaps the best placed agent Moscow Centre ever had.

He was not a product of the undergraduate disillusionment with Capitalism and the West. Far from it, his Cambridge days coincided with the Attlee government, and like many young men of his generation he saw the New Britain as a fresh beginning, rising out of the ashes of a war-ravaged Europe. A Double First had been his passport into the Civil Service, ambition and the pursuit of power his fare.

Llewellyn Jones became a traitor for money, and a lot of it. He was no ordinary spy, filching and photocopying documents and handing the results to a contact. Not for him the clandestine dead-drops in parked cars and out-of-the-way places, the furtive pre-arranged meetings down darkened side-streets. Llewellyn Jones was the ultimate agent of influence whose identity was known only to one man, code-named Victor, who ran the anonymous Dept 12, First Chief Directorate, K.G.B. Victor's identity in turn was known only to the Head of the K.G.B. himself.

Contact between Victor and Llewellyn Jones had been made only three times in twenty years. The first time Llewellyn Jones made the approach, knowing full well that Victor was a rising K.G.B. man who would do very well in future. Normally, an agent of Victor's ability would shy away from any direct approach in case the offerer was a double agent, about to be planted. Yet Victor had a sixth sense about his man which proved to be correct.

Payment was always channelled into a Swiss bank account and a charitable trust had been set up to pay for Llewellyn Jones's three children to be educated. Expensive preparatory schools, Winchester, Benenden,

44

Cambridge, the Sorbonne and U.C.L.A. were the order of the day. The trust also owned the farm in Sussex, the mews house in Mayfair and a villa on the select end of the Algarve. The holiday cottage in Wales had been sold discreetly to a young local couple when the arsonists started work.

Llewellyn Jones had been positively vetted twice. But a security investigation is only as thorough as the resources allotted to it and the calibre of the men carrying it out. The trust had supposedly been set up by Llewellyn Jones's great-uncle who had made oil money in the United States. But the Moscow Centre forgers had done their work so well that even the I.R.S. would have had difficulty disputing its bona fides.

In return, Llewellyn Jones only acted when he felt it safe to do so. Victor was clever enough to know the value of his agent. The late Alexei Svetkin had failed to carry out Nimrod successfully. Victor had achieved Nimrod's desired objective without one drop of blood being spilled. Llewellyn Jones would never overplay his hand and Victor would not allow him to do so. His agent would never be blown by a chance defector from Centre, would never be caught out by British watchers. The only danger to Llewellyn Jones was if someone played a hunch and managed

45

to obtain the highest political authority for total investigation. Even then, Llewellyn Jones had his contingency plans.

Caldicot or Unit Alpha presented a problem. But Llewellyn Jones would deal with that problem and come out of it with an even greater reputation. Moresby's joker was isolated. His Master was dead and the security apparatus overhauled. The poor fool has nowhere to turn, Llewellyn Jones smiled to himself.

★   ★   ★

At 10.15 that evening, Richard Lansbury lay sprawled on the sofa of his North London flat listening to the stereophonic sounds of James Last through a Celtic mist of whisky. The D.G. of Five had summoned him that morning and told him that his services were no longer required and that early retirement at fifty-three with no loss of pension rights was not such a bad fate after all.

Lansbury could not believe his superior. After twenty-five years in the service, twenty-five years of limited family life, missing out on the children growing up, the long, mind-shattering hours, the danger, he was out in the cold. And all thanks to the new Head of Special Services.

The rumours had been bouncing like Asdic from floor to floor of Five's Headquarters. At S.I.S. they had christened Llewellyn Jones 'Stalin' on account of the purge that had good men dropping like sprayed flies. Lansbury had accepted three fingers of the D.G.'s malt and two refills—the proper article, not the discount brand kept for unwelcome callers and staff. He had been floating on a sea of alcohol ever since. The last order he gave as Director of Operations was to his driver:

'Bill, come and get me from the Oasis Club. I'm pissed.'

Lansbury knew that getting drunk was a pointless exercise. But his life had lost its sense of purpose. His wife had chosen that week-end to visit her sister in Scotland and there was no-one home to sober him up so he carried on. He did not hear the front door open. He had not put the security lock on. Up to that evening he would never have been so lax. Now he was singing uncomplimentary songs about Llewellyn Jones and waving his hands in an attempt to conduct the music.

Suddenly, the music stopped.

'So you wrote all those rugby songs.'

The voice was Alpha's. He stood there, overcoat open, Browning automatic in his hand. Smiling he holstered the gun.

'Come to gloat, have you, you shadowy sod?

47

Have a drink.'

'You've had enough for the whole of Totteridge. I'll make the coffee. Sober up time.'

It was a long process. Lansbury's capacity for alcohol was phenomenal. So was his intake of the strong black coffee. He gibbered at Alpha about being thrown out of the service and having people spying on him. Alpha ignored the remarks. He marched his inebriate charge up and down the lounge, destroying a coffee table and two glasses in the process. After two hours, almost a gallon of coffee and several trips to the lavatory, Lansbury had achieved seventy per cent sobriety.

Alpha had searched the flat for hidden microphones. He had gambled by visiting Lansbury and was about to gamble again. Time was running short. Already his computer defences had alerted him to the enquiries being made by S.S.D. Moresby's executor needed another man, a back-up.

'Read this, D.Ops,' he handed Lansbury a copy of the legacy.

'I'm not bloody D.Ops any more.'

The legacy hit Lansbury like a wall. His first instinct was one of self-preservation.

'You weren't followed, were you?'

Alpha shook his head. Then he spoke

seriously.

'I've come to you because I'm in trouble. I took this to Beauchamp at the Cabinet Office and got the brush off. For all I know, he has told L.J. S.I.S. had an all stations alert out for me and two Special Branch boys tried to pull me last night. Llewellyn Jones is getting close to me. Now, it may well be because under the reorganization my face doesn't fit. That is of course a legitimate reason for his action. I have him under surveillance from some private enterprise I know. Here comes the crazy part.'

Lansbury was puffing away at his old briar. The mournful look was back on his face and his eyes were bloodshot but alert.

Alpha continued:

'You remember that wreath at Moresby's funeral, the one with Valhalla on it? According to Moresby, that was Wyatt's coded reply to the word "Friday". Assumption: Wyatt sees Moresby has died. After that Nimrod business he is nervous, assuming our Centre chums have taken revenge. He is next on the list. So he scatters. Now, the difficult part. Either he has genuinely disappeared or Moscow Centre did get him out of spite. But that Valhalla codeword gives it away. He thought there was something fishy about Moresby's death and he left that message for Moresby's successor. You know how close those two were.'

'Crazy idea, Alpha. But it makes sense.'

Lansbury was by now scared. He lit his pipe again and resisted the temptation to take another whisky. If Alpha was correct, the safest side to be on was the other one. There was no concrete proof of course, except for the unusual word Valhalla.

'How do we find Wyatt?'

'Official channels are closed, aren't they?' Lansbury replied. 'But there is a chance, a slim one, that the Mossad might help.'

'You know official co-operation has been cancelled. Foreign Office disapproval over the Lebanon,' Alpha objected.

'Well, I just happen to know that the lovely Ruth who runs a small network out of London helped Wyatt not long ago. There is just a chance she might talk to me.'

'We need him. Remember he started the Aberinvest Corporation and they have considerable interests in Bakar. He might have some idea what Moresby meant.'

Lansbury took his decison. Alpha had never seen Lansbury scared before. The tall ex-policeman walked over to a bureau and unlocked the bottom drawer. He took out a notepad and biro which he handed to Alpha and a Ruger Security Six .38 Special in a belt clip holster.

While Alpha wrote the message for Wyatt, Lansbury went into the next room, turned off the light and checked the street. There were no watchers. He should report Alpha's visit to his superiors. That was laid down in the new procedures. Any allegations had to be reported. But Lansbury was no longer employed, although still bound by the Official Secrets Act. It was time to look after himself and leave his ex-colleagues to look after themselves. They were being paid for it.

'You'd better stay out of sight,' he warned Alpha.

'I shall be going to ground, never fear. Unless of course something comes up. I'll be in contact.'

Alpha left by the fire escape.

CHAPTER FIVE

Prince Asif bin Said, Chief Minister of Bakar, arrived at Heathrow Airport on Friday 17th September at 9.30am. He had travelled incognito, using a diplomatic passport and a privately chartered Grumann Gulfstream from Zurich. The Ma'an 500 S.E.L. limousine, exported from the U.S.A. and now kept in

London for the Prince's exclusive use, chauffeured him to the private house in Belgrave Square.

His father, the legendary Abdullah Said, had forged Bakar from the remains of Turkish withdrawal, aided by the fired-steel loyalty of his Akrize tribesmen and a fighting reputation justly gained with T. E. Lawrence. Abdullah had married an Austrian countess in 1930 against the strict precepts of Islam. Their only son Baquoos, Asif's elder half-brother, was ten years old when his mother died, tragically young. For political reasons, Abdullah had married again into a neighbouring royal family in 1945. Ten years, Asif and several daughters later, Abdullah himself died, mourned by his family, a grieving people, and the Foreign Office to whom the old warrior had been a good friend.

Abdullah had brought Bakar into the twentieth century. The kingdom was firmly established in the British sphere of influence; a stabilizing factor in the region, as was the new King, Baquoos bin Said. A tall, dark-haired desert eagle of a man, Baquoos was educated academically by British tutors and militarily at Sandhurst. Idolized by his people, expert marksman, horseman and falconer, he had inherited from his mother a respect for Western ideas and philosophy.

Bakar's vast oil revenues were spent on all the Bakaris—the best medical, economic and social facilities anywhere in the Middle East. The King was pro-Western, a playboy who could govern and a Muslim in name rather than in observance of strict religious custom.

Half-brother Asif, born in 1946, a small, fat baby, grew to be a small, fat boy. Inherently vain, selfish, and possessed of a cruel streak, he did not endear himself to his father. The old King did not like the boy and shuffled him off to an expensive preparatory school in England at the first opportunity, thence to Eton. On Abdullah's death, Baquoos became responsible for his half-brother's education and acceded to Asif's choice of University— the Sorbonne. In 1965 Asif decided Cairo was more to his liking. Baquoos did not object— he was too busy fighting a rebellion by the Drua, a Marxist-backed Muslim sect who had imported Yemenis to do their fighting. Baquoos led the British-officered Bakari Scouts from the front and won. But he failed to act on advice to proscribe the Drua. Asif meanwhile was in Moscow, learning subversion and revolution.

Baquoos had no love for his half-brother, but made Asif Chief Minister in the hope that responsibility would temper the young man's fanatical Muslim ways. Asif hated Western influence in Bakar and his brother for controlling all dealings with commercial interests. The West only used Bakar for its resources and strategic position. But he stayed silent. One day he would depose Baquoos, seize the oil, lead a Muslim revolution, a Jihad against the hated Jews and restore the Arab world to its rightful owners.

Baquoos further incurred his brother's hatred when the King's English wife produced a son, Feisal Khaled bin Said, who automatically replaced Asif as heir to the throne. In 1971 Britain had withdrawn military protection. Baquoos was well able to defend the area with British weaponry, the Foreign Office had reported. The Treasury was delighted at the fiscal saving.

The young prince Feisal Khaled abhorred violence—mainly as a result of being kidnapped by a P.L.O. fringe group as a five-year-old. Asif had given the terrorists his blessings but proof was not forthcoming.

The King had paid the ransom not in the millions demanded, but in the blood of the boy's kidnappers. A young British officer leading four other men had snatched the young prince from under the noses of two hundred terrorists and inflicted terrible casualties.

Asif had been lucky. He decided to bide his

time. No longer did he vociferously oppose the King's continued support of the West, particularly at O.P.E.C. meetings and Arab summits. When the Shah fled Iran and the mullahs seized power, Asif did not utter a single word of support. Baquoos believed his half-brother had found wisdom. Asif had dismissed his Drua advisers and Bakari money, creamed off by Asif, no longer found its way into the coffers of terrorists. Asif had changed. The Western embassies in Bakar reported a new understanding between the King and his Chief Minister who was given more responsibility.

But Asif had not changed. He had secretly attended a meeting in Tehran aimed at the destabilization of the Gulf. Muslim fundamentalists were already at work in Kuwait. His presence at this meeting had been suspected by one of his staff. The man had telephoned the British Embassy in Raza wanting to speak to Barrett. But Ablett-Green had taken the call. The call had been recorded at the Chief Ministry by Asif's shadow, the Lebanese Habish. The German had been despatched to kill the informant and the young British diplomat. Asif could not allow any lapses. The wheels of his *coup d'état* were already in motion.

Now he had to ensure that once installed as

King, he could defend his government against the more powerful Saudi forces who might be tempted to counterstrike against him if they felt his espousal of the revolutionary cause threatened their own stability. For this purpose he required British political influence and weaponry. Which was why he had come to meet Charles, Seventh Viscount Penmayne.

Habish announced the arrival of a Rolls-Royce Silver Shadow bearing Penmayne and his personal assistant, Martin Brett. The Lebanese was a tall, dark man with a lean moustache and predatory blue eyes. Of shadowy antecedents, he had once trained as an economist at Prince Asif's old alma mater, Patrice Lumumba University. His economic education had gone no further than the production curve of a Kalashnikov rifle. A manipulator, clear-thinking and ruthless, he would arrange the death of an opponent and carry out the task himself. To outsiders he appeared a silent, somewhat subservient man who never spoke unless Asif addressed him. So neutrally polite was he in his dealings with anyone from Ministers to servants that people mistakenly assumed Habish to be part of the Royal furniture. Immaculately and expensively dressed, he smoked Sobranie cigarettes incessantly, even in his master's presence, and he moved around meetings like a silent ghost. Responsible for Asif's protection, he was accompanied by a young German who had a cigarette lighter that never worked.

Martin Brett was the first man through the door. Twenty-seven years old, slim and dressed like a tailor's dummy, he had initially been dismissed as a lightweight by Asif. The Prince had met similar public relations men, mouthpieces for the real power, public school ladies' men with flowery manners and obsequious attitudes. But this shifty-eyed old Etonian was a different breed. Someone had groomed him for real power. The young man knew exactly what he wanted and the most direct way of obtaining it. The preliminary discussions had taken place some weeks before in Bakar whither Brett had been dispatched by his master to bid for concessions on the lucrative Marine and Ekara oilfields and the Kariz mineral deposits. Asif had hinted that such concessions were not within his gift as Chief Minister but if the King were ever to abdicate it would be a different story.

Charles, Seventh Viscount Penmayne, Chairman of the ultramarine-blooded merchant bank, Penmayne Harcourt, had taken the hint and suggested further discussions which had culminated in this, the first personal meeting between himself and Asif.

The Chief Minister greeted Penmayne warmly. The introductions were soon over and coffee was taken. Asif signalled to Habish who handed Brett a document.

'The contract for your development company to build the three new hospital extensions in Ad Said. By way of a gesture of good faith.'

Charles Penmayne liked the twenty million pounds' worth of good faith. A silver-haired, grey-eyed man of fifty, he was dressed in a dark Savile Row three-piece pinstripe that accentuated a lean, hard, athletic frame. He ran three miles daily—jogging was a recreation for amateur businessmen pretending to be athletes. Brett had tried to keep up with him one morning and had to be chauffeured the last mile, exhausted. Penmayne smiled, a handsome, aristocratic smile that disguised a personality as hard as cut diamond and almost as many-sided.

'Your highness is most gracious,' Penmayne observed.

'As you know, Lord Penmayne, I would be pleased to deal further with you if my brother Baquoos did not control the concessions you require. Invariably he grants those concessions to the Aberinvest Corporation. At their renewal next month he will undoubtedly do the same.'

Get on with it, you unctuous little creep, Penmayne thought. State your price and see if I can match it. What is it? Bend a Minister's ear or set up an offshore slush fund to finance your revolution? Send you a clutch of Mayfair call girls for your harem or the Brigade of Guards to watch your back?

Asif signalled again to Habish who passed over a thin folder. Penmayne flicked through the document and smiled.

'So you require a Wolverine missile system and technical expertise in Bakar by the 27th of this month. And I gather from this document that you cannot approach the makers direct because they are a subsidiary of the Aberinvest group and the King deals personally with Aberinvest. You also have a slight problem in that the missile system is on restricted sale for Britain and the United States only at this stage.'

'Exactly,' Asif replied.

'So you want me to approach the Ministry of Defence, obtain clearance and some experts to work the thing and have it delivered to Bakar by the 27th of this month. Forgive me for being blunt, you don't want much, do you?'

Asif's brown eyes flashed angrily.

'Neither do you in the way of concessions.'

'Point taken.'

'So you can help me.'

'I think you can safely say that you will have your Wolverine.'

Penmayne's mind was working overtime. It could be done. Anything could be done if he put his mind to it, did not worry about the price and was not concerned about the legal niceties.

*   *   *

By 11.30 Penmayne was standing beneath the portrait of Penmayne's Harcourt's founder in his first-door office overlooking Lombard St. Algernon Penmayne had first opened the family merchant bank shortly after the South Sea Bubble burst. A soon-to-be-stilettoed rumour credited him with siphoning off a large proportion of the proceeds. Ennobled by George the Second in 1744, reputedly in return for a contribution to the Privy Purse (empty, it was said, after a public relations exercise to lead the troops at Dettingen), Algernon Penmayne bought nine thousand acres of Cotswold land near Cirencester and built the forty-room country house of Arlingford which was now his descendant's home but not his only residence.

Now, Charles, Seventh Viscount, controlled an empire—insurance, property, oil, real estate, mining and commodities, and even a Liberian shipping line, half of it laid up owing to excess world capacity. By nature he was a predator, stealing through the City jungle ready to pounce swiftly on unsuspecting lame ducks. And if the ducks were not lame—there were ways and means. A master of the dawn raid on any undervalued company with assets worth realizing, he allowed a string of personal assistants with their own companies funded by Penmayne Harcourt to take the political and social disapproval while he took forty-nine per cent of the profits.

Day-to-day decisions were left to the deputy chairman and to Martin Brett, a promising and malevolent young entrepreneur, while Penmayne oiled the wheels. Politically unambitious, he was reputed to donate vast sums to politics. One journalist had described him as the ultimate power broker and not too particular where the commission came from. The journalist had shortly afterwards received a redundancy notice. A newspaper proprietor owed Penmayne a favour and did not want to see valuable advertising revenue go elsewhere.

Brett arrived in the office to be given a whisky.

'Seen your arms broker friend?' Penmayne asked.

'Later today.'

'I don't trust that little wog. But you'd better invite him to Arlingford for the weekend. Say tomorrow at four pm. Then we can present him to my political influence. In the meantime, see if you can find out what the rush is for this Wolverine by the 27th. I'd like to have something on the swine. Take him out tonight to a casino, he'll like that.'

Brett had other plans for the evening. But Penmayne would not like to hear about those.

'And Martin, tow some sort of present along with you. Arabs like titled whores. Gives them a sense of vicarious revenge. Might give us some information.'

'Shall I acquire some shares for you? The concessions will make our own bullish when the news breaks.'

'I'll make my own arrangements thank you. Make sure no-one can shout Insider Trading.'

★   ★   ★

Brett did not stand up as the girl approached the restaurant table. A waiter with better training if not manners held the chair for her.

'Late,' Brett announced.

'Woman's privilege, darling.' The word

came out as 'daahling'.

    She took a cigarette from a slim gold case and waited for Brett to offer her a light. The waiter, a small Italian quick on his feet, already had a flickering Colibri in his hand.

    'Thank you,' she smiled, looking him up and down. The look brightened his day.

    She was tall, elegant, her blonde hair hung loosely over the shoulders of a dark-blue, coutured blazer. The white silk blouse was open three buttons down. Light brown eyes stared at Brett and a smile played on the corners of her wide mouth. Her perfume was prohibitively expensive and she was confident of her beauty, her breeding and underlying sexual aggression that occasionally broke to the surface. She knew it annoyed Brett so she played on it.

    'Pâté and chicken salad to follow. Glass of house wine. Now lovable reptile Brett, I haven't seen you around. Into schoolgirls now are we? You're turning into a cheapskate, darling. I lunch at the Savoy Grill, not some down-market spaghetti house, even if they do have beautiful waiters.'

    Brett did not rise to the bait. She flirted with the waiter who brought the pâté. Brett sipped his gin and tonic.

    'Finished flirting with the cooking oil?' he demanded.

'Thinking of doing more than flirting with him. So why buy me lunch?'

'We'd like you to do us a favour. A client of ours has an important visitor who could do with some well-bred, cultural company.'

'You're trying to procure little Vanessa for one of Charlie Penmayne's house parties are you? Old goat doesn't have the neck to ask me himself?'

Brett's hand clamped on the girl's knee underneath the table. He was hurting her. She winced.

'An emissary from the Gulf,' Brett smiled.

'All right, pax. Vanessa behaves herself.'

She rubbed the leg to restore some circulation then demanded:

'Not some oily little bazaar trader is he, masquerading as a friend to the West?'

'The real article. A powerful man.'

'Like in chopping heads off powerful?'

Brett nodded.

'Now you're talking. And I suppose as well as whore for you Vanessa has to put on her gumshoes and be inquisitive. It'll cost you.'

'There'll be a little extra something from Cartier in your Xmas stocking. Make sure you get it right.'

'I'll get it right,' she giggled.

*　　*　　*

Martin Brett parked the Aston Martin outside a block of flats overlooking Hyde Park. A light was on in his penthouse lounge and the curtains were drawn. It was 7.45pm and he had to wine and dine Asif at nine.

She was wearing his bathrobe and lying on the lambswool rug, a long left leg arched to reveal golden-tanned skin. A martini glass balanced between the slender fingers of her left hand while a cigarette smouldered in the long ebony holder in her right. Thirty-two, willowy, ash blonde, and married to someone else.

'I have to go out again,' he announced curtly.

'Screwing one of your hot little secretaries?'

'Entertaining one of my employer's clients.'

'What's it like to be a tame puppet, Martin darling?'

He was angry at the remark. His eyes seemed to change colour—now blue, now green. His eyes were the first thing about him she had noticed, that week-end at Arlingford. Smiling eyes, wicked eyes, ambitious eyes that had watched her swimming in the indoor pool early that Sunday morning when her husband had been summoned away the previous night. The rest of the guests were all fast asleep after a famous Saturday night of gourmet hospitality. She had emerged from the pool as he watched teasingly then took a towel and dried her as she lay on the sunbed. Soft, almost feminine hands had caressed her, nimbly unclasping the bikini. Strong, demanding hands had held her as they made love gently, firmly, then violently. She had seen the look in his eyes as he climbed off her. He had the same look in his eyes now.

'Bitchy remarks annoy me,' he laughed coldly, taking the cigarette from her hand. 'And you know you should not annoy me.'

He took the drink. The eyes were now arrogant. He was becoming angry.

'You do look macho. Done a good deal today?' she teased.

His hands seized her thighs, forcing them apart. His eyes were filled with vicious expectation. He tore the bathrobe open and forced her head back, kissing her violently. His weight crushed her and she struggled. The hands went to her breasts. Sharp pain seared through her whole body and she cried out. God he was rough. Brett, you bastard, you're hurting me. She fought him but he kept on driving into her hard. Brett, why is it like this with you? Yes, more, more, more.

Minutes later, she lay back, gasping.

'Cruel bastard,' she cried out.

He was lying on one elbow and laughing.

66

'You like it. You wouldn't be here otherwise.'

'Arrogant,' she giggled as he slapped her backside hard.

'Time to go and do the boss's dirty work. I've had his wife so now I'll try and have his job.'

'You'd never let on, would you?' she asked, a curious frightened look in her eyes. 'I think he knows I have lovers, but bedding the employees is very bad form.'

'So how did you get out tonight?' Brett demanded.

'Someone important coming to dine. Said I was out with a girlfriend. He expects me in the small hours. I'll wait for you to come back if you won't be long.'

'By twelve. I've lined up some amusements for the client. I think he'll like her.'

'You keep your hands to yourself.'

'Listen, Lady Annabel Penmayne, you get into bed and wait.'

CHAPTER SIX

Charles Penmayne's Portman Square town house had belonged to the family since the idea occurred in their architect's head. The butler greeted Gareth Llewellyn Jones at the door and ushered him across the hallway into a drawing room that boasted a glittering chandelier, Chippendale furniture and Persian carpets. Llewellyn Jones felt immersed in the elegance of a bygone age, cocooned from the twentieth century. Even the heavy velvet curtains excluded London's darkness.

Penmayne was seated at a Louis Quinze escritoire, working on some papers. He greeted his guest as the butler poured dry sherry. Llewellyn Jones always took dry sherry and the butler always remembered. Penmayne waved his guest to a chair and then sat opposite him. The frilled cuffs of the dress shirt, his silver-grey hair and sharp, decisive jawline conjured up in his guest's mind the perfect picture of an eighteenth-century merchant prince. The carriage clock struck eight as Penmayne announced:

'Annabel will not be joining us, L.J. I believe it is her night for seeing her lover.'

Llewellyn Jones was always taken aback at Penmayne's almost brutal directness. Silence was the most diplomatic reply.

'Very statesmanlike silence, L.J. How are the corridors of Power?'

'Like the starting gates at Newmarket.'

Penmayne smiled. It was time to indulge in some mental swordplay.

'I hear the security services are being reorganized, not before time. Lots of nasty little Red pansies and child molesters being winkled out of the closet. I was up at College last week. Senior Common Room very aghast at all the dead wood you have cut jockeying for fellowships.'

Llewellyn Jones parried the humorous threat.

'And the City, still bullish?'

'Treasury seem to be working the oracle for the dealers. About time too, considering this is the first decent government since Salisbury. Got to keep them in, L.J.'

'As you know, I never offer an opinion.'

'But if the other lot get in, you'll be out on your well-padded arse, won't you? They do not love you for leaking to the Press that news about their doe-eyed nancy boy Lefty and his Russian schoolboy chum in Split.'

Llewellyn Jones was about to reply that the disclosure had been mere expediency when the muffled metallic echoes of a dinner gong sounded.

The dining room was the drawing room's high-ceilinged twin. A small table in comparison to the size of the room; Llewellyn Jones realized it was not the usual dining table. The meal was to be confidential. No shouting from end to end of a banqueting bench.

Avocado stuffed with prawn was served on Wedgwood by two attractive housemaids, a light hock in Waterford crystal goblets by the butler. The staff then withdrew. Conversation was political, mainly about Europe. Sole bonne femme arrived immediately Penmayne rang a small silver bell positioned six inches from his left hand. The staff withdrew once more and the conversation turned to industry. Llewellyn Jones expected the proposition he knew to be in the offing with the sweet, but Penmayne pre-empted him. It came with the second glass of claret and the Chateaubriand. The butler had left a plain white envelope on a silver salver near Llewellyn Jones's left hand.

Penmayne was being theatrical, not for the first time in their long acquaintanceship. Both had used each other's positions to mutual benefit in the past. The morality or even the legality of the fact had never been mentioned by either man.

'Something towards the future,' Penmayne announced. 'I need a Wolverine missile system by the 27th of this month for export to a discreet destination. Can you provide the necessary paperwork and stop any silly questions being asked by nosey persons from media and suchlike?'

Llewellyn Jones sipped his claret and

thought rapidly. Wolverine was on a restricted list. He knew. On his advice it had been placed there pending a N.A.T.O. re-evaluation.

'Don't go all stuffy, L.J. Open the blasted envelope.'

Inside was a pass document giving one Andrew Lloyd access to a Zurich bank account containing one hundred thousand pounds sterling. The Welshman smiled.

'I think you had better elaborate, Charles.'

'Bakar, in the Persian Gulf, sorry you know where the place is, require a Wolverine. If I get them one I get in on the goodies. Jobs, L.J. Exports. Money for us. Only my contact wants the deal kept quiet.'

Llewellyn Jones was thinking about the report Unit Alpha had sent in on Bakar. After reading that he had sent for a Foreign Office update on the Gulf situation with particular reference to Bakar. All was politically quiet, economy expanding but Britain short of contracts there. Aberinvest Corporation were the favoured party there. And they were Swiss based for the purposes of the exercise. Arms were already supplied in accordance with the terms of the 1971 treaty. Hawk jets, Scorpion tanks, Rapier missiles. What did Unit Alpha know about Bakar?

'Didn't know you had interests there. I

71

thought Aberinvest were receivers of all Bakar bounty, Charles.'

'Not now, old boy. Wyatt is dead and the King might be losing his touch. But they'll keep it in the family.'

'I didn't hear that, Charles.'

'So you don't want to hear about my safety device for catching you if there is some kind of row.'

'Such as?'

'A seat on my board, a salary of two hundred and fifty thousand per annum tax free for the next five years. Plus the usual block of equity in trust for the children. Say forty thousand A shares currently at £4.97. They will double within twelve months.'

'It is going to get dirty, isn't it,' Llewellyn Jones observed. 'Tell me more.'

It was past midnight when he left Portman Square, glowing with best Napoleon and the comfortable feeling of being very, very rich. He did not notice a thin, philosophical man in an Austin Allegro taking photographs with a camera fitted with an image-intensifying lens.

*   *   *

A C.I.A. controller had once described Alexander Hamilton Coburn as a human stick insect. The description bore no resemblance

72

to his physical appearance but referred to his ability to blend into any background, from the jungles of South East Asia to the grey, depressing streets of East Berlin.

Coburn walked through the door of Martin Brett's penthouse exactly five minutes after Lady Annabel Penmayne had left.

'Martin, you sure are no gentleman,' Coburn observed, 'letting ass like that find its own cab home.'

'Discretion, Alex, is a gentleman's watchword. Tonic water?'

Coburn settled himself comfortably in the lounge. A thirty-nine-year-old, balding, chubby New Yorker of medium height and twenty pounds overweight, he could have been an overfed corporate lawyer or a broker who took four martinis before dinner. To casual acquaintances he described himself as something on Wall St dealing in negotiable securities. Well, he rationalized, arms were negotiable securities.

Coburn received the tonic water and the file on the Wolverine missile system simultaneously.

'I want one of those set up, and working with trained personnel, in the Gulf by the 27th. And I don't want the makers to know of its destination.'

'My Aunt Luella's fanny you do,' Coburn

replied. 'This system is Brits and Uncle Sam only. I had to use Company influence to get in on the trials. What do I do, hide one under my coat?'

'So there are problems. Enumerate.'

'One—restricted system. You'll need end user certificates and export licences. Two—availability. Three—a rapid approach from a private outfit will look suspicious. The timescale is wrong. You don't buy this stuff like cornflakes.'

'Solutions?' Brett asked.

'One—legitimize derestriction with the politicians. Two—use a vital executive in the manufacturers. Bribe or threaten him to keep his mouth shut. You don't need loose talk. Availability you can't buck. By the way, it'll cost.'

'Can you handle it for us?'

'With a great deal of help.'

'Good. You can come and meet my employer tomorrow. A real English country house party. I'll pick you up around midday. Where are you staying?'

'I'll come here,' Coburn replied. 'Who is your employer?'

'Tomorrow Alex, all will be revealed.'

★　　★　　★

Coburn already knew that Brett worked for Penmayne Harcourt. He also knew Charles Penmayne. The association went back to 1975 when Coburn had first left the C.I.A. and had helped Penmayne deliver a consignment of arms to a rebel faction in a newly-independent African state. The rebels had become the government and Penmayne had become the first Western banker to do well in a now prosperous one-party state. Which had all happened a long time before Martin Brett joined Penmayne Harcourt.

Coburn had spent ten years with the Company, serving in Laos, Cambodia, Chile and Berlin. He might have become a deputy director one day had it not been for the post-Watergate crisis of confidence that brought Congressional enquiries into the C.I.A. One of these had uncovered some private work Coburn had done on the side for an American conglomerate. Going private had its advantages. He would broke politically sensitive arms deals which could embarrass an Administration. He would set up an internal security system for a Latin American country who needed Uncle Sam's help but not the United Nations' censure of its withdrawal of human rights. And whenever his deals might be contrary to his former employer's interests, Coburn knew exactly how to play the system.

Coburn took tonic water on the sprawling terrace at Arlingford. Penmayne had sent Brett to ensure that Prince Asif and Habish were being settled comfortably into their rooms. He had promised to join them for afternoon tea which would be taken on the terrace in an hour. Meanwhile, he wanted to talk to Coburn, alone.

They walked around velvet green lawns and down the wide stone staircase towards the lake. Coburn wondered how many gardeners Penmayne employed to keep the ten acres of ground immediately adjacent to the Georgian country house looking like an advert for *Homes and Gardens*. He even found himself unwilling to discard his cigarette stub in case it looked out of place.

'You've seen our visitors, Alex. You can guess the proposition. Interested?'

'How much?'

'I thought a fee of one hundred thousand pounds for securing the Wolverine, set up and working in Bakar. I would then be prepared to offer a further fee of one hundred thousand per annum for the next three years as an insurance against my oily little olive-shaped friend Asif going back on his deal.'

Penmayne smiled. Coburn replied:

'Chickenshit.'

'Now what did you have in mind, Alex?'

76

'First the Wolverine. Brett briefed me fully on the situation. The company that makes it, Tectrokite, is a subsidiary of the Aberinvest Corporation who are very big in Bakar. If they suspect where it is going, there'll be questions. We have to move fast to obtain one and ship before they catch on. That could be tricky. But someone might have to get hurt if they don't co-operate. I'm talking about a full covert operation here and possible executive action.'

'If you mean you might have to kill someone please say so. Executive action is a phrase open to several interpretations. Just don't get caught. Continue.'

'Right now, I'm very big in Libya which gives me a handle on Asif. His son is over there studying to become another mad little Muslim revolutionary. I can have him covered every step of the way by one of my boys out there. I also have a team put into Bakar to work the Wolverine and run Asif's security. First wrong move from Asif and click, click. This costs you, Charles. One million up front, one million per annum for the next three years. Alex is getting too old for all this nonsense. I want a quiet life on some island beach, and a parcel of money in Gnomesville, Switzerland.'

Penmayne thought carefully for a moment.

The insurance proposition was tempting. He smiled:

'All right, Alex. But no foul-ups as you say. And you help me sell the proposition to Asif.'

Both men had just rounded a corner of the orangery when Brett appeared:

'You ought to hear this. The lovely Vanessa has just told me that Asif is planning an assassination in London on the 27th.'

'Give her a big kiss from me,' Penmayne instructed, smiling at the American. Brett caught Penmayne's glance which said 'Thank you, Martin, you can go now.'

As Coburn watched Brett walk away he lit another cigarette and said casually:

'Did you know he was screwing your wife?'

Penmayne's horrifed look told Coburn he had just broken bad news. Coburn had himself broken one of his own age-old rules. Never tell a man his wife is having an affair. Either he knows and hates you for making his silence cowardly or he does not. In which case he spends money on lawyers and ends up a very unhappy man who no longer requires your friendship. But Coburn did not trust Brett. There were already too many players in the game. And Charles Penmayne was a man who hated strangers touching any of his possessions.

'Is he really?' Penmayne remarked

nonchalantly. 'Thank you Alex, we'll have to put a stop to his little games. Pity, my vet is on holiday this week.'

Coburn saw the look of malicious hatred in Penmayne's eyes as he spoke. The American drew heavily on his cigarette and said no more.

★ ★ ★

Alpha looked at the photographs. The flat was in darkness except for the pool of light an old anglepoise lamp cast over the table, showing up the scratch marks and the lack of polish on the stained surface. Alpha lit another cigarette and looked up at Pavel. Tuesday 21st September, 2am.

Pavel had done a first-rate job. The photographs were all dated and arranged in order. There was no doubt as to where Llewellyn Jones had been or with whom he had been meeting. Pavel had produced an itinerary. Friday night, dinner at a house in Portman Square, owner Viscount Penmayne. Saturday night and Sunday, week-end at a large country house near Cirencester. Other guests had included a young man, two young women and two Arabs. Pavel's associate Gador had made some discreet enquiries of a gardener at Arlingford in the village pub. He had been told to get lost. Lord Penmayne's business was his own. Alpha did not recognize either Arab, although the Ma'an 500 S.E.L. limousine could provide a clue. The registration number was noted in Pavel's report.

On Monday, Llewellyn Jones had gone to his office. Close surveillance had proved impossible and on two occasions Pavel had decided not to follow the official car. During working hours, Llewellyn Jones was escorted by plainclothes members of the S.A.S. Alpha was disappointed but could understand Pavel's caution.

'We need more men,' the thin, philosophical man had announced. Alpha had to agree. But there was no-one else he could trust.

The following morning he telephoned Lansbury. Three consecutive rings followed by hanging up the phone and dialling again. Just in case anyone was tapping Lansbury's phone. It was agent rules, now, no messing around. Lansbury walked to a call box two streets away and waited for Alpha to dial the call box number. Lansbury made a note of the vehicle number and asked a friend in the Metropolitan Police to check the vehicle's ownership. Not an official request, more for old time's sake. He waited around the call box for Alpha's return call. Vehicle registered to the Bakari embassy.

'By the way, I have had a reply from my enquiry through our friends in the Middle East. You'll be pleased to know that Mr Wyatt is on his way back.'

CHAPTER SEVEN

The helicopter picked us up from the beach at Freshwater West. Fallon's people had sent over a Sea King from the North Sea run. Sea Kings never look out of place in Pembrokeshire. The Services run them from Brawdy on Air Sea Rescue. I did not want any attention drawn to our arrival.

The beach was deserted on a clean, windswept evening. The surf rolled in angrily, crashing and foaming up the beige sand. An inflatable launch had brought us in from Sean's boat that lay half a mile off-shore. We had wet feet and Peter Fallon, the razor-cut, blond whizz-kid who ran Aberinvest, was still feeling seasick. The three of us stretched out in the monster's metallic belly as the Sea King lifted off. In twenty minutes we would land at Ty Newydd.

'I feel like some kind of illegal immigrant,'

Fallon protested. He had not taken kindly to sneaking back into the country. Concorde and V.I.P. lounges are more his style.

'Wrong colour,' came a voice from the corner, its owner's location pinpointed only by the lighted Gauloise.

'Bloody Hungarian,' Fallon complained teasingly. 'They should have sent you back long ago. Can't think why we brought you.'

'He can handle a gun,' I replied.

'That's what I love about you, Wyatt,' Fallon announced. 'You always look on the bright side.'

Then he lapsed into silence. He knew Johnny had found the bomb someone put on our plane and that it was sensible to let everyone think we had disappeared over the North Atlantic. Canada was a safe place to hide. Although he found it difficult to run Aberinvest through the anonymous offshore outfit he was prepared to try. But when I decided it was time to come back he wanted a place on the boat. I didn't think the bomber had meant to kill anyone except me and possibly Johnny. But a bomb is an indiscriminate weapon and there were three women on that plane as well as ourselves and the pilot. I don't subscribe to all that political terrorist crap about there being no such thing as an innocent civilian. They call a different tune when one of them gets banged up in solitary and his visiting rights are cancelled. That is deprivation of human rights!

I had come back prematurely because the Mossad had tracked me down to deliver a message. You can hide from anyone except the Mossad. They practised on Eichmann and got it perfect stalking the guys who killed their Munich Olympic athletes.

The message contained a codeword and could have been written by Sir Philip Moresby's ghost. It said simply: YOUR VALHALLA ENQUIRY RECEIVED. FRIDAY CONFERENCE ESSENTIAL. OUR EUROPEAN REPRESENTATIVE AT THE LANSBURY WILL ARRANGE VENUE FOR ALPHA CONSOLIDATED HOLDINGS PROJECT.

Which meant that a private, deadly recluse known as Alpha was the executor of some kind of legacy bequeathed by Moresby. Richard Lansbury, Director of Operations, M.I.5, was the cut-out. By implication, something was still very rotten in the state of Security.

Not my problem, except that two days before he died I told Moresby that if he ever needed my help again to pass the word— Friday. My response would be Valhalla.

When I heard he had died, my first reaction was that the boys in the K.G.B. had taken their revenge over the Nimrod business. I had shot dead one of their top nasties and some lesser fry. They had started it by framing Moresby and then killing a civilian and threatening his surviving family. I'd have called it quits where we left it. But with Moresby gone I thought it safer to take a long holiday. Before take-off, we found the bomb. They were trying to kill me and did not care who else they took out. So I arranged the wreath. Valhalla was an appropriate valediction for Moresby. It also let anyone he trusted enough to know its significance realize that I was still around.

I had spent some hours considering my next move when the message had arrived. Although I wanted to stay where I was, I had given Moresby my word. He must have thought Alpha was going to need help, otherwise he would have let my promise die with him. And you cannot break your word. Nor can you duck the responsibilities your word commits you to, however dangerous.

We landed at Ty Newydd at 9.30pm. The air was cold and clean and I could catch a whiff of the sea breeze coming in from the Cardiganshire coast almost two miles away. This green and pleasant land, as the poet said.

I had bought the estate in the days when I ran Aberinvest Corporation. I lease most of it to the Company for conferences, week-ends and as an out-of-the-limelight place important people can come incognito. In these security-conscious times it rates as a very safe establishment. The security staff are experts—mostly from my old mob. Closed-circuit T.V., infra-red, tactile and sonic alarms cover the ten acres of grounds. Then there are the dogs: two sniffer Alsatians and the brothers Khan, Genghis & Kublai, two of the friendliest psychopathic Dobermanns any intruder could wish to meet.

The Home Farm, set in six thousand acres, has its own stables and a string of company-sponsored horses, Fallon's tax-loss play-things. There is also a helicopter pad at the bottom of the garden. It makes a change from fairies and I got used to travelling that way as a soldier. For the top business executive it is the only way, faster than an unreliable train and very difficult to kidnap. A helicopter can land almost anywhere, depending on the pilot's skills. And Aberinvest pilots must be the best in the world—ex Royal Navy.

My suite of rooms is on the first floor, overlooking the grounds and the farmland. On the way up, I bumped into Mrs Eluned Harries, my middle-aged, motherly housekeeper, who burst into unrestrained tears when she saw me. No-one had told her we were alive. Cover had to be preserved. Housekeepers are prone to gossip. I extricated myself from her welcome and walked into my study. Johnny had decided it was not safe to return to my cottage at Dysant. A pity, because the woods are peaceful and the Falls Pool is sometime home to the wiliest salmon in Wales. I own the land for a mile all around. It is leased out to the local farmers, but they respect my privacy and I respect their professional need to use the soil. Dysant would have to wait until I had seen Alpha.

Johnny came up and accepted a whisky. He had watched my back for years, that seventeen-stone, quarry-faced Hungarian— one of my very few friends. The knife scar still showed across his forehead and the close-cropped dark hair was beginning to show flecks of grey. Former brother officer, mercenary, faster than deadly with gun, fist or knife, he was still alive at forty-eight. At six foot four he towered above most people, my five foot nine included. He had left Hungary back in 1956 after the only engagement he ever lost—against the Red Army. I suspected the name he went under, Jan Szczelskowski, was Polish. I never asked the reason and he was known to all as Johnny, mainly because no-one we knew well had a degree in either Polish or Hungarian.

He savoured the whisky and sat in the armchair opposite my desk. I lit one of my thin Havanas and waited for the question followed by the inevitable warning:

'You sure you want to do this?' he asked. 'Not getting any younger, remember. Boys today are probably better than they were and the odds are getting shorter all the time on you getting killed.'

I love a man who thinks positively. His logic is that of a man who rationalizes that the more often you cross a street, the more likely it is you will be hit by a bus. You can never argue against the actuarial figures. But you can stay lucky.

I poured myself a whisky and raised my glass: 'Don't let the bastards grind you down.'

He grinned: 'I'll drink to that. When do we move?'

'After I have slept. I'm jet lagged.'

*   *   *

Midday, Wednesday 22nd September, we were breathing the monoxide poisoning that passes for London air. I hate cities, the noise, the traffic and the rat packs of crowds scurrying nowhere. Lansbury was playing a game of tag around the lunchtime stripperamas and the drinking clubs. Each

87

one we visited he had left ten minutes earlier with a message to follow to another one. So he was being very careful. Because every time we left each salubrious establishment a Volkswagen Golf followed us at a discreet distance. Either the opposition was short-handed or it was Lansbury's man watching our backs. I guessed Lansbury's man. Unless any opposition was on a shoe-string budget there would have been a squadron of watchers.

At three we were in the kind of place you never take elderly aunts from Bournemouth. Cheap vinyl, red carpets, down-market bouncers from the local Borstal and low lighting so you can't see the short change. It had the stale aroma of girly bars the world over—tobacco, cheap perfume and clammy sweat. The floor show was a mile the wrong side of obscenity and the whisky tasted like the flat ginger ale it probably was.

The dirty raincoat brigade were ostrich-necked at the far end of the bar. Next to them the simple tourists were being relieved of their money by fixed-smile hostesses and cartel-priced fizzy water that came in champagne bottles. Two fifth-rate heavies in off-the-peg monkey suits were leaning on the bar. As I moved towards a corner stool Johnny was beside me and stiffened slightly at a signal

88

from one of the apes who had noted our arrival. But the only trouble that materialized was the company of two late-teen girls wearing too much make-up and almost topless dresses.

'Hello,' the blonde's voice was pitched artificially low. She had probably seen all the Bogart movies on T.V. and thought this was the way to do it. Cash register eyes noted my expensive suit, Turnbull and Asser shirt and the John Lobb shoes. Her friend was telling Johnny what a big good-looking fellow he was.

'Like to buy me a drink?' the blonde asked.

I almost told her that in these feminist times a working girl was supposed to buy her own. But I never gratuitously insulted a lady, even if she did look like a hooker.

'Do you know the proprietor of this wadi?' I asked Johnny. He nodded an affirmative reply.

'Tell Aristide Briand behind the bar two large ones of the proper stuff and whatever the ladies are having. Then we can sit down and wait for our Uncle Richard.'

Thirty seconds later the barman, a gay character in silk cravat and French-style shirt, received the message. I wandered over to the corner table and invited the girls to sit with their backs to the room because I wanted the corner seat.

89

'I'm Cynthia,' Johnny's friend announced.

Her friend smiled at me.

'I'm Louise.'

'He's Hungarian and I'm not,' I replied, nodding in Johnny's direction.

They started drinking the champagne and were surprised it was the real article. But you get what you pay for in this world. The blonde could have been attractive without the red lipstick and the excess mascara and she was under the impression I might be laying out some more money in her direction if she appealed to my wallet, and my vanity.

'Not your sort of place, this,' she observed.

'No. But the Queen is still at Balmoral, or so I'm told, so tea at the Palace is out.'

They both thought that was funny. Then Lansbury emerged from a knot of amateur flashers and signalled it was time to leave.

'But I can see Prince Philip may be back and I have been summoned. This has been very pleasant, ladies, and we must do it again one day soon.'

Louise held my hand disappointedly as I passed her. I smiled farewell and followed Lansbury's tall frame towards the exit. In my right hand was a card with the girl's telephone number on it. Even the working girls went in for professional marketing in hard economic times.

'How is your security?' Lansbury asked as we re-entered daylight.

'Good enough to notice your tail in the Golf,' I replied.

Johnny drove the Sierra. Lansbury had his old briar pipe clenched between his teeth. He looked more like a bereaved spaniel than ever as he told how Alpha had come to him the previous Friday with a story he would never have believed if he had not been four sheets in the wind and no longer employed. There was a copy of Moresby's legacy, a straight computer print-out which could have been forged. Moresby's inimitable style scotched that suspicion. The word was: 'Watch Llewellyn Jones and events in Bakar.' The only trustworthy contacts were Sir Russell Beauchamp and yours truly.

It was one hell of a story. The difficulty in dealing with Intelligence people is sorting out the good guys from the bad guys. Because they all play the same game and often employ the same tactics. They will invert the truth to confuse you, and fabricate fairy tales the Brothers Grimm would have been proud of to cover themselves and drop you right in the treatment works. I had first met Lansbury

91

fifteen years before and he had always played straight with me. Besides, he was scared and carrying a gun. Most ex-coppers dislike firearms and Lansbury was no exception. Yet here he was, dodging around the dives of Soho with a short-barrelled Ruger Security Six under his coat.

The meet with Alpha was scheduled for four at a house in Bayswater. Lansbury had been given the address by Alpha over a payphone so security was tight. Everyone was playing safe. Not a bad idea with Gareth Llewellyn Jones's name on the scorecard. I had met him once for lunch at his club; not a social occasion, he wanted something. I trusted him about as far as I could throw the House of Commons at Division time on a busy night.

We parked the Sierra a street away. Bayswater is very familiar territory to Johnny. He once had a girlfriend there. So I sent him to look for the back door. It was one of those tall Victorian houses where you expect to see an aspidistra in the ground-floor front window and have the bell answered by a retired spinsterly schoolteacher surrounded by well-fed cats and knitting bags. Lansbury rang the doorbell while I waited to one side. Old house-clearance habits die hard. Never stand in front. The chances are some bastard has booby-trapped the other side.

A woman answered. She knew Lansbury.

'Come in, Mr Lansbury. Bring your friend with you.'

Not the retired spinster but a girl in her early thirties, five six with close-cropped blonde hair and the brightest emerald eyes I had ever seen. Alpha you old fox, I like your housekeeper. More magnetic than beautiful. Maybe it was the boots, the tight leather trousers and the roll-neck sweater that did it, but she looked like a girl who could handle herself. As she closed the door behind us and stood with her back to it, a hard, calculating look crossed her wilful face and I knew we had a problem. There was nothing I could do about it because I was not carrying. Anyway, Lansbury was in front of me and partially blocked my line of sight.

The two men appeared simultaneously. One from a doorway in the long entrance hall, the other on the top of the stairs. They both had short Smith & Wessons pointed at us. They looked trained and useful. Lansbury must have flipped because his hand was reaching across for the Ruger. I clamped my hand on his left wrist before he could get to the gun.

'What the hell?' he exclaimed.

Over my shoulder I could see the girl

holding a Remington double derringer that had miraculously appeared down the sleeve of her roll-neck sweater. Very proficient.

'Doc Holliday you're not, Richard,' I advised. 'And I expect they already have enough colanders in the kitchen.'

Always try and inject some levity into the proceedings, even if no-one appreciates it. Gives you time to think. The first man holstered his gun and moved forward to take Lansbury's pistol. I watched the girl. Those eyes were hard and the smile unfriendly. Covered by two guns and three people we were well outnumbered. Where the hell was that bloody Hungarian? Send him round the back way and he gets locked out.

The girl had taken her eyes off me. Movement at the top of the stairs distracted her. The derringer came up as she shouted a warning. Johnny dropped the man at the top of the stairs with his broadsword-edged left hand to the man's neck.

'Charge, Lansbury,' I shouted and grabbed the girl's gunwrist, my fingers feeling for the pressure point above her wrist. The Remington clattered to the floor as I put an S.A.S. necklock on her. She struggled and tried to elbow me in the stomach. But I had used the hold where you jam your hip into the small of your opponent's back. She had no chance.

'Cool it, or I snap your lovely neck,' I ordered.

She would not be told. She tried running her heel down my shin. So I put my left hand on to her left breast. Sexual moves in unarmed combat almost always throw women. They don't expect you to fight foul. I always do. It's the only way to win. She went limp as if shrinking away from something horrible. I felt the judo tap on my arm—the submission signal.

Lansbury had flattened his man with a quick right cross. He collected the hardware. I still held the girl. I felt comfortable with her against me.

'Miz Vennaway from Special Services,' Lansbury announced. 'Put her down, Wyatt. She doesn't like men.'

Which was a pity. I released the hold and before she could move out of range slapped her backside.

'Rude to point guns before you've been introduced,' I remonstrated. She glared back and rubbed her throat. I took the two .41 calibre bullets from the breech of the derringer Lansbury gave me and handed her the empty gun.

'Nifty piece of hardware,' I observed. 'Where is the tenant of this establishment?'

'Francis,' she ordered Lansbury's punchbag. 'Look after Cadogan.' She looked upstairs to where Johnny still stood, the big .45 Colt automatic never wavering from her breastbone. I nodded to him. He holstered the gun and picked up the fallen Cadogan like a bear picks up a recalcitrant cub.

'Come with me, Mr Wyatt,' she ordered. 'You too, Lansbury. The tenant is upstairs.'

We followed her up the staircase. Lansbury muttered:

'Lovely rear end on it, Wyatt.'

'View from the front is fair,' I replied.

In a first-floor room overlooking the street, someone had arranged a black plastic sheet in the middle of the floor to cover a human-sized object. Blood and brain matter had been spattered liberally around the surrounding ten feet of carpet. A faint smell of cordite lingered in the room, mingling with Vennaway's perfume. The mixture seemed appropriate.

There were two brass cartridge cases that glowed a burnished yellow in the electric light of the room. The heavy curtains had been drawn closed. I had this premonition before the girl drew back the plastic sheet with the words:

'If either of you are squeamish, don't look. But I would like to know who this man is.'

I remembered his physical shape only

vaguely and the dark hair more definitely. I would have recognized his face if I had seen it again. But the corpse had no face, only the remnants of an outline. The space at the front between the ears was a bloody, gaping mess.

'Jesus Christ,' Lansbury swore and had to make an effort not to turn away. The girl was waiting for me to throw up but I disappointed her. In six years of soldiering I had seen a lot of bodies with no faces. You never get used to it but after the first few times you learn to hang on to your breakfast.

She was looking down at the shape of what had once been a deadly recluse called Alpha. I noticed the gold ring on the little finger on his left hand—an unusual ring, with an ecclesiastical seal set in it. The cross of Lorraine topped by a crown and the Latin inscription. Este Fidelis. Be faithful. You tried Alpha, hell you tried.

'May I?' Lansbury asked, and took a pencil from his pocket.

'Forensic are on the way over,' Vennaway replied. 'Put it back in the exact position.'

The ex-copper had reverted to type. He lifted one of the cartridge cases and examined it. Then he held it in front of me.

'Automatic,' he observed.

You did not have to be Sherlock Holmes to deduce that fact. Rimless cartridge, slight scratch marks on the brass. Also, it had been ejected and left in the position where it had been thrown from the gun, a .45 calibre automatic that took an Auto Colt Pistol cartridge. Two shots. A professional killing. Except they had left the shell cases behind. Obviously they were not worried about someone finding the murder weapon.

'Forty-five, Auto Colt Pistol,' I confirmed. 'Heavy bullets, probably hollow point to make that mess.'

'Ring any bells, Mr Lansbury?' Vennaway asked.

'Yes. Usual Moscow Centre method for disciplining traitors. Department Five trademark. Dum-dum bullets to the face.'

'Exactly,' Vennaway agreed. She was standing, arms crossed, watching me.

'So, gentlemen, what are you doing here?'

'Visiting,' I replied.

'Your man on the stairs carries a big auto. Forty-five, Mr Wyatt?'

I looked down at the body. Whoever had shot Alpha shot him from the window side of the room. He must have known his killer.

'Not more than two hours ago,' Lansbury suggested.

'Leaves my man out,' I announced. 'He was with me, and half the alcoholics in this town, doing the rounds of the down-market boozers.'

'Dressed like you are, Mr Wyatt?'

'We country yokels always dress up when we come to the big city. I had to buy a new pair of wellies for the occasion.'

'So you don't know who he is?'

'Do you?'

'Why do you think I'm asking you?' she replied.

The emerald eyes never wavered. Either Vennaway was telling the truth or she was a very practised and polished liar.

CHAPTER EIGHT

The next move should have been for someone to call the police. But the funny people hate size twelve feet worse than those awkward questions in Parliament. Positive vetting has such a high failure rate, so the forensic team was private enterprise. Then a squad of searchers arrived and started tearing the house apart.

Vennaway made no comment about how she came to be there. She did warn us not to contravene the Official Secrets Act by mentioning what we had seen to any third party.

'You can go now,' she announced, showing us the door. 'But I want to see you all again, separately.'

'Go jump in the Thames,' Lansbury grunted. Being familiar with the law, he knew his rights. With dozens of them and only three of us I felt the invitation to be provocative, but Vennaway ignored him.

'I'm at my best around midnight,' Johnny remarked. 'You can come and tuck me up in bed any time.'

'If Mr Wyatt lets you out,' she replied, coldly.

A charming personality, Vennaway.

'No smart remarks from you, Mr Wyatt?'

'My scriptwriter has arthritis. I'll be in touch when he improves. Your number?'

'My office number,' she emphasized, handing me a card.

The door closed behind us and we were out in the street. Vennaway believed in putting people firmly in their place.

'Calculating little dyke,' Lansbury muttered, then turning to me. 'They've killed that poor bastard and why? Because he knew something else rotten in the system. Us next, I expect.'

Not if I had anything to do with it. I lit a thin Havana and walked back to the Sierra. Johnny was checking the car for unauthorized devices attached in our absence. He found one: a radio transmitter, small and magnetized, to fit under the bodywork and emit bleeping signals to tell someone where we were.

We left it in the cistern of a public convenience at Queensway tube station.

*   *   *

We were gathered in the top-floor office of the Aberinvest building near St Paul's Churchyard. The Press were baying at the door because they wanted any update on the conference Fallon had given at midday to announce our survival from the plane crash. The television boys were gathered in the car park, all cameras, duffle coats and cord trousers, sheltering from a cold breeze behind the outside broadcast van.

I read the legacy again. Llewellyn Jones under suspicion but facts not proved. Watch events in Bakar and then the report about the death of a young Mr Ablett-Green in Ad Said which looked kosher cardiac failure but Alpha had been suspicious enough to send Llewellyn Jones a copy. Then someone had killed Alpha. And Vennaway had been at the meet to greet us. Janus alias someone called Beauchamp had also been party to Moresby's suspicions and we all knew Janus was a two-faced Roman. Well, Lansbury didn't till I pointed it out to him.

He sat there, occasionally fortifying himself with Scotch from the directors' drinks cabinet. Johnny was sitting in a swivel chair, gently rotating himself through forty-five degrees and saying nothing. I just wished I was a trained detective, instead of some wayward ex-soldier who couldn't find his way out of a police station without a map.

'Alpha was a Hungarian, wasn't he?' Johnny asked Lansbury, more for confirmation than in hope of learning something new.

'More than likely. He did not officially exist. Moresby's joker, remember, the man who watched his back.'

'And Moresby ran S.I.S. Eastern Europe once upon a time,' I observed.

Johnny handed me a note and walked towards the door.

'Be careful,' I ordered.

He was going to look up a few old émigré chums. If Alpha did not exist he could not use British service personnel for his observation on Llewellyn Jones. Who would he use? Probably someone he trusted from the old days. Sound thinking, Johnny. Not just an ugly face.

'I'll pay Janus a visit,' Lansbury suggested.

'No,' I replied. 'You're former service personnel. You could have an accident. We leave Janus alone for a while. Where is your wife?'

'Couple of ex-mates are keeping an eye on her up North.'

'Go and join her. That way you're still close enough to be useful. But shift the location. Aberinvest have some remote farms up there on the Dales. If I hide you at Ty Newydd someone might go looking for you. Not that they'd get you but I might have to leave my lads a bit thin on the ground down there which means shooting to kill. My local police chums would not want that.'

'I don't duck out,' Lansbury replied.

'You're walking evidence. If I don't make it you have the option. Leave home or get stuck in.'

'And you?'

'I'm going hunting. But first I want to know the ground rules. So I'll ask Vennaway.'

'Watch her, Wyatt. She is viperous.'

'I have my snake antidote,' I replied.

★　　　★　　　★

I rang the number Vennaway had given me. At six-thirty I did not expect a reply. Then a

103

cold, businesslike voice said:

'Yes?'

Enthusiasm for the sound of my voice meant it had to be Vennaway.

'Wyatt. We should talk. Where would you like to dine?'

'On my own,' she replied.

'I know why our mutual acquaintance had an accident.'

'Go on.'

'We'll try the Etoile D'Or. Where can I collect you?'

'I'll make my own way.'

Which she did. I was at the bar, talking with Georges who used to run a Resistance group for the S.O.E. and now does the same in Aberinvest's restaurant holdings. The Etoile catered for the gourmet, not the pseudo bon viveur who visited such places for kudos and did not know what he was eating. Like similar establishments the Etoile was expensive, but you were paying experts to cook and serve the best food.

She did not smile as we sat at a corner table. Always the corner, Georges knew that. You can watch the room. Vennaway's tight leather trousers were still in evidence, as were the boots but in black this time. A pair of gold earrings had been added and the sweater exchanged for a white, frilly-cuffed shirt. A

104

gold medallion hung in her cleavage, playing musical chairs with small breasts that lacked visible means of support.

She accepted a thin Havana and asked where I obtained them. She preferred Irish whiskey to champagne and it was no macho act. This was pure Vennaway. I discovered her first name was Naomi and told her mine was just Wyatt. She ordered the pâté maison and lobster thermidor. I would not have given the lobster odds even before he went in the pot. She went straight to business and I had the impression I had lost on points before the match began.

'So why did Mr Caldicot get his face shot off?' she asked.

'The dead man in the Bayswater house I take it. I knew him as Alpha.'

'We knew him as Caldicot. He ran Unit Alpha, one of Moresby's creations.'

That figured. Moresby had been a cagey old buzzard. One of the reasons he stayed alive for forty years.

I decided to fly a dramatic kite and see what reaction I had: 'Then you'll know Moresby told him Llewellyn Jones was suspect. Alpha was told to call me if he needed help. He called me.'

She did not bat a long eyelash. The eyes were carborundum hard as she sipped the white Bordeaux. I was relieved to see her hands still free of knuckledusters. She said nothing for a while and finished her pâté. I was working overtime trying to calculate her game and whose side she was on.

'How did you meet Alpha?' she asked.

'He turned up with the cavalry as some Centre hoods were trying to crêpe Suzette me.'

I deliberately left Lansbury out of the picture.

'On Moresby's last operation?'

I nodded.

'Then your plane disappeared after Moresby died. Today you suddenly reappear.'

'Someone put a bomb on the plane. But we found it.'

'Probably Centre wanting to retaliate,' she rationalized.

'Or someone on your side publicity shy.'

'We do not operate like that,' she objected.

'And I believe in fairies.'

In view of old Lansbury's remarks about her, perhaps not the most appropriate reply. But what was a chromosome or two between friends?

She broke the lobster's claw with more enthusiasm than she would have done my neck:

'How did Alpha find you?'

'Through a mutual friend.'

'And you came back?' she asked, as if I were the neighbourhood nutcase.

'I'm old fashioned and naïve enough to keep my promises.'

'You had better go back where you came from. Don't they have any companies out there you can go and play with?'

'I'd rather take you to the casino.'

'I don't gamble, Wyatt.'

And for the first time I saw a flash in the emerald eyes. Imperceptible almost. Now it was my turn to ask a question. So I started with an awkward one.

'What were you doing chez Alpha?'

'Trying to track him down. He had ignored requests to report. I arrived there and ten minutes later you walked in. By the way, if you ever touch me again, I'll break both your arms.'

For the first time we had met, she smiled. I made sure my arms were on my side of the table and well out of her reach.

'Blame my old unarmed combat instructor. He told me: Fight dirty or lose. I am a poor loser.'

'According to Special Services records you used to fight very dirty. But that was a long time ago. The world has moved on since then.'

'Yes. The terrorists have become respectable, as always. They end up as politicians spouting fine principles about freedom and the right to exist. They forget about the way they casually cancelled those rights for others on the way. The people like you make sure they stay there, by fair means or foul.'

'You do believe in fairies,' she replied. 'We took Alpha's safe house apart and found some very interesting material. Evidence exists to suggest he was a double agent. You may yet be locked up under Prevention of Terrorism.'

'After dinner, please.'

The emerald eyes were seeking the centre of my soul. She said nothing until the Armagnac and coffee arrived.

'The Gascon brandy,' she observed seriously. 'You're not tall enough to be D'Artagnan.'

'You'll do as Milady de Winter.'

I lit thin Havanas for us. Round One to Vennaway. I had told some of the truth. She had given away nothing. But you can't win them all. Now it was time for her to tell me I should be a good boy.

'An enquiry is being launched into the business of Alpha. The security apparatus is already under siege. The Left are baying for public accountability in Parliament and those media fools are fanning the flames. Centre's disinformation campaign is far enough advanced to warrant their blowing a good agent last week just for the well-timed embarrassment of an Old Bailey trial. Several accusations have already been made about Llewellyn Jones ranging from trivia to treason. Go home, Mr Wyatt, before you are caught in the crossfire.'

'And you?'

'I do as I am told.'

'By whom. Centre?'

She did not smile.

'Can I offer you a lift home?' I asked.

'You're not my type, Mr Wyatt.'

As I watched her walk towards the Escort XR that contained her two babysitters I had a strange feeling that the next time we met could be across gun barrels aimed at each other.

Hers could well be a Russian AK47.

★   ★   ★

I was on the river just as dawn was breaking. The water was murky after a Wednesday night downpour but the West Wales air was now clear. Going to be a bright day. The black scampering shadows of the half-light became a pair of white-tailed rabbits playing tag with each other on the short grass at the edge of the wood. Down wind of me I could smell fox so I sat silently at the base of an old oak tree and stayed very still.

He came footpad-crafty around some blackthorn clumps and waited. The bright eyes of hungry fire had homed in on the playful rabbits. He lay flat against the brown earth, so still, his red-brown coat blending in with the ground's colour, you could have tripped over him before noticing.

The plaintive call of a young and hungry buzzard floated down on a spiralling air thermal. The rabbits stopped, sat upright on their haunches, noses twitching and ears cocked like expectant radar antennae.

Fox did not move.

The buzzard was above me now and gliding down towards another tall oak at the end of the wood. His tactic was simple. Move closer step by step. If the rabbit had not moved by the time he was in a position to strike— breakfast time. The hawks have to eat every day, especially in winter. If not, they die quickly.

But as the buzzard cruised in, a mottled grey harbinger of sudden death, the farthest rabbit bolted, out of my sight. The other ran towards the wood. Straight at the blackthorn.

Fox crash-tackled him. The rabbit arched

into the air and fell, twitching, the eyes glazed, the neck broken. Fox picked up the rabbit and slid away.

I stood up and the buzzard moved off.

There was a lesson in that, somewhere.

CHAPTER NINE

Sir Russell Beauchamp handed Gareth Llewellyn Jones a glass of dry sherry. His daughter, Camilla, was taking notes. Thursday 23rd September, 10am in Beauchamp's Whitehall office and Llewellyn Jones was in a jagged mood.

'Here is documentary evidence that the spy you set on me was working for the other side,' the Welshman announced coldly.

Beauchamp looked at his daughter and then looked back at Llewellyn Jones with the air of an injured archbishop. He took the files and sat behind his heavy leather-padded desk.

'Furthermore, Russell, I don't like you setting your dubious girlfriends to tittle-tattle on me. Vennaway told me what she had been asked to do.'

Camilla Beauchamp lit a cigarette and asked:

'Do I minute that, father?'

'Yes, you do,' Llewellyn Jones replied. A briefcase lay beside his chair and his own concealed tape-recorder was running. So these people wanted to play games. The Prime Minister would have a full account if necessary.

Llewellyn Jones lit his own cigarette and sipped the sherry. He watched Beauchamp's eyes as the pages of each file were flipped over rapidly.

'My God!' he exclaimed: 'You even found cipher pads. If this has been going on for long, Moscow have got the lot.'

Llewellyn Jones smiled to himself. Beauchamp you fool, you are about to swallow it wholesale. How long before you get to the tricky part?

'What I don't understand, L.J., is why they killed him. If he was their man why not keep him to discredit you. I mean he did a damned good job with all that cobblers about Moresby's legacy. Took me in I must admit.'

'Because they had no further use for him. He had created the doubts about me. Therefore we should be fighting amongst ourselves for a very long time, none of us knowing who to trust. But if we did catch up with him, Centre was probably afraid he would crack under interrogation and not only admit this was all disinformation but probably give us a lot else besides.'

'I don't suppose we can keep this amongst ourselves, can we? The P.M. is bloody enough over the last lot and with this Old Bailey business coming up next month.'

Llewellyn Jones smiled. He pretended to consider the possibilities as he finished his sherry.

'To what purpose? You acted in good faith. No, it has to be reported and in some detail. You see this is why we must have centralized control over Intelligence and Security matters. If Alpha or Caldicot's operation had to go through the Directorate I would have known about it. We could have stopped him in time and all this unnecessary embarrassment to you and to me would never have occurred. I'll let you have a preview of what I say about your part in all this. It will look good, don't worry.'

Sir Russell Beauchamp opened the door for Llewellyn Jones. Then he breathed very heavily as it closed.

'Camilla, I think I have been very lucky. Decent of L.J. to pop in and put the record straight.'

His daughter smiled at him.

'I am inclined to agree.'

*   *   *

Half an hour later, Vennaway was summoned to the presence. She walked into Llewellyn Jones's inner sanctum and he smiled at her.

'I have just been reading the Riot Act to Beauchamp, in the nicest possible way. You did a very good job in locating Alpha. I also understand Mr Wyatt has returned to Wales. Do you think he got the message?'

Vennaway nodded.

'Well, Naomi, I hope he takes your advice.'

'I think he will,' Vennaway replied.

*   *   *

Llewellyn Jones attended the reception given at the Russian Embassy for their visiting trade delegation that same evening. It was not a sinister or suspicious thing for him to do. The Foreign Office people were there in force, so were the Department of Trade & Industry. Besides, he had taken the precaution of minuting his visit in the Directorate's record that afternoon. A delicate negotiation regarding the exchange of an American agent caught in Russia and one of their London Embassy attachés who had been careless enough not to lose his watchers needed the very professional touch. It also enabled him to meet Victor.

The Russian was a slight, asthmatic figure

114

of medium height, who wore evening dress that had last fitted properly five years before. The discussion took place in a deserted drawing room protected by anti-bugging devices. Victor was not young, neither would he ever look old. He had a nondescript face and brown eyes that seemed dull and almost glazed. He smoked American cigarettes incessantly and his voice rarely rose above a hoarse whisper.

'How was Beauchamp?' Victor asked.

'Convinced,' Llewellyn Jones replied. 'Alpha's death was the only really difficult part. But blowing his face off was a neat brush-stroke.'

'He was Hungarian, you know. Defected in Moresby's day. We have long memories. So Sir Russell Beauchamp is now testing every statement made to him against a possible disinformation theory? Good. I understand Mr Wyatt has surfaced.'

'Vennaway has warned him off. She does it so beautifully.'

'He is not to be allowed an old age, but that can wait. There is another matter on which you should be briefed. Bakar is shortly to have a change of government. We would appreciate your help in ironing out any political reaction which may be adverse.'

'I don't think the Arabs like us very much

at the moment.'

Victor laughed. He said nothing for a few moments, as if waiting for Llewellyn Jones to say something. He handed his guest a glass of champagne.

A mental game of poker was being played by the two men. Victor knew his opponent's hand. Somehow, Llewellyn Jones realized and smiled his understanding.

'You should have been a Russian, L.J.'

'Let's just say I have an investment in a change of government in Bakar. Who is your man?'

'The Chief Minister Asif bin Said is an old friend. He is advised by another old friend. It is time the Gulf situation was stirred.'

'About the Americans?' Llewellyn Jones asked.

'No publicity. Our removal people will be in touch. We will have Comrade Alexandrovich transferred to filing duties in the Index. Good for his character, I think. There will be no more doubt against you in your own service?'

'I think I can safely promise you that. Thank you for the protection.'

Victor said nothing. Llewellyn Jones really ought to be thanking Victor's second best-placed agent. But she was a lady who probably would not appreciate it.

116

On Thursday 23rd September, Alexander Hamilton Coburn made his well-researched approach to obtain a Wolverine. To assist him he had received the benefit of information provided by Penmayne Harcourt's Intelligence Unit.

Computerized information and analysis was kept on every Western and Far East company employing more than fifty people. Share prices and performance were closely monitored. Regularly updated profiles existed on all companies operating in areas of the remotest interest to Penmayne Harcourt. Included on those profiles were data on all top executives.

The manufacturers of Wolverine were Tectrokite, a wholly owned subsidiary of the giant Aberinvest Corporation. Aberinvest always detached one of their own executives to control overall direction and finance of any of their subsidiaries. In this case, John Yardley was the man. Described on profile as forty-four, aggressive, capable and tipped by some pundits as a future director of Aberinvest itself, Yardley's business record was brutally impressive. He had come from nowhere to top management in just over twelve years. No degree, no good school to put him on the ladder. Just drive and ambition.

The computer did not record Yardley's personal weaknesses which were Coburn's real interest. That was Huggitt's job. Used anonymously by Coburn on several previous occasions for digging up information, Huggitt was a good man for the job.

He had answered his telephone through the early morning alcoholic haze and the flailing, waking arms of his teenage sleeping companion. The caller told him where to find two hundred pounds in cash. Instructions would follow. Sober enough to realize this was paid work, he rolled out of bed and ducked his head under the cold tap. The cramped bedroom was a mess. Clothes, empty gin bottles and the contents of an ashtray were scattered indiscriminately. He shook the girl awake.

'Coffee, you slag, now.'

The girl blinked and meekly obeyed. She was a sixteen-year-old runaway who had left Coventry for the bright lights on the previous Wednesday. She would find a job in London and earn money, find her own flat maybe. On the Thursday she had met Huggitt.

He had once been a first-rate policeman; a vice squad sergeant suspended on a corruption enquiry who took fast legal advice and resigned before taking himself to South Africa for a vacation on the proceeds of his unofficial pay packets. The climate was better than England and the air freer than Wormwood Scrubs. In a Johannesburg nightclub he had been recruited by the then B.O.S.S. into a section that specialized in sexual entrapment to discourage liberal politicians and others from protesting too liberally about apartheid. The Immorality Acts provided the pressure and Huggitt the evidence. His vice experience was well rewarded before he lapsed into his old habits of purloining indecent material for street resale. Huggitt was advised to leave rather than fall out of a tenth-storey window of a certain building in Pretoria.

The dust had settled in London and he set up a small enquiry agency handling the kind of business the bona fide firms would not touch: strong-arm repossession, squatter-bashing and surveillance on prostitutes cheating on their cash returns. He made enough to keep himself in food, betting money, drink and a succession of young runaways he then passed on to a pimp in Brixton for a commission.

Huggitt received a further five hundred in expense money with the instructions. His undercover skills were formidable, aided by his medium height and build, nondescript, almost characterless, face and indeterminate age. These enabled him to transform from a polished, high-pressure, three-piece-suited salesman to a piece of human flotsam, reeking of methylated spirits, with comparative ease.

He had checked into a private hotel in the more select area of Redland with its redbrick Victorian terraced houses and air of solid if faded respectability. He had not worked the Bristol area before but with the aid of a street map and a year-old hired Vauxhall Cavalier he soon found his way around.

Target: John Yardley. Residence: Sneyd Park—where the wealthy Bristolians overlooked their own rural scene, the Downs, acres of rolling parkland stretching to the edge of Clifton Gorge and Brunel's Suspension Bridge. The house was detached, early 1920s, set back thirty yards from the roadway in its half acre of garden and screened from the roadway by conifers. Daily woman to clean three hours for five days. Handyman to play gardeners three days. Wife, a childless, morose and sullen woman in her late thirties whose mornings were taken up visiting neighbours for coffee. Her afternoons consisted of emptying sherry bottles down herself to the accompaniment of Radio Two. Yardley, never home unless necessary, took business acquaintances to a local hotel. His spare time was spent at the Clifton flat of a long-legged brunette practising for the sexual Olympics. They ate out in discreet places that knocked big holes in Huggitt's expenses. Yardley only smiled when he was with the girl, whom Huggitt would have taken for a call girl of the high-performance, high-price variety had he not checked out her identity as being that of a History student at the University.

Mrs Yardley was not ignorant of the girl's existence. Domesticity chez Yardley was not so much a series of explosive rows as one long guerilla campaign. Her main pleasure in life was telling Yardley he could have a divorce to marry the 'academic whore' and ten minutes later swearing she would ruin his career and bankrupt him with settlement demands if he tried. Huggitt reckoned Yardley would have had better companionship from a dog and a dog would have been easier on Yardley's eyesight.

Huggitt wrote a full report, including weak financial status and enclosed photographs of the almost nightly triathlons at the Clifton flat.

At 9am on Thursday 23rd September, armed with the information, Coburn moved. He arrived in Bristol at 11am and went to a house in the Clifton area. The top-floor flat was occupied by two heavily built men who were in shirtsleeves and lightweight trousers. A pair of binoculars stood on a tripod behind muslin curtains. Coburn left five hundred pounds in cash on the table.

'Any time within the next two hours,' Coburn ordered.

'She is in there now,' the first man replied in a heavy Bristolian acent.

'Go and frighten her. On no account hurt or damage her in any way. Just scare the hell out of her. You understand your job.'

'Certainly,' the second man replied.

They waited for Coburn to leave then crossed the road to the girl's flat.

*　　*　　*

John Yardley was in the bar of the restaurant by twelve noon. He was anxious to meet Mr Coburn. The man's introductory credentials were impeccable. Conarmco Sales was held in high esteem by the Pentagon and the Ministry of Defence had dealt with them on several occasions. Efficient, good payers and honest. Yardley was looking forward to doing business with Coburn.

The American arrived and shook hands with Yardley, a short, stocky red-faced bulldozer of a man with a rasping Bristolian accent. Yardley insisted on buying the drinks and Coburn took tonic water. Yardley had a large gin and tonic. As they sat down to a seafood cocktail, Yardley smiled effusively. He was doing his public relations best to impress the American about Tectrokite's quality control, reliable delivery schedule and advantageous financial arrangements. The American said little in reply. He was more interested in the quality of the food. By the time the cheeseboard arrived, Yardley tried to steer the conversation in the direction of some commitment to Wolverine.

'I'm sorry, John,' Coburn apologized: 'This food is something else. I can see why you eat here often.'

The statement surprised Yardley. He was puzzled.

'John, my people know a great deal about you. Good executive. You could make the main board of Aberinvest very soon. A good sale would help.'

Surely the American was not angling for a bribe, or in the terminology of the arms trade a 'sales commission'. Yardley was momentarily lost for words but Coburn ignored the silence and continued:

'You have a Wolverine available for immediate delivery. I want it in London, crated for transport by 6am on Monday next.

27th September that is. Forget the performance bond. This deal is what we call covertly legitimate. Why we came to you direct instead of involving the Ministry in the negotiations. My people in the U.S. military want the deal kept quiet because it does not go through the Senate appropriations committees.'

Yardley nodded his understanding of the situation. He had heard of such deals. Coburn looked like the type of man to front such a purchase. Chubby, friendly, but with an air of mean confidence. He handed Yardley a folder.

'We have provided end user certificates to the Ministry copies of which I have attached to the export licence which is in here.'

Yardley thumbed through the folder. Contracts for a Wolverine system and the international bank references were all in order. A nominee account with the full purchase price of a Wolverine system had already been set up, less ten per cent. Coburn had not bargained but had arrived at the exact figure Yardley would have agreed on for cash terms.

'All very much in order.' Yardley smiled, not really able to believe his luck. Orders like this never came out of the blue. They usually required uphill sales work, test firings and government assistance with finance. Wolverine was on a restricted list and the speed of the approach would have made Yardley suspicious except for the fact that all the Ministry paperwork was in excellent order.

'John, I told you this deal was confidential. The Ministry security people wanted to come down and talk with you but I told them you were a man who could keep his mouth shut. Our governments, not to mention your parent company, need this kept confidential.'

'I understand. Only myself and Anthony Lannerson of Tectrokite need to know about the contracts.'

Coburn raised an eyebrow.

'Positively vetted, Alex. First-rate engineer. Wolverine is his baby.'

Coburn handed an envelope to Yardley, smiling as he did so.

'Now we know this deal will put you to some inconvenience so inside are details of a little piggy bank we opened for you with the cuckoo clock people. Twenty grand as a sign of good faith. A further twenty will be deposited in there when the Wolverine is delivered. Outside in your car will be a further ten thousand in cash to tide you over that temporary cashflow shortage on account of your friendship with Christine.'

Yardley could not believe he was hearing this. They had been watching him, checking up on him. He was angry and Coburn could see that. But he was also afraid for his position and did not articulate his feelings.

'If you have to pass on any of that cash to Lannerson as an inducement, telephone me at this number. I'll reimburse you. But John, one word of this leaking out and my people can get very irate.'

Yardley drove back to his office. He had heard about deals like this one before. It was wise to say nothing and do as you were told. It was all legitimate according to the paperwork. So he was doing nothing wrong and being well paid for it. If Coburn wanted to give him a small gift to show appreciation, where was the harm?

Christine, his girlfriend, called five minutes after he arrived at his desk. She was almost hysterical. Two men had called at her flat and had been carrying guns. They had looked around the flat and explained in graphic detail how they would hospitalize the girl if her boyfriend did not do exactly as he was told.

Twenty minutes later, Coburn called and apologized for his people being so excitable. It was all a mistake. But they had not even touched the girl, had they? No harm done then, but Yardley knew exactly where he stood, didn't he?

CHAPTER TEN

Anthony Lannerson had arrived at the Tectrokite factory just outside Gloucester at 7.30am that same morning. Habit of a lifetime, being an early riser. It went back to the days in his parents' terraced house in the back streets of Manchester just after the war. He was always poring over texts and newspapers, books and plans in the cold front room on winter mornings. University had been a struggle for them and he had succeeded brilliantly to become a top electronics engineer. Thirty years, a daughter, a divorce and a bankruptcy later the habit was still with him.

Tectrokite had been his dream. Fifteen years before, almost to the day, he had set up the small factory with sound finance, inspired designs and a rock solid partner. Ten years later, the same partner undermined the foundations of Lannerson's life bringing everything crashing down. He had run off with Lannerson's wife, Deborah, the contents of all bank accounts and even the firm's petty cash. Bank guarantees were called in and

Lannerson had lost everything: house, family, company and self-respect. Inevitable bankruptcy was followed by suicidal despair and humiliation. Lannerson would have ended the entire sorry saga of his life had his eighteen-year-old daughter Josephine not arrived at his lonely rented cottage very early one morning. Her father needed her more than the V.S.O. project in Somalia did, so she had come home unannounced and unaided.

She put him back on his feet psychologically and even tried socially. A month later she went up to Sussex University. He fought the emptiness as hard as he knew how, refusing to descend again to the haunting depths of self-pity that could again so easily become his refuge. In this he had been helped by the arrival of Peter Fallon.

Lannerson thought the twenty-six-year-old, slim, boyish, speaking calculator was a trainee asset-stripper. He looked the part: psychedelic tie, silk shirt, Gucci shoes and hand-made Italian-style suit. Fallon had climbed out of the Ferrari like a fast-jet pilot who had successfully tested a prototype. He had grinned, surveyed the overgrown garden and general air of untidiness and dilapidation as if scenting a prey. Lannerson almost disbelieved him when he announced casually that he was the Managing Director of the mammoth Aberinvest Corporation. Aberinvest was a multinational so vast that it made Britain's largest company look like an up-country general store. Fallon had said only:

'We've just bought what's left of Tectrokite. Heard you used to run it until you had some bad luck. If you fancy another go, be at the factory tomorrow morning at eight.'

With that young Fallon had climbed back into the cockpit of his Ferrari and drove off.

A successful year later Fallon had visited the factory. With him was a slim, dark-haired man whose dark brown, almost black eyes took in everything around him. The lean, gaunt features, tanned and characterful, seemed out of place with the man's dress— Savile Row, hand-made shirt and shoes. An old combat jacket that he put on against the biting wind seemed more his style. He had listened, followed Lannerson quietly as a cat and said nothing at all until he was on the point of climbing into the Aberinvest helicopter.

'Remarkable progress, Anthony. Aberinvest is a fair-sized outfit and sometimes we can lose touch. If you ever need me, don't hesitate to call.'

The man had smiled then climbed aboard. Lannerson asked Fallon who was some distance behind:

'Who was that?'

Fallon had raised his eyes to the skies:

'Don't suppose he even introduced himself. That was Wyatt.'

Lannerson watched the helicopter lift off. So he had met the Chairman of Aberinvest. Lannerson never forgot the meeting or the words or the manner in which they had been spoken: quietly, but Wyatt had meant what he had said. Lannerson could tell. There had been a look of almost dangerous determination in Wyatt's eyes. He had not seen Wyatt since.

Lannerson controlled operations at Tectrokite and his real love—Research and Development. Wolverine was his design. A recent lull had left two systems in storage but in three months the order books would be full again. Expansion could even be on the cards. But that was Yardley's job—to find and finance the orders. Yardley had telephoned at 3pm to say he had done just that. And at 4.30pm he had walked into the office, rough-voiced and ebullient.

'Got it processed?' Yardley demanded reaching for Lannerson's desk telephone. Yardley always spent most of his time on the telephone.

'Bit sudden, isn't it? Paperwork all in

order?'

'Of course the bloody paperwork is all in order.'

Yardley threw a file on to the desk. The customer was Conarmco of Detroit. The name seemed familiar. Had his daughter, Jo, now a journalist, mentioned it to him?

'How do we manage for the performance bond, John? No mention of it here.'

A performance bond was a very large sum of money which arms suppliers would put up as collateral against breach of contract or delivery schedules. Tectrokite had not dealt with Conarmco before so logically the customer should require one. Lannerson asked because at a previous board meeting recently, Yardley had rounded on him about cashflow and the fact that R. & D. costs on a new project were running over budget.

'Look, do you want the sodding business or not? Leave me to worry about the arrangements, you just get the bloody Wolverine delivered. As it happens they don't require one. Received good refs from the Ministry.'

Lannerson was surprised by the aggression in Yardley's reply. He was used to a surly attitude but this was something else.

'John. Is there anything wrong with this deal?'

131

Yardley rounded on him, his face mad bull-red and his hands unsteady.

'Just do as you're frigging told. I'm under pressure from Head Office and the security people on this one. And keep the bloody gossip quiet. Conarmco work for the U.S. government. They are very touchy about weapons publicity right now. Okay?'

'No need to shout, John,' Lannerson replied coolly. 'It's just that arms sales can so easily go wrong. You hear a lot of informed stories.'

'Not about this one,' Yardley snapped. 'I'll call you tonight at home. Make sure we are up together.'

*   *   *

Yardley was in his girlfriend's Clifton flat at 7pm. He mollified the long-legged Christine by the promise of a late dinner and a night club. Then he sent her out of the room and telephoned the number Alexander Hamilton Coburn had given him.

'I've got a problem. It's not my fault. Lannerson is nosey.'

'Listen very carefully, John. This is what you do.'

Hearing the calm voice on the other end of the line Yardley was reassured. It was no

132

problem. Lannerson had merely misunderstood the situation. Where did he live? What kind of man was he? Did he have any family? After twenty minutes Yardley put the telephone down. He had cleared himself of any comebacks. He suspected he had let Anthony Lannerson in for some problems. But forty thousand pounds was a lot of money, his girlfriend's safety was precious to him. And he was not his brother's keeper.

*   *   *

Anthony Lannerson answered his door at 11.15 that night. He was surprised to see two men standing there. The first, a chubby, balding man wearing dark overcoat spoke with an American accent:

'Tony Lannerson? Sorry to call so late. I'm Alex Coburn. I'm with the C.I.A. My identification. This is Mr Summers. He is with British Security.'

Lannerson took the identification card Coburn handed him. Attached to it was a Ministry of Defence Security pass in the American's name. Lannerson was so taken aback with the announcement that he did not ask to see the other man's identification. Coburn had counted on that happening.

'May we come in?'

Lannerson ushered both men into the small but comfortable lounge of the cottage. Coburn walked to the mantelpiece and looked at the photograph of an attractive brunette.

'I guess this will be your daughter, Jo. Fine-looking young lady. Journalist as I recall with the *Red Widow* or some such magazine. Not that we take much notice of youthful ideals even if they do freak towards Communism.'

Lannerson was frightened. This man knew everything about his daughter. And the implication was clear. She could be a security risk by virtue of her political views. It had not mattered when he was positively vetted by the British, but . . .

'Again, Tony, may I call you Tony, sorry to call so late, only we have this problem and the boys at the Ministry said you were a regular sort of character they could rely on. That so, Summers?'

The big, heavy man nodded and sat down.

'May I?' Coburn indicated the sofa and only sat down when invited to do so.

'Tony, I'm with Conarmco of Detroit. I saw your Chairman a Mr John Yardley today.'

'He told me about the Wolverine.'

'Then you know all about the need for secrecy. Say, can Summers check this place over for listening devices?'

'Surely you don't . . .'

'Tony, you would not believe. Look I omitted to tell Yardley I was with the Company and this deal has the full backing of both our governments and, needless to say, your people in Aberinvest. See Yardley looks like a drinker and not to put too fine a point on it, his private life, well . . . you know how it is. Can we rely on you?'

Lannerson was overwhelmed by the American's confident, efficient approach. He was also frightened by the mention of his daughter and the big man ferreting around the cottage.

'Yes of course, but why hasn't someone else from Aberinvest been in touch with me if you don't trust Yardley?'

'Because the fewer people that know about this the better. You weren't in on the original list of those with a need to know but I revised my opinion on it when I realized you were the guy who designed the Wolverine. Hell, you're not stupid. Yardley told you that story and you must have thought he had flipped. Tony, I apologize.'

'That's okay.'

'Just promise me you can keep security on this one. It is vital.'

'Yes.'

'Thank you. No problems with delivery?'

'Had to reschedule some work but nothing

too difficult.'

Coburn handed him a package. Small, wrapped in brown paper and sealed with clear tape. He also handed him a card.

'Any problems, call me. What's in there will compensate you for the inconvenience. I insist. Hell, we had to spread money for the transportation our end, so why shouldn't you have a tax freebie? Yardley's had his commission. Why not you?'

Coburn left ten minutes later. He smiled on the way out. Summers, the big heavy man, did not. He had just looked at the photograph of Jo Lannerson and grinned unpleasantly.

Lannerson lit a cigarette and opened the package. It contained five thousand pounds in fifty pound notes. All the notes were used and had serial numbers that bore no sequence to each other.

He did not know what to do. He had heard stories of deals like this. Aberinvest were a multi-national and all multi-nationals had interests that transcended frontiers and even political beliefs. The identification had seemed genuine and both men looked as though they were used to this type of work. He did not know what to do. He was worried about his daughter, so even though it was gone midnight, he telephoned her.

'Of course I'm all right,' she replied. 'What

about you? You sound in a bit of a state.'

'Are you coming down tomorrow?' he asked, anxiously.

'Of course. We were supposed to be having lunch. And you are buying so we'll go to the Courtyard restaurant in town. I was planning to see you there at twelve-thirty. Are you sure you are all right?'

'Yes. No-one has been following you have they?'

'Not that I have noticed. Why?'

'Tell you tomorrow, darling. Goodbye.'

Lannerson put the telephone down. He poured himself a brandy which he drank quickly. Then he took another one and started thinking. Why had not anyone in Aberinvest, apart from Yardley, spoken to him about this Wolverine business? It was strange and frightening. There had been the hints about his daughter, that man Summers looking at the photograph, and the money. It was not right. But he could not go to the police. If British Security were involved he would look foolish and maybe even lose his job.

He sat for some time feeling very alone. He drank more brandy and the problem seemed worse. Eventually he remembered a man called Wyatt and the only conversation they had ever had. But Wyatt was no longer Chairman. In fact there had been some strange news about him recently. His plane had crashed and then later it turned out he had survived. Did that have anything to do with Coburn? And why would the C.I.A. admit buying arms? If they were up to clandestine deals why would Coburn admit it?

He remembered Wyatt's words again. If you ever need me, don't hesitate. So on impulse he checked the Aberinvest London Office's telephone number in his desk diary and dialled. There would be no reply of course, but if he left a message on the answering machine and then called again in the morning from his own office, perhaps someone would know how to get in touch with Wyatt.

Confused by the machine and by now a fourth brandy, Lannerson said.

'This is Tony Lannerson of Tectrokite. Please ask Mr Wyatt to call me. This is an urgent message. Thank you.'

Unknown to Lannerson the call was overheard by Summers who was sitting in an old van two miles away. Instead of checking Lannerson's cottage for hidden microphones, Summers had planted several. He did not work for British Security.

CHAPTER ELEVEN

Charles Penmayne received Coburn's call at 7am. It did not wake him. He had already run his three miles and was emerging from the cold shower at his Portman Square house. He listened with interest to Coburn's report and the hitch that had occurred with Lannerson. The name Wyatt had also been mentioned. Coburn was told to stand by for instructions.

Gareth Llewellyn Jones was breakfasting on his usual three cups of coffee and the first cigarette of the day while reading his daily appointments, always arranged for him the last half-hour of the previous day. He received Penmayne's call and listened very carefully to the developments.

'I'll be in my office in half an hour. Have Coburn to stand by for what they call executive action in his language. He will understand about it. Lannerson has to go and quickly. But we need what Coburn would call a patsy.'

The main reason for Llewellyn Jones's brilliance as an adviser was his ability to think out a plan of action and to implement that plan with effective speed. Once at his office he consulted the records. The Directorate's absolute powers over operational security matters had necessitated the installation of computer links to his office. Within thirty seconds he had M.I.5's profile on Jo Lannerson in front of him. She was on record because of her previous membership of the Communist Party, her involvement with the Marxist periodical *Red Widow* and two convictions for disorderly conduct at demonstrations. Within two minutes Llewellyn Jones had made a quick character assessment and his decision. He called Penmayne back.

'Kill Lannerson before he can meet his daughter today and have the finger pointed obscurely at Mr Wyatt. If the girl's relationship with her father is what I expect then there are no further problems. Mr Wyatt will not be in a position to have the concessions in Bakar renewed on a personal basis. A hedge against the Bakar business going wrong for you, Penmayne. That way you can always ingratiate yourself with the King at a later stage and get the same concessions out of him.'

Llewellyn Jones omitted to add that he would also be doing a Russian named Victor a considerable service. Even if the girl were unsuccessful in killing Wyatt he would probably kill her. Because he was expecting someone to try for him after Alpha's death. And Wyatt had proved before that as a killer of men he had few equals. The only gamble was the girl's reaction to her father's death, and if not violent it would certainly be noisy and probably journalistic. The Wolverine would be clear of the country long before any repercussions and he had kept his involvement in the acquisition of export licences to a minimum. The trail of paperwork led through so many departments that an enquiry would take six months to trace its source.

He finished another cup of coffee and summoned the official car to take him to the first meeting at the Ministry of Defence.

★   ★   ★

Anthony Lannerson kept dialling the Aberinvest London Office every ten minutes. He knew it was a futile exercise. No telephonist would be on duty until 9am at the earliest. Even then it would be highly unlikely that they would know where Wyatt was. It could take days to reach him and the Wolverine would be despatched in less than seventy-two hours.

He had slept only fitfully, dreaming of Yardley's angry red face, the smooth, matter-of-fact, chubby American, talking pleasantly yet menacing his little girl. He had seen large men carrying anonymous coffins to bleak churchyards with his name on all the gravestones, and pools of blood surrounding his daughter's wrecked car. Money had fallen from a Tectrokite, speeding skywards towards a Jaguar fighter and a television news announcer had reported questions being asked in Parliament. They had put him on trial at the Old Bailey and sentenced him to thirty years in prison where no-one spoke to him. The terrifying montage of confused nightmares was still with him.

He tried to shake off his fears, rationalizing them as extensions of a bad dream. Eventually, he managed to work. When his severe middle-aged secretary who had been with him since Tectrokite started came in he asked her to book a table at the Courtyard restaurant. He also asked her to contact Aberinvest's London Office. She kept coming back with the news that the number was engaged.

At twelve noon he left the factory. A short drive and he would be at the restaurant well before twelve-thirty, in time for a quick drink before his daughter arrived. She would put his irrational ideas in perspective.

He did not notice the Ford Granada that

142

followed him from outside the factory gates.

★   ★   ★

Jo Lannerson, was a capable, twenty-four-year-old, blue-eyed brunette who stared angrily across her battered typewriter at Roger Daniels, a neat, bespectacled and well-meaning young barrister.

'You've taken the balls out of my first three chapters,' she objected. 'What else do you want to emasculate?'

Daniels had a conservative lawyer's distaste for vivaciously attractive young women who wore battered denims and used forthright language. The distaste increased whenever he met Jo Lannerson because he was in love with her. The object of his clandestine fantasies was not supposed to behave like some butch liberationist at a street meeting.

'Jo, I've told you before. We have libel laws in this country which are supposed to protect people from unwarranted diatribes like your first three chapters.'

'Christ, Roger. I am dealing with multi-nationals. You know the people? They screw work out of blacks for less than living wages and condemn them to racial oppression. They con their political puppets into an arms race that only they profit from and they cheat the people of this country by their tax-evasion, their control of the media, and their manipulation of the system.'

'That is an opinion to which you are entitled under British law. But you are not allowed to state it as fact, naming names and companies without the relevant evidence to back it up. I grant you there are some indicators, but your publishers have retained me to make sure that the lawyers won't drive us all out of a living.'

She threw her hands in the air.

'I bloody well give up,' she shouted, walking from the untidy office. 'Well I might just try and find some evidence.'

By the time she had reached Gloucester she had cooled her temper down. Tony was buying her lunch and it would be good to see him again. She had been working too hard on the book and meetings with Roger always annoyed her. He was so complacent and yet so persistent in trying to invite her out. She always refused. One broken relationship in the last six months had already taken its emotional toll. And Roger was not to be the start of another.

At 12.40 on Friday 24th September she walked into the Courtyard restaurant. Aptly named, the courtyard of an old coaching inn where good food was served al fresco, weather permitting. Clear blue skies, a surprisingly

144

warm autumn sun, checkered table cloths and striped umbrellas made the place look like a Continental bistro. Several heads turned to watch the long legs encased in tight blue jeans as she passed the first few tables. She looked for her father among the diners but the view of some tables was obscured by a knot of people gathered around one table. Other diners now craned inquisitive heads to gaze, uselessly. A thin, fussy man in dark trousers and white shirt, bow tie and an ostrich neck, shooed people away.

Involuntarily Jo Lannerson ran towards the group. She knew her father was in some kind of trouble. Even before she saw him lying on the ground, convulsed in a desperate struggle for his very life, she knew he was badly hurt.

'Tony,' she screamed, clawing and kicking her way through the throng, pulling a woman away from beside him by her hair. She fell down, seized his shaking arm, her face close to his grey death mask.

Dull recognition gleamed in his eyes. His trembling hand pulled her closer to him, desperately, as though his life depended on it.

'Jo. Listen,' he fought for the words. 'Wolverine. Aberinvest killed me.' The words were a hoarse muffled whisper now: 'Get Wyatt.'

His eyes rolled upwards. The deathgrip

tightened on her arms, a final effort to cling to life. His lips were very blue. His body twitched and he lay very still. She could hear nothing but his last words.

Over and over again she heard the words. A klaxon sounded and a stretcher rolled noisily over the cobblestones. Voices hushed, then were raised again. Ambulance doors slammed and she was inside. Radio clacking voices chattered meaninglessly. More sounds, doors again and heels clicked on tiled floors, echoing the squeaking of stretcher wheels. She sat lonely and far-away, afraid yet senseless, half-listening to the sound of cups. She tasted sweet, sickly, tepid tea. Somewhere a telephone rang, hollow-toned and unanswered for a long time. Skirts rustled, doors closed. Her trembling hands failed to light a cigarette.

A young man in a white coat, soft-eyed, kind and understanding, nervous yet in control, took her hand.

'I am sorry. We did everything we could. But the cardiac arrest was so massive.'

The words trailed into a long silence. Disbelief and fear mingled with the emptiness she felt. She had known, long before the doctor spoke, that Tony was dead. He had died after the words 'Aberinvest killed me. Get Wyatt' had left his cold, blued lips. She knew but could not believe. The one constant

146

in her life had gone, leaving only what seemed like an illusion. She clung now to the way she would always remember him. Not as a dying man but as she had known him in childhood: happy, smiling, loving.

'Please come and sit down.'

The words brought her back to the present. The young doctor was still holding her hand.

'I'm sorry. I understand. You tried.'

She wanted to cry, to scream, to run to her father.

The young doctor knew. Experience of death, emotionally as well as clinically, had tempered his youth with understanding. He really did know how it felt. His own father had died young, wasted by cancer. A reason he was now a doctor.

'Is there anyone I can call?' he asked and knew it was a stupid question. The girl was alone. She had made no phone calls.

'I'll manage if I can call a taxi,' she replied.

Jo Lannerson was in no state to notice a tall, blond German who was waiting in the reception area of the hospital. He followed her out and sat in a Ford Granada. As the taxi drew away, the Granada followed.

*   *   *

The cottage seemed so silent when she awoke

on Saturday morning. There had been no real alternative to spending the night there. Returning to London seemed like running away from the problem. She had telephoned of course, to the magazine and to a friend in the research department on one of the popular dailies. She wanted information on Wyatt.

The morning was taken up collecting her father's belongings from the hospital and arranging with a local undertaker to bury him. A severe yet sympathetic man, he noticed a strange look in her eyes, not of bereavement but of something akin to hatred.

The Tectrokite factory was a place she felt unable to go. They could find out about her father their own way. Aberinvest would already know. They had driven him to death, if not actually caused it. But the manner of his death was not as important as her avenging Tony. During the day it became an all-consuming hatred.

She did return to London by 6pm. Instead of going to her flat she drove straight to see Mac.

McIver was a hard-nosed, hard-drinking sub-editor who had worked every daily in Britain at one time or another. He sat in the bar of the Horse and Hounds watching her fiddle with the gin and tonic. She had told him of her father's death while he remained silent, like a wise old bear.

'No point in grieving, is there Mac? Won't bring him back, will it? So help me with my book. Some background, maybe?'

He did not buy the change of subject. An intuitive journalist, he had brought her up in the wily ways of the Press. He was still a little in love with her and admired the stands she took on matters of principle. Good to be young enough and willing to starve for your principles, he would tease her.

'Aberinvest Corporation. Anything dirty?'

'For that line of country they're pretty clean. No Lockheed-type scandals there. But they're big, diverse, and very powerful.'

'Man called Wyatt, used to be their chairman.'

'Don't tell me you're going for the exclusive interview. He won't talk to anyone from the Press. The Street has been trying to locate him for the last week. He survived a plane crash.'

'I want to ask him some personal questions.'

McIver thought there were tears in her eyes. She took one of his Capstan cigarettes and coughed.

'Come on, Mac.'

'He started Aberinvest. Came from nowhere with some Arab money and a lot of the right connections. Four years ago he jacked it in and went to live in Wales. Met him once at a Press launch for something or other. He spent all his time closeted with that smart blonde Italian piece that writes for one of the heavyweight Continentals on finance. Bet she got a really exclusive interview.'

'Mac, cut the El Vino reminiscences.'

'Sorry, love. He's a quiet fellow, listens a lot and moves like a bloody cat. Wally Duncan served under him in the S.A.S. before they became fashionable. No bullshit, Wally reckoned him the best officer anywhere. Unorthodox, brilliant and none of this gung-ho, we-can-walk-on-water attitude. Oh no. Thinking man's professional. Knows when it's healthy to be scared. Minimizes the risks then moves fast. Worth a few million now. Still owns a big chunk of the company.'

'So he could influence decisions?'

'Obviously.'

'Possible Intelligence connections, with his background?'

'Possible.'

'So he could kill?'

'Certainly.'

*   *   *

Big Ears Simms had acquired his soubriquet in Wormwood Scrubs. The nickname had
150

nothing to do with his radar-like ability to pick up most criminal gossip south of the river. It was prompted by the foolishly large ears that stuck out almost at right angles from a curly mass of dandruff and black hair. Big Ears had started as a small-time burglar. Twenty years and two stretches later he was a small-time fence who was still a burglar at heart. But the kids had made burglary an impossible game. While the police were concerned that housebreakers averaged thirteen years of age, Simms viewed the matter as a diabolical liberty. The little ingrates had no finesse, never cased a drum properly and always left a disgusting mess. He blamed the parents, teachers and truant officers. Unemployment did not help. His own father had made him stay at school for a proper education. 'Something to fall back on, son.'

He had acquired the gun from some little brat as part of a job lot. Shooters were dodgy business, but a quick turnover to a reliable customer and there were no problems. The girl looked reliable, if nervous. Probably a model—long legs, brown hair cascading over a blue denim jacket. Shirt was silk and the tight denim jeans faded. She spoke like a toff and clutched the shoulder bag apprehensively. Her boyfriend had walked out on her. The girl in the next-door flat had been attacked by an intruder and she was scared. She was positive she had seen a masked face at her window the previous night.

Ten minutes after she handed him the three hundred pounds wrapped in newspaper inside a supermarket carrier, Big Ears Simms finished his mild and walked out.

Jo Lannerson thought he might walk off with the money. An unprepossessing villain emanating B.O. and a sly sideways look, Simms might have conned her out of the money. Alternatively, he might now be telling a policeman that a girl who was probably an urban terrorist had tried to buy a gun from him. She obeyed his instruction to go to her car, parked in a darkened side street.

He was already sitting in the passenger seat. She knew the car had been locked.

'Lots of dishonest people about, Miss,' Simms observed, pocketing his skeleton keys.

A big gun, Simms had nodded sagely. Colt Python .357 Magnum. Stop a bloody rhinoceros. Know how to use it? Point at the middle of the target and brace yourself. Kicks like a Tiller girl. But you wouldn't remember them. Be lucky, Miss.

Then he had vanished into the pale half-light of the deserted street. A creature of the shadows. Simms watched her drive off. He shook his head. Bloody awful times to live in. Girl like that not safe on the streets. Bloody rapists and sex maniacs. Ought to have it cut off. He lost no time in making his next delivery—a sawn-off shotgun to an old mate. Later that night he thought about the girl and wondered in passing if her story was true. Then he counted the three hundred pounds again.

*   *   *

Jo Lannerson saw him through her binoculars at 3.15pm on Sunday 26th September, just as McIver had described him. Ten minutes later she was twenty yards from him. A slim, dark-haired man, dressed in khaki green, his quilted armless jacket was the same colour as his fishing waders and the trousers underneath. He was crouched over a fishing rod, tying a lure to the nylon line. She walked through the gap in the brambles, ignored another 'Private' sign and casually strode towards the river bank. He had heard her, despite the fact his back was to her. Then he glanced over his shoulder, said: 'Good afternoon,' and began burrowing in an old fishing bag. She walked closer, returning his greeting and stood five yards from him. Her heart beat quicker as she took the pistol from beneath her denim jacket. Her mouth was dry. She had found the man responsible for her father's death. 'Get Wyatt,' he had said.

He was oblivious to the danger and she felt somehow sorry for him being in such a defenceless position. But her father had been shown no mercy. The gun that would stop a rhinoceros was pointing at him now, held in both her hands. Her feet were very slightly apart, more to stop her knees from knocking together than from any conscious attempt to brace herself for the recoil. She centred the sights in the middle of his back and prayed: God, let me kill him. He murdered Tony. Yet she had to tell him why he was about to die.

'Mr Wyatt,' she called.

He turned and saw her. No look of surprise or even fear registered on his tanned face. Younger than she expected—late thirties perhaps, and his face did have character, suggesting experience and something darker, more purposeful, that flashed in those brown eyes as he spoke:

'Do you have a licence for that?'

The voice was firm, calm and slightly mocking.

'I'm going to kill you, Wyatt. Raise your hands.'

His eyes never left hers as he quietly obeyed. Then he smiled. And he was not a

154

bad-looking fellow. Why did she think of that? No explanation. Then she tried hard to remember her father's dying words. God, please help me. I have to kill him. But first I must tell him.

'Don't you want to know why I'm going to kill you?'

'I'm sure you are about to tell me,' he replied, still with a smile.

That damned smile made him so human, likeable even. Why didn't he look evil, guilty and murderous? She steadied the gun.

'You murdered Tony Lannerson, you killed my father.'

The name elicited no response, no reaction. Not a glimmer of recognition, no excuse, no justification. Instead he moved a step or two towards her.

'Stay there,' she snapped. He obeyed. The palm of his hands bunched into fists then relaxed again. She hated him now, for being so calm, so steady and not begging for his life. She tensed to fire the gun as he spoke.

'No, I didn't do that.'

At the same time his left hand closed again. A loud explosion sounded to her right. No, her gun had not fired. As she turned a weight flattened her to the ground, driving the breath from her body. The gun fell away. She tried to drive a knee at him, uselessly. Her flailing

155

arms were pinned to the ground above her head. She kicked out fiercely and was rewarded by a hard, stinging slap to her face. Tears filled her eyes. By the time she could see anything again he was standing five yards from her. The gun was now in his right hand. She thought another man was standing to her right.

'Don't move,' Wyatt ordered, his voice cold and commanding. 'Place your hands on your head and kneel down.'

The voice had to be obeyed. She felt sick doing so. Her hands trembled and her whole body shook. She had failed Tony and would die for it. Black dizziness overwhelmed her. She fought the feeling and the fear, searching desperately for some defiant last words:

'Kill me then.'

She did not remember but must have closed her eyes. Die like a helpless animal. Please God. Don't let it hurt.

The gunfire echoed in one long, rolling blast. Yet by some miracle she was alive. Her eyes open, she saw Wyatt standing, not facing her, but crouched and firing to his left. An old tree stump virtually disintegrated.

He stood up. Then hands seized her from behind. Her wrists were tied behind her back and she was pushed face down on the ground. Hands ran swiftly over her entire body, from

156

the top of her head to the boots she wore beneath the jeans. The boots were pulled off, then the belt from her jeans. Not tied and helpless. No, not this way. Oh God please. She screamed at her searcher.

'Can't you get a woman any other way?'

She was rolled over on to her back. A short, square apparition with slab Mongolian features and shiny black hair seemed to be grinning at her. She kicked out at him then he landed on top of her, his weight pinning her hips to the ground. Her legs were tied with the belt and she was turned to face Wyatt. Thank God, she was not to be raped . . . yet. She was now in a sitting position, arms and legs tied and very helpless but at least she had all her clothes on. The oriental-looking man took out a short knife.

Jo Lannerson started screaming.

CHAPTER TWELVE

By now it was common knowledge that I had returned from the dead and we were expecting trouble. So it was no real surprise that on Sunday 26th September at 3.27pm I was looking down a gun barrel. From my point of view, the wrong way, and it was a big gun barrel. The length does not realy count. It is the size of the black hole pointing at you that matters. This one was at least .357 Magnum, maybe bigger—the kind that makes a neat little entry in the front, a gaping mess the size of a Mansion House banquet tureen at the back, and does one hell of a lot of damage in between.

At such times I tell myself I really should have given up this kind of nonsense years ago. The other kind of nonsense I willingly and actively indulge: this one was five seven with steady blue eyes, tight blue denims and a wild, if carefully dishevelled, hairstyle. She could have been modelling perfume, or sex in the wide, open spaces and lost her photographer. No such luck. The look on her highboned, haunted face told me she was not joking.

She announced she was going to kill me. And somehow that did not fit with my expectations of a professional who just shoots you, usually from behind cover, without the social niceties of an introduction. No, this girl was an amateur, and they sometimes do a lot of talking before actually pulling the trigger. I was curious, so I started a dialogue.

The matter appeared personal. I was supposed to have killed her father. That did not make sense to me. None of the bastards I had taken out on that cold mountain a month

158

before would have had offspring the requisite age, let alone the obvious quality, of this girl. Distraught relatives are not usually expert with handguns and this girl was definitely in the novice category. She was doing a good imitation of all the double-handed pistol grip stances she had seen on all the T.V. shows. Her feet were wrong and her limited weight was out of balance. If and when she squeezed the trigger of that Magnum, the recoil would land her flat on her slim backside. Although she was only five yards away, she could not hold the muzzle steady. It wavered around my middle region. She might have hit me, but the odds were high against it. And at five yards, the makers of the quilted jacket I wore had sworn their product would stop a .41 Magnum. The tests I had seen had been very impressive.

I moved in closer and got to within nine feet before she said: 'Stop.' There were tears in her eyes now; tears of rage, of lost love, of the gods knew what. There was no more time to indulge my curiosity or gamble unnecessarily, even with those high odds in my favour. She was ready to shoot.

I gave the pre-arranged signal. A Browning long-recoil shotgun was fired harmlessly into the air, twenty yards off. I had already started talking—an old distracting trick. I had moved my hand again—another. The sound of the shotgun confused her. Then, of course, she had not cocked the Magnum, which meant she had to fire double-action—at least a four pound trigger pull.

All the split seconds, the distractions, added up. I moved fast. And I can move very fast when I have to. My weight flattened her. No, I am not fat, just bony and quick. She lost the gun which I picked up before slapping her face, hard. By the time she was aware of what had happened, I was standing five yards off holding her gun, a Colt Python .357 Magnum. A big gun for such a little lady. She knelt down obediently and thought I was about to shoot her. Brave girl, she told me to get on with it. I liked her style.

I thought maybe a demonstration of how to use the gun properly might convince her of my genuine intentions. I crouched, swung right ninety degrees, and let go six, rapid-fire, at an old tree stump twenty yards away. The echoes rolled into one long blast. Every crow not disturbed by the shotgun going off decided there must be somewhere else for a quiet afternoon nap and scattered into the blue yonder.

Ko then tied the girl and searched her for any more weaponry. He had fired the shotgun on my signal. A careful man, Ko. The girl thought he was about to do something else when she lost her boots and her belt. She saw him take out his knife and let out one long scream.

Ko had that effect on people. If you did not know him you could think he was contemplating you for lunch. Five foot tall, squarely built, with shiny black hair so bright many believed he polished it, Ko was a Dayak. He looked like a slab-faced Mongolian, and not too pretty in his natural state—short bow and arrows slung on his back, Browning shotgun in hand and sheathed machete at hip. How he joined me is a long story with origins in Sarawak. Dayaks were headhunters and first-rate trackers. Ko could track a lizard across rock and his hobby was creeping up on ghosts and scaring them witless. He worked out on the Ty Newydd estate as assistant gamekeeper to Bill Grant. We did not have any poaching problems.

'What happens now?' the girl asked. 'Do I get put in his cooking pot or do I become the tribal plaything?'

Brave, muddy-faced, bright-eyed kid, she was giving as good as she got. The R.T. in my fishing bag crackled. I answered. Tom Watson, my other look-out, reported:

'I heard the Browning then you playing silly buggers with a handgun. No-one else is

161

around. I found the girl's car. Renault Five parked in the gateway of Long Hill Meadow. Driving licence and insurance documents in the name of Josephine Lannerson. Also a Press Card and Union membership. I'll take the vehicle in. Land Rover coming for you in ten minutes. Do you require the Old Bill?'

'Not yet.'

'You knew I was coming?' the girl demanded, puzzled.

'I was expecting some kind of trouble. That saved your life. Had I been alone down here, I'd never have let you get close enough to point guns at me. Now, what makes you think I killed your father, Josephine?'

'My name is Jo,' she replied, petulantly. 'And if I answer that question, you'll probably kill me.'

Ko observed pertinently:

'Missy, if Tuan going to kill you, you be dead by now.'

Not exactly the confidence-building character reference I needed, but true. Ko realized he had said the wrong thing and lapsed into silence. And some people said he was insensitive! He took a tin from his pocket and started rolling a foul mixture of tobacco into a cigarette paper. I nodded. He handed me one. Determined girl, man-stopping cannon, nasty few minutes; I needed a cigarette.

'You like tobacco, Missy?' Ko grinned.

Jo Lannerson nodded. Ko put a cigarette between her lips and, with a sweeping motion of his left hand, cut her wrists free. She almost counted her fingers. Then she coughed as the tobacco took effect. Whatever brand Ko smokes would give an iron lung cancer.

I was trying hard to remember. The name Tony Lannerson did not register. Faces—I've a photographic memory, but names...

'What makes you think I killed your father?' I tried again.

'Get stuffed,' she replied.

'You're no professional, that's certain. But you're determined and you've got guts. Now unless you tell me who Tony Lannerson was and what gave you the false idea that I killed him, we'll pass you on to the police. Attempted murder, possession of an unlicensed firearm, you'll probably do five years.'

'I expected you to own the police as well.'

The remark was bitter, like she really believed it. The tears were there now, tears of grief and failure. She was shaking and feeling very alone.

The R.T. crackled. Tom Watson again:

'Wyatt. There's a letter here in her car which will interest you.'

163

'Read it.'

'Addressed to Tony Lannerson at Tectrokite in Gloucester. Dear Tony, re: Wolverine. Further to Yardley's instructions, ensure Wolverine ready. Failure will result in your employment being terminated. The word "employment" is in inverted commas. On Aberinvest notepaper dated Thursday and it looks like your signature. Anyone who didn't know you better might conclude you'd been dropping subtle hints about removing Lannerson permanently.'

I looked directly at the girl. She looked back hate.

'My father's last words, Wyatt: Wolverine, Aberinvest killed me. Get Wyatt.'

I inhaled tobacco too deeply. I had neither dictated nor signed any letters in weeks. Something was rotten in the state of Aberinvest now. And instinct told me it might not be a coincidence.

$$\star \qquad \star \qquad \star$$

An hour later Jo Lannerson was standing in my study at Ty Newydd. We were alone and she had cleaned her face up. Now all of her looked good. I poured two measures of malt, large ones, and she accepted a cigarette.

'I blew it,' she admitted. 'You and your

164

millions have won. You've proved influence and this whole stinking rotten system can crush the ordinary people and get off scot-free. My father never hurt anyone—I hate you.'

In impotent fury she threw the glass. I ducked successfully. I was getting used to her aggressive attitude now. But the attack was half-hearted. As I caught her the aggression gave way to grief. She buried her head against my shoulder and her hands clutched my shirt. Maybe she had not really cried for her father before.

I am not good with the bereaved. There is no easy way and there are no words. You cannot bring back the dead. She had done what she thought was the next best thing. She had come after me to avenge her father. More courage than I would have had in her position. She had come alone, face to face, no backshooting or hired pros. Foolish but brave. I admired her for that. And now the poor kid had run out of steam. I was something human to hang on to. I stroked her curly hair and kept my mouth shut.

I remembered Tony Lannerson. I had met him once. A straight, honest, hard-working man the sharks had taken to the cleaners. He had lost family and business. Fallon hired him back to run the business he had lost. Good organizer, Lannerson, but none too strong on business politics which are dirtier than the other kind. I had once told him if he needed me to get in touch. His last words to the girl. 'Wolverine, Aberinvest killed me. Get Wyatt.'

Not Kill Wyatt, the poor mixed up kid, just get him to help me sort this problem out. Too late. Then there was the letter. Now that was a forgery but taken with her father's death circumstantial evidence neat enough to convince her I was guilty of something.

She cried for some time, then apologized, the way people do. I smiled at her. Maybe I had not been there to help her father. And maybe I did have another problem on hand. But to con a girl into going up against pros like me and the lads at Ty Newydd was tantamount to murder in my book.

'They meant you to think I had killed Tony, Jo. I promise you I didn't. But I'm going to find out who did.'

★   ★   ★

Johnny had called in at 5.30 to say he was on his way down and had there been any developments. With the death of Alpha and the passing of Moresby I was the only protagonist of the Nimrod business left alive and the way things looked it was only a matter of time before someone tried for me. Which was why Jo Lannerson had walked into a carefully laid trap.

The thought had crossed my mind that she was telling stories and that maybe she did work for those who did not truly have my best interests at heart. If she did then she had made about as big a mess of taking me out as someone had made of Alpha's face. I had immediately started checking up on the story. Sunday or not, quite a few people were working overtime.

Johnny had some information that would prove very relevant to Alpha's death. We would confer when he arrived. Meanwhile I was alone in the study with a telephone, a notepad and a computer printout. The terminal at Ty Newydd had been busy since 4.30pm. Fallon was handling the Aberinvest in-house enquiries from London. We were spending a lot of money buying information at short notice.

I had Lannerson's last words written out in front of me. Wolverine, Aberinvest killed me. Get Wyatt. The poor bastard had run out of life before he could say any more. The hospital had diagnosed massive cardiac arrest. Why was everyone dying of heart attacks? I wrote that down on the notepad.

Wolverine was the very latest in

sophisticated missile hardware—the ultimate defence system. Relatively inexpensive and considered ten years ahead of its time it could knock down anything from an incoming aircraft to an artillery shell. The revolutionary detection device built into the system could see in areas blind to radar and locked the Wolverine on to its target at a range of up to fifty miles. A ten-year-old with a Ph.D could operate it. Tectrokite and the Ministry had a restricted sales list. H.M.G. and good friends only. It occurred to me that Wolverine was the ideal defence system for any small-time dictator or neighbourhood nutcase who wanted to shove his weight around and then show two fingers to any threatened retaliation by air or sea.

Arms sales were big business worldwide. The computer printout showed me how big. World overseas arms sales in 1969 were worth 9 billion U.S. dollars. By 1978 at constant prices they grossed 19 billion. And by 1988 the projection was 40 billion plus. Tectrokite had a tidy slice of the cake. The human race seemed intent on practising self-inflicted genocide. The big arms deals were the new diplomacy. Jobs and foreign exchange depended on them. Politicians acted as salesmen and were not averse to trundling the occasional Royal around while the M.O.D.

168

sales boys made their pitch.

No-one liked talking about the dirty side of the business. Covert purchases, smuggling, blackmail, the slush funds all necessitated the knife-in-the-back deals and the dead bodies.

We already had one dead body.

I am no detective but I jump to a good conclusion. It looked like Aberinvest were into a Wolverine deal that necessitated killing Lannerson. But he had suffered a heart attack.

By 7pm I was on my fourth cup of coffee and confirmation of Jo Lannerson's background and profession. Journalist with marked Marxist leanings. Writer for the ultra-left *Red Widow* and working on an exposé of multi-nationals. My informant told me to be careful. 'She'd like to castrate Aberinvest and probably you too, Wyatt.'

I had a name in front of me. John Yardley, the chairman of Tectrokite and an Aberinvest executive working out of the Bristol regional offices. According to all the Tectrokite paperwork I had managed to lay my hands on via the computer link, Yardley and Lannerson were the only two characters needed to decide a policy for Tectrokite and then carry it out. Yardley had to be the man to see. I wrote his name down on my notepad.

The computer link was churning out more

169

paperwork when the telephone rang. It was Fallon.

'Tony Lannerson left several calls for you at the London office. Damn fool of a secretary did not sort them out properly from all the press requests for interviews. The first call was left on the answering machine sometime after midnight on Thursday. Then he followed that up with several more around 8am on Friday morning. After that nothing. Sorry Wyatt.'

So was Lannerson. He had tried to talk to me and I hadn't been around. Maybe if I had seen him the pressure would have been off his heart. I poured another cup of coffee.

Before I had time to drink it, the noise of the helicopter coming in to land told that Johnny was back. Within two minutes from touchdown he was in my study. He looked like he had not slept since we last spoke. He helped himself to a large vodka and lit a Gauloise. The brown Manila envelope in his hand landed in front of me.

'You'd better look at that,' he said. 'I've been halfway round Europe for those holiday snaps. They were taken by Alpha's man. I told you he was a Hungarian, so who else would he use but someone he could trust, someone from the old days. He used Pavel and Pavel is running very scared. I paid him

170

twenty thousand in cash for those pictures. If they aren't worth it, tough.'

The photographs were all dated and marked with a location. They showed Gareth Llewellyn Jones going into a house in Portman Square. Further shots showed a country house and cars arriving. I recognized Llewellyn Jones and a short, tubby Arab who resembled a stuffed olive. Prince Asif bin Said, Chief Minister of Bakar. The house was called Arlingford and belonged to one Charles, Viscount Penmayne, darling of the Royal enclosure and a man you'd never shake hands with because you'd always have to count your fingers afterwards.

Moresby's legacy. Watch events in Bakar. Johnny was already at the study door.

'Where are you going?' I asked.

'To pack my keffiyah and sandals. Tom Watson was with you in Bakar, wasn't he? I'll take him if that's all right with you.'

I nodded.

'Stay close to King Baquoos,' I ordered. 'I'll have the jet put on standby now. Be careful, Johnny. Asif is a slippery little excrescence. He'll have some useful talent watching out for him. And he carries a knife, left-handed.'

CHAPTER THIRTEEN

I saw Detective Chief Superintendent Dan Caswell at 8.30pm. He was leaning on a walking stick and his piercing blue eyes spoke of some inner pain, coming from his right foot by the look of the odd shoes he wore. A man in his late forties, wiry and dark-haired with the foxy expression of a senior plainclothes man who knew exactly what he was doing, Caswell sank into the armchair in my study and accepted the Scotch.

'Got the bloody gout,' he grimaced.

'Serves you right for being a crafty old politician,' I replied. 'Should you really be drinking?'

'And why not? I suppose you think it is an old piss artist's disease. News for you, it isn't. The vet of a police doctor prescribed something useless. My own quack is on a month in the Bahamas. Scotch at least makes the pain bearable. And hobbling up here to the master's private quarters has not helped. Well now, I have spoken to the girl.'

'And?'

'Advised her if she made a complaint it would be investigated. I would also require authority from her to have an autopsy performed. I don't really but it will speed things up.' He coughed and lit one of his Capstans:

'I am in possession of the note she alleges was found at her father's cottage. I am also in possession of your statement denying the letter was written by you or on your behalf. Don't you know any other policemen?'

'Why?'

'You could go and use them for your crazy schemes. By rights I ought to lock you and the girl up and take it from there. I probably would too except she would howl "police brutality", and the county would go broke when it received your claim for damages alleging wrongful arrest. You should make a complaint against her for assault with a firearm.'

'No.'

'Thought not. You are using me aren't you? Sort of Uncle Caswell in case things go wrong. Do you think I could have the entire sordid truth from the time you arrived back in this country to this moment? The last time I got mixed up with you my inflation-proof pension almost went to my next-of-kin.'

Caswell, fox-crafty and cunning, would have been burned as a witch not so long ago. He listened as I told him the whole truth and nothing but the truth. Then he held out his glass for more Scotch and winced at another twinge of gout.

'If I didn't know you, I'd suggest you be committed under the Mental Health Act. Low Celtic speculation gets you one common factor in all this—two heart attacks. One for the diplomat, the other for Lannerson. Very long shot. Stories about traitors in high places and the murder of Alpha are outside my regional province. So why don't you forget about all of it and go back to Canada? That way if someone does kill you another policeman will have the privilege of nicking the miscreant.'

Practical man, Caswell, he always gave sound advice.

'No can do. I gave Moresby my word I'd stick with Alpha. And I once told Tony Lannerson that if he ever needed me, get in touch. Apart from which, the King of Bakar is one reason for our being able to sit here in such rustic splendour quaffing twelve-year-old malt at today's prohibitive prices.'

Caswell lit another cigarette. 'I was afraid you would say something like that. This conversation never took place. Could your cheque-book medicare wake up a pathologist and put him to work? Saves me embarrassing the local nick before I have to. Can I smell Mrs Harries's cooking?'

'I suppose you had better stay to dinner.'

'I take it that I will soon be sticking my neck out on your behalf, then?'

'You take it correctly.'

'In that case pour me another Scotch.'

*　　*　　*

At almost 1am I was walking the grounds. The night was yellow with moonlight and cloudless. The Khan brothers, Genghis & Kublai, were stalking the area like black demon footpads. I heard movement behind me and I was too late to do anything about it. Or I would have been if the dark shape had been hostile. It was Ko. It had to be. The Khan brothers had made no aggressive moves. Then another figure appeared from behind him—Jo Lannerson.

'Tuan,' Ko nodded sheepishly, looking uncomfortably at me then at the girl: 'I go now, Missy.'

'Ko—Thank you,' the girl called out. But Ko had gone.

'Why did he leave so suddenly? When he saw you, in fact?'

'Ko saw me long before you did and before I even knew he was there. You were holding on to his arm, so he was embarrassed. Warrior, you see. Doesn't do that sort of thing in front of the other warriors.'

175

'Or his Tuan, his master?' she asked scathingly.

'Just a name. Like all true primitive warriors, Ko will only follow if he wants to go. Very democratic, you see.'

'He is no ignorant savage,' she objected.

'I said true primitive warrior, meaning he has an absolute sense of right and wrong. Something we educated white men have lost the ability to distinguish in many instances. Ko lives by a code.'

'And he respects you. He says you would never have had my father killed.'

'Really?'

'He says you would have done it yourself. And that policeman Caswell says that heart attacks can be induced, that the Russians used to kill their dissidents that way. Do people like you blame all the world's ills on the Soviet Union?'

'No. About sixty per cent.'

A silence. Maybe I had said the wrong thing. We leaned on the paddock fence. Somewhere in the distance a horse snorted. She hung on my arm and tensed.

'Only a horse,' I reassured her.

I could see her blue eyes in the moonlight. There were tears beginning to well. I took out a handkerchief and wiped the tears away.

'Ridiculous, isn't it?' she whispered.

'Tough little lady journalist who doesn't know where she is or who to trust. Ko says someone is trying to kill you. You say they set me up to do the job for them. And I can't see the truth. I just wish my father had been left out of all this. But I know that there are no innocent people, that we are all guilty by association.'

'Rules of engagement say combatants only. Your father was no combatant, he was used, you were used and for all I know someone is using me. All you can do is fight it.'

'And what do you win at the end of it all, Wyatt?'

'Probably my peace of mind.'

'Why not just walk away. The soft option. Enjoy all this obscene wealth?'

'Because I gave my word. To your father among others. And I'll nail the bastard who killed him, if he was killed, and I'm almost sure he was. No moral crusade with the people deciding in committee what to do. Just a dirty fight, probably between professionals. Meanwhile you can stay here and make notes about big, bad millionaires for your forthcoming book.'

She said only: 'Will you take me inside now, please?'

★   ★   ★

I did not go to bed. It was my move in the surrealistically sinister chess game. I had this irrational feeling that the deaths of Ablett-Green, the diplomat in Bakar, and Tony Lannerson were parallel ploys in some enormous game. There was no evidence and the only other person even to guess was Caswell. Low Celtic speculation he had called it. I put it down to Celtic instinct. Which can often be wrong. I know. I am part Celt.

There are two ways to encourage a man to do something he knows he should not do. You frighten him badly enough, or you buy him. The true conspirator uses a combination of both. Lannerson had called his daughter on the Thursday night, late. She knew he was worried. As it turned out she blamed herself for not going to him that night. He had left calls for me that same night. So I reckoned someone had put the frighteners on him, through threats to his daughter. Then they had killed him almost in front of her. And a letter implicating me had been left conveniently among his papers. If they were this well organized, they had to have something against me to leave so many pointers. They must have kept him under surveillance. And they had probably nobbled another Tectrokite executive. The key man was John Yardley. I needed some proof.

178

We hit Tectrokite's factory outside Gloucester mob handed at dawn. Jo Lannerson had insisted on coming. Fallon wanted to be nice to the Press, even the fringe Press, so I told him he would have to keep an eye on her. Bleary-eyed, he was wearing the acceptable face of capitalism and asking her what a well brought-up young lady was doing with a bunch of self-interested anarchists and misfits like the *Red Widow*.

I was deep in a last-minute briefing with Bill Grant and Noblett, the Aberinvest Chief Security Officer who got airsick in helicopters.

Bill Grant was there to watch my back, under secret instructions from Johnny, I suspected. A quiet, soft-spoken Scot, my own age, fifteen stone of unobtrusive muscle, he wore a sympathetic smile and a 9mm Browning. Reputed to be the highest-scoring entrant ever to enter the S.A.S. 'killing room' at Hereford, Bill had done it for real during a little-publicized hijack attempt at Cairo. The court administrators did not need to reschedule their cases to try any surviving participants. There weren't any. He had come to Ty Newydd after his time was up. A boyhood spent in one of the Scottish sporting estates made him the natural choice for head keeper. He sat puffing on a Peterson pipe and nodding silently at each instruction.

Noblett was sixty, thin, grey haired and bespectacled, frail even. To look at him you would think he could not cross the road by himself. He used to fool the Gestapo that way, running a Maquisard group for the old S.O.E.—Moresby's generation, and a sly old pro. To see him indicating the location of buildings on his map you'd have thought he was still out there. The instructions were clear and crisp:

'I'll grab the gatehouse and send the factory S.O. to you at the R. & D. Buildings entrance. You young gentlemen can secure the main switchboard and operate the security switch to ensure all calls are routed through that switchboard. If they do have a man keeping tabs, he'll have to leave via the main gates and I'll be checking all passes and vehicles until Yardley arrives. What time is he due, Mr Fallon?'

'Sorry, Nobby, not paying attention.'

Noblett repeated the question patiently.

'Eight-thirty. We calculated forty-five minutes from Bristol. I told him not to be late. It was a matter of urgency that we decide on Lannerson's replacement by mid-morning. Board meeting this afternoon at Aberinvest. He'll buy it.'

'Telephonist?' Noblett asked, looking

directly at Jo Lannerson. 'Vital chore. Not exciting, but vital.'

Noblett has a considerable understanding of people. He wanted to involve her.

'I can operate a P.B.X.'

'This one's a piece of cake, then. You must clear all outgoing calls with Wyatt, who will then have a chance at all the hidden paperwork, if any. Right, I'll go up front and tell the pilot to anounce me just as we touch down.'

Bill Grant was first out as the rotor blades whistled to a standstill. He glanced around the perimeter fence, eyes scanning the grey mass of buildings and noting the high points. Noblett flitted towards the gatehouse, like a jinking woodcock in the half-light. By the time we reached the R. & D. Building, security men in dark blue uniforms were saluting everything that moved.

The factory S.O., a short, balding man with a Cockney accent, buzzed around us like some demented Uriah Heep until I thanked him warmly for his efforts in opening the offices and told him Noblett wanted him at the gatehouse. 6.15am Monday 27th September. All to plan . . . so far.

If you can get up in the morning you can always be ready for those who intend to be ready for you.

181

Bill Grant was poking around the offices with a pocket-sized device that emitted a low whistling sound. Fallon looked on distastefully. Hooligans like us had no business in well-furnished offices.

'E.C.M.,' I replied to Jo Lannerson's questioning glance. 'Electronic counter-measures. Detecting hidden and direction-finding microphones zeroed in on us.'

A world full of surprises, the technological area. Industrial espionage is very big business, R. & D. costs being what they are. But the offices were clean, although there were some scratch marks inside the receiver of Lannerson's desk telephone, where the mouthpiece was wired in. Bill Grant and I looked at each other. I was right. They had kept Lannerson under surveillance. Who had planted the inside bug? Noblett interrupted the proceedings by calling through on the internal phone system to tell me the bad news:

'One Wolverine system. Contract No CX 140/4293/83 already delivered to the freighting area at Heathrow at 6am. Customs clearance was immediate because of the M.O.D. clearance code. Charter aircraft departed immediately. Provisional destination Tripoli.'

We all knew which neighbourhood nutcase lived there. 6.45am and the Wolverine was airborne. I checked the paperwork.

182

Conarmco, a highly-regarded American company, were the purchasers. Export licence granted by the Department of Trade. End user certificates provided by Conarmco. The end user certificate is a device whereby the recipient guarantees the system will not be used contrary to the interests of the supplying government. If you believed that you really did believe in fairies. All you had to do was sign your name on the dotted line and declare your friendly intentions. As Fallon said: 'You could sign one Mickey Mouse and they'd probably accept it.'

Bad news never comes alone. Caswell was on the line. I sent Fallon to be with Jo. I did not expect her to burst into tears. She had reconciled herself now.

'Traces of prussic acid found in Lannerson's stomach,' Caswell announced. 'So I looked up the method.'

We were about to hear chapter and verse from: 'A Rustic Copper's Reminiscences on the Methods of Foul Play.'

'1959. Russian dissidents or rather Ukrainian émigrés, Rebet and Stepan Bandera, murdered by one Bogdan Stasshinsky, Department Five, K.G.B. in West Germany. Stasshinsky later defected and told all. Gas pistol discharged into faces of victims. Heart attack induced by sprayed prussic acid. Bit old for present day operatives, though.'

'No patent on ideas like that, Dan.'

'Well you watch yourself. And wait until I arrive there with the local bobbies. I have received a complaint. I will now investigate.'

Dan Caswell had a one hundred per cent clear-up rate on murder. But I was here first. I made the appropriate noises and put the phone down.

'Bastards,' Bill Grant murmured.

'Take Jo out to her father's cottage and have a very good look. Noblett will give you a man to watch your back.'

'I'd love 'em to try,' Bill replied and wandered off.

I was reading the paperwork and making notes on Swiss banks and guarantees for the contract price of Wolverine already paid when the door opened. A hatchet-faced old harpy, grey-haired and exuding the bureaucratic sang-froid of the old-style typing-pool Gauleitress, marched in. I told her who I was and found the Scotch. I put glasses in front of us both and told her Lannerson was murdered, I was interested in a particular Wolverine contract and I wanted all the answers she could supply.

Like most people who have worked a long time for one company, she felt she was part of

184

it. So I recognized the fact and told her a few white lies about how indispensable she was. Her manner thawed from deep-frozen to gas-cooled. Maybe it was the Scotch going down or my charming personality. Hell! I am good with old ladies. I used to frog-march them across High Streets as a Boy Scout.

She remembered exactly when Yardley came to Tectrokite. He had called on Thursday and again arrived Friday afternoon, late, in the company of an American who wanted reassurances about the Wolverine. News of Lannerson's death must have travelled very fast. His secretary had not known about it until 4.30pm on Friday. Security had informed her via the local hospital.

Which gave an outsider the opportunity to enter Lannerson's office, in company with friend Yardley.

Then the intercom rang. Fallon had heard, via Noblett, that Yardley's Daimler was at the gatehouse. I told Fallon to stay out of sight and take the old harpy with him.

I did not want any witnesses to my conversation with John Yardley.

CHAPTER FOURTEEN

Yardley bowled into the office with all the confident ebullience of a front-loading dumpy truck. Early forties, short and heavily built he reminded me of a prize-fighter who had got just a little too fat. I could see the aggression in his swivelling eyes and heavy face, the surge of his powerful shoulders as he bulldozed towards Lannerson's desk and pressed the intercom.

'Miss Johnson. Come in here and get this pigsty cleaned up. Scotch bottles and glasses all over the damn place. The Managing Director is due here any minute.'

The voice was rough Bristolian, rasping and unfriendly. I had been watching him through a crack in Miss Johnson's office door. So I walked in.

'Who the hell are you?' he demanded, glowering at me like a mad old Charolais bull.

'You have blood pressure problems,' I observed quietly.

He stood up and walked towards me. Swivelling eyes took in my generally affluent appearance and the thin Havana. His confidence appeared momentarily dented, but it was a bluff. The heavy hands were at his sides, fingers working slowly.

'I asked you who you were?'

I smiled and kicked him straight in the groin. A real ball-busting kick, bang on target.

He doubled and dropped like a proverbial stone. The yell came from his stomach but I never heard it as such, just a gasping grunt as he rolled on the Axminster clutching his offended parts and groaning. The colour had drained from his face.

I poured myself a Scotch.

'No bullshit, Yardley. When you can articulate, tell me all about the Conarmco deal on the Wolverine. Lannerson was murdered by someone trying to implicate me. I am on a very short fuse right now, as you can feel.'

He pulled himself up using the desk as a prop. The swivelling eyes were bloodshot and scared. I wanted him terrified, just like they had terrified Lannerson. I wanted him friendless and alone, in fear of his life, dreading my next move.

I let him have another kick while his left hand was stretched out to the desk. As he collapsed again, the word 'bastard' was forming on his lips. Given the chance he would like to tear me to pieces. But he was not dealing with the meek design executives now, the poor sods like Lannerson who get kicked around by the corporate bullies of the world. He was dealing with me, Wyatt. Genuine twenty-five carat indestructible aggravation. And he deserved it.

I sipped the Scotch. He was taking longer to recover this time. The intercom buzzed. I stepped around the stumbling mess and answered. Noblett's crisp voice announced:

'We've checked all typewriters within a five office vicinity of Yardley. The note implicating you was typed on his secretary's machine.'

He hung up on me. Yardley was by now hanging halfway up the desk. The eyes pleaded with me not to hit him again. He was caught between two choices. Tell me or clam up. I had provided the pressure for him to tell me. In the back of his mind was a very good reason for clamming up. If his overweight hide was the only thing at stake he should have been blubbering out his story. The bullies of this world are like that.

'Yardley, I'm waiting.'

'They'll kill me,' he objected.

'And I won't? You really must be the bookmakers' friend.'

'It's not only me.'

'You start talking. I can arrange better protection than the Mafia.'

'I believe you can. Promise me they won't

hurt her.'

'Wife?'

He shook his head. Heavy trembling hands searched for a cigarette. Time to let up on the creature. I handed him a Scotch which went down in one. A crisis drinker. And Fallon told me Yardley was a candidate for the main Aberinvest board. Peter, you are losing your capacity for judgment.

The story came out. With some prompting from me and the aid of more Scotch he whimpered about being threatened by an American called Alexander Coburn who wanted the Wolverine. He knew it really was not a straight deal because of the money he had been offered. They had also threatened to cut up his girlfriend. Two heavy men had visited her and given her a very nasty shock. No violence, only soul-rending intimidation that had scared the poor kid witless. He confessed to giving Coburn the background on Lannerson, aiding Coburn to plant bugs in the Tectrokite offices and typing the letter incriminating me. Which was the point where he knew the American's story about a clandestine deal having Aberinvest support was bullshit. Too late then to get off the roller-coaster of nastiness.

When he had finished the sorry tale, I switched off the tape recorder hidden in the desk. I called Noblett and told him to ensure Yardley called the contact number he had been given for Coburn and to repeat the message I had written down.

It was time to see if these brave boys could scare me and Bill Grant.

*   *   *

The lovely Christine lived in the elegantly decaying part of Clifton where the unwashed rubbed shoulders with the students and the little old ladies who never went out alone at night. She was surprised to see us come in the back way.

Yardley had told the truth. She sat drinking coffee, long legs curled underneath her on an old sofa. An intelligent, good-looking girl, a student. Probably flattered by the attentions of a well-heeled bon viveur like Yardley. He spent money on her and she confessed to preferring older men. They had more experience of life. She was gradually realizing they also caused more problems.

'So if the doorbell rings, I just leave it?' she asked nervously. 'But the last time they came...'

'We weren't here,' Bill Grant observed. 'I promise you lass, they'll never come back.'

Ten minutes later the doorbell sounded.

Bill had been watching the street. Two off-the-peg nightclub types had emerged from a red Jaguar. They looked useful. Minutes later the front door was kicked in and I heard a Bristolian voice shout:

'Come on, darling. We know you're in there.'

The footsteps lurched down the passageway. The door was kicked open. As they entered the room a girl's hand tightened on mine. The first one was stocky, five eleven with short fair hair and the kind of face that had spent its thirty-odd years walking into things. The second was taller, heavier and older. He took off a pair of leather gloves and walked towards us.

'Beat it, lover boy,' he invited.

Never, ever let a bigger man outmanoeuvre you. I shrank back, visibly afraid and he took one step forward. His mate had turned and seen Bill Grant standing against the wall. I let the big boy have a cup of scalding hot coffee in his face and let go with my left foot.

I was a fair kicker in my rugby days and I let him have enough power to put a thirty-five yard drop goal straight between the posts. He went straight down, sightless and in absolute pain.

Bill Grant had hit his man three times before the ape knew the attack had started.

Ten seconds after the first gut-busting jab, the man was eating carpet, his hands cuffed behind his back.

'You were saying?' I asked.

But he wasn't. Bill soon had him trussed and both men searched. Wallets, car keys, a razor-sharp switchblade and credit cards even. I picked up the phone. Within five minutes, Noblett had arrived with an old van. The two incapables were removed and I thanked Christine for her co-operation. The wallets had contained two hundred pounds in cash. I reckoned that was fair compensation for disturbance. Fallon arranged for a carpenter to fix the front door.

'You deserve better than Yardley,' I told her.

★   ★   ★

The helicopter hovered two hundred feet above an angry Bristol Channel. The grey sea was whipped by a thirty-knot wind and it was a good day to be at the Boat Show. Our two acquaintances were propped up in the belly of the helicopter. The hatch was open and Bill Grant stood, the slipstream blowing his hair, strapped securely on a trailing line fixed to an anchor point on the bulkhead.

'Not very conversational,' he admitted.

192

They realized what was about to happen. In those seas they would have lasted half an hour, if that. The bravado had gone. They were two frightened creatures who realized they would soon be very much out of their depth.

'It's murder,' the first one yelled. 'For God's sake. We'll drown.'

'That my friend is the general idea. You are of no use to us. This way we ensure you never bother the girl or anyone else again. Vermin like you has forfeited its right to exist. Come on, Bill. Get the big bastard out.'

'I can't swim,' the big man whimpered.

'So what?' I smiled. 'The fall will kill you.'

He looked down at the bone-chilling water far below.

The story was not long in coming. They had been hired by an American to watch the girl and frighten her. The instructions for that day had been to mutilate her but of course they would not really have done it. No, they did not ever do that sort of thing.

There was no lead to Coburn, only the telephone number. Noblett was currently checking that out with a bent telecommunications person. Fifty quid bought you the address to go with the number. The two yobboes were just dumb, mindless muscle. The kind of trash that works for manipulators the world over. They enjoyed hurting people but when it came to an even fight you never saw the bastards for dust.

Bill blindfolded them. They screamed as we forced them through the open hatch at gunpoint. They had told us all they knew. Now we had gone back on the deal. To give them a sporting chance, Bill untied their hands.

'But the fall will kill us,' the first man shouted, wetting himself as he went through the hatch. His partner followed.

'Bye-bye,' Bill waved.

They fell only ten feet, into about five feet of water less than thirty yards off-shore. But they would have a long, wet walk home. There was not a house for miles.

CHAPTER FIFTEEN

Charles Penmayne had breakfasted at 6am on Monday 27th September. Now he sat alone in the study of his town house watching a video film. He had left orders not to be disturbed. His wife was in the country at Arlingford and he thought of her, fleetingly. She would have to see the film of course.

The quality was excellent and the sound reproduction very faithful. It showed the interior of Prince Asif bin Said's study. Martin Brett was being courteously welcomed. Habish, the silent Lebanese, was standing just behind Brett's chair. Penmayne turned the sound up for a better understanding of the conversation.

'Here are the papers for Lord Penmayne,' Asif smiled.

As Brett reached forward to take them, Asif smiled again. Habish had moved forward quickly and crushed a lighted cigarette on Brett's outstretched hand which had been forced down on the table. Habish smashed a ringed right hand into the Old Etonian's face. Blood spurted from a split nose.

'Someone told me you are working for British Intelligence,' Asif shouted, unaware of the deliberate unreliability of Penmayne's information. 'Well, Mr Brett. They are going to be under-manned.'

Brett had no chance of surviving the vicious onslaught in any state to be able to defend himself. Habish pulled him to his feet and jerked a knee into his groin. As Brett rolled on the carpet, sharp toed, steel capped shoes kicked a series of penalty goals into his kidneys and ribs. Sick, dizzy, Brett could not focus his watering eyes. The taste of blood and the pain soon had him retching. He tried to scream but no sound came. His mouth was

195

swollen and his tongue cut. He curled vainly into the foetal position to protect himself. A crack like a pistol shot filled his head. He relapsed into the relief of oblivion.

Asif ordered: 'Take him where he won't bleed on the carpet. Find out what he knows and what he has told.'

The film cut to the interior of a cellar. Brett had been suspended from a beam in the ceiling by handcuffed wrists that bled from the pressure. If he stood on his toes he could just reach the floor but not well enough to do more than alleviate a little of the pain.

Habish was an expert in interrogation. His university course had been refined by practical work for the P.L.O. on captured Israelis. A bucket of cold water stood in the big, square, drip-stained porcelain sink. A cassette recorder stood on a small table in the corner. Habish took off his jacket and tie.

Brett was not a brave man. Revived several times by cold water he mumbled incoherently as the tape ran. Even a brave man who has had his jaw broken in two places, several ribs cracked and whose testicles felt like medicine balls will say anything to avoid more pain. He babbled about Vanessa Rogerson being introduced to Asif and how on Monday 27th September, Prince Feisal Khaled, heir to the throne of Bakar, was in for a nasty surprise

196

when he visited London.

Habish left the room. Then a tall, blond German dressed in a beige safari suit reversed a chair so that the back faced Brett. The German sat, legs astride the chair, smoking a cigarette. Brett's shirt had been ripped off. The German leaned over and stubbed the cigarette out on Brett's stomach. The pain and the smell of burning flesh made Brett scream until he had no breath left. He was in a world he did not understand, in the grip of a soul-rending nightmare. He prayed the pain would end or that they would kill him.

Habish had discovered what he wanted to know. For him it was enough, a detached professional who would use any means to reach the required ends. But the professionals often attracted helpers like the German who enjoyed hurting people. Schroeder was such a man.

'Pretty boy, eh? Fast cars, fast women. Not so pretty now,' he laughed.

Another cigarette burned Brett's pock-marked flesh. But the cellar was soundproofed. Only the videotape and Brett's brain could hear him screaming.

The film ended. Penmayne sipped his coffee.

'That'll teach you to play around with my wife, you little upstart.'

Penmayne was about to turn the film off when the screen flickered to life again. He recognized a giggling and very naked Vanessa Rogerson with Prince Asif in a circular bed. The conversation was quite clear:

'More of your films, darling,' she laughed.

Asif had switched on a remote controlled video at the foot of the bed. He lay back on the pillows. Penmayne breathed in as he realized Asif was showing the girl the same film he had just seen. He heard Vanessa pleading with Asif who forced her to watch the film. Then he hit her several times around the face. Within minutes the girl was tied, face down on the bed, arms and legs outstretched.

'I execute spies,' Asif laughed.

What followed was too brutal for Penmayne to watch. He closed his eyes as Asif fell on the girl.

'Jesus Christ,' Penmayne exclaimed when the screaming had stopped, after what seemed to him hours.

Asif had his hands around the throat of Vanessa Rogerson's lifeless body.

Penmayne was perspiring. His hand trembled as he poured a very large brandy. All he could say for the next few minutes was: 'Jesus Christ. That Asif is a madman.'

*　　　*　　　*

198

The bodies of Vanessa Rogerson and Martin Brett would be discovered ten days later in a Surrey wood. Detective Chief Inspector Alan Cockcroft would regret the fact that his wife had got up especially early to cook him a very large breakfast. After some weeks he would identify the mutilated bodies. The case would go into the unsolved file. The bodies and their discovery would become the subject of a security 'D' notice.

*　　*　　*

Prince Feisal Khaled bin Baquoos, heir to the throne of Bakar, arrived at the London Embassy in Queen's Gate at 7.30am on Monday 27th September. The visit was not even officially classified as private, although the Ambassador and staff had been aware of his departure from Paris earlier that morning.

Something about the young man's bearing impressed the forty-year-old uniformed sergeant of the Diplomatic Protection Group who stood guard at the top of the ten steps that led to the Embassy's front door. A happy, brown-eyed smile greeted the sergeant who stood to attention and saluted the tall young Arab dressed in lightweight suit, silk shirt and tie.

'Good morning sergeant.' The Prince spoke excellent English.

'Good morning, sir,' Sergeant Arthur Lambert replied. Although unaware of his visitor's identity he realized the young man was important.

The second man to emerge from the Rolls-Royce Silver Shadow was an entirely different proposition. Tall, bearded and grizzled—a desert warrior in full dress if ever Lambert had seen one. The old Arab's war eagle eyes flashed, questioning any movement or glance directed at or near the young man. Lambert decided he would not like to meet this character in a dark alley or anywhere else for that matter and felt comfortable with the weight of a regulation-issue Smith & Wesson at his hip.

The chauffeur unloaded the luggage as the visitors entered the Embassy. Lambert's radio crackled. Message from the local station. They would relieve him in one hour for refreshments.

Inside, the Ambassador had lined his staff up to meet the Royal visitor. Prince Khaled courteously, if informally, greeted everyone and retired to the guest suite. His old Akrize protector took up position inside the suite's main doors. The fifty-eight-year-old Zaraq had protected the Prince for fifteen years and regarded the young man almost as a son. Khaled in turn looked upon Zaraq as a second father. He would often tease the old warrior for his protective obsession but would never call into account the Akrize's judgement.

'London, Zaraq. It is good to be here. Is my uncle Asif in the building?'

'I understand he calls later,' Zaraq replied, stiffly.

'Relax, old friend, we are in the Embassy, in London, among friends.'

Zaraq had never liked Khaled's uncle. He felt uneasy in the man's presence. Loyalty and law prevented his voicing distrust for the Chief Minister. They never prevented extra vigilance whenever the Chief Minister was in the vicinity. And Prince Khaled never made a bodyguard's task easy. He trusted all and talked continually of the need for peace and understanding between people. In many ways un-royal for a Bakari, his easy-going nature and desire for informality, his open-minded approach towards people and their problems, were qualities the conservative Zaraq found hard to understand.

'I will be with the Ambassador,' Khaled announced.

Zaraq knew this meant the Prince would be walking around the Embassy and grounds, sauntering in and out of the kitchens, joking with the office staff and when it opened, wandering into the visa section and talking incognito with the public. Thereafter the young Prince would probably decide to go shopping and not tell anyone, especially not Zaraq. The old man nodded and followed his master.

'You can stay and rest, Zaraq.'

'I rested on the flight.'

★   ★   ★

Twenty minutes prior to the Prince's arrival at the Embassy, Habish had entered the back way. Habish was well known by the staff as the Chief Minister's most trusted aide, and his five companions rated only a cursory glance from the security man on duty at the rear door. Extra protection for the Prince, Habish had explained in passing.

He kept an office at the Embassy, locked when not in use, entry forbidden to all but the Ambassador. At 7.43 Habish and the five men entered the room. They synchronized watches. Habish rolled back the carpet and from a six foot square, three foot deep floor cavity he took five Czech-made Samopal 62 machine-pistols. Each man received one and five spare thirty-round, detachable box magazines. The Samopal was nicknamed the

Skorpion and a favourite terrorist weapon, being only eleven inches long when the butt was folded and weighing only three pounds unloaded—an easily concealed weapon.

The five men had flown into London earlier in the week from differing points of departure. They all carried passports declaring them students or tourists. Habish and the London office of a political front organization had ensured they were well hidden and entertained until needed. Each man now loaded his Skorpion with practised efficiency and waited for the signal. They could hear the conversation between the Prince and Zaraq in the upstairs suite. Habish had hidden a bug there. The Lebanese selected a Soviet-made Kalashnikov AK 74 short assault rifle, considered by many experts to be the finest of its type in the world. He instructed the gunmen to await his signal.

By 8.00am the majority of the Embassy staff were taking a delayed breakfast. The Ambassador was sitting nervously in his first-floor study. He was under Habish's strict orders not to come out. But the Prince did not walk towards the Ambassador's room. Instead he came down the stairs. As he came into view, Habish's men deployed around the marble-floored hallway and raised their Skorpions. At that moment Zaraq appeared on the stairway.

Khaled saw what was happening and threw himself flat on the small landing a third of the way down the stairs. The range was less than fifty feet and the air hissed death as bullets ricocheted around him. Zaraq's leathery hands seized the Uzi submachine gun from beneath his flowing robes. Cruelly outnumbered and outgunned, he went into the attack.

The first gunman was stitched from groin to scalp by 9mm Parabellum bullets, his body torn and smashed against a pillar as heavy lead hail cut him down. The second attacker returned Zaraq's fire as the other three scampered for cover beneath the stairwell and behind another pillar. Zaraq was now prone on the small landing, shielding his prince with his body. Khaled had been shocked and surprised by the attack. But he had trained as an officer in the Bakari Scouts and knew his protector was making the right moves.

'Fire escape in the suite,' Zaraq ordered.

Khaled's move was dictated by Zaraq's covering fire. As the Akrize sprayed bullets around the hallway, the Prince moved. He felt a searing pain in his left shoulder and tripped. He had been hit. Zaraq took two bullets of the burst in his upper left forearm. Plaster and banister splinters filled the air as he returned fire. The Uzi was a weapon that could be used single-handed. A second gunman died in a lethal rain of lead as the third fired, covering an attacking rush by the other two. Zaraq had no option but to stand and draw their fire, away from the Prince. He knew it took a brave man to fire at a second target when the first was throwing death. Zaraq paid for his bravery with three bullets in his abdomen. But he had killed a third man. As he and the Prince retreated again up the deadly staircase he sprayed the hallway indiscriminately. Falling against his master, both men lay prone as Zaraq changed the Uzi's magazine.

The attackers were now questioning the choice of weapons. The model 62 Skorpion fired a 7.65mm automatic pistol cartridge, a load of only marginal combat effectiveness. Zaraq had been hit five times and although bleeding badly he was still in the fight. Sheer firepower ought to have been enough. But legend had it that an Akrize could take his own weight in lead and still fight on. As the fourth gunman moved forward he wished he was holding the model 68 that fired the man-stopping 9mm Parabellum round that Zaraq's Uzi fired to such deadly effect.

Habish had waited in the side doorway to his office. As the Bakari security guard at the rear door came rushing to the fray Habish fired a fully automatic burst from the Kalashnikov at point blank range. The Bakari's head disintegrated.

Khaled was meanwhile trying to drag his protector along the landing out of sight of the hallway. But the two gunmen below still had sight of the last short flight of stairs. Zaraq knew there was only one chance. He caught a fleeting glimpse of Habish below.

'Go, little Prince,' he ordered. 'Run. Trust no-one. Find your soldier friend.'

Zaraq pressed a Browning pistol from beneath his robes into the Prince's hand.

'Promise me. Go when I fire.'

There were tears of rage in Khaled's eyes. They had killed his friend, a friend who had died for him. He nodded.

Zaraq bellowed a terrifying war cry and rose as the last two gunmen opened fire. Uzi levelled, brass cartridge cases littering the staircase. The fourth attacker died as the war cry became the dreaded Akrize death cry. The fifth man dived for cover. Spitting blood from a punctured lung Zaraq ran forward, his last magazine empty. Habish appeared, Kalashnikov in hand, and smiled. Zaraq shouted.

'Lebanese whoremonger,' and drew a long-bladed knife.

Habish would never believe you had to kill

a man so many times. The Kalashnikov's heavy bullets finally halted Zaraq. Habish ran over the body towards the suite, shouting at the last gunman.

'Kill that policeman.'

Sergeant Arthur Lambert had radioed in at the first shots. But the encounter had taken only thirty-eight seconds from start to finish. He had run bravely towards the opening doorway as the last gunman shouted: 'Help. In here quickly.'

Smith & Wesson only half out of his holster, Lambert ran into the hallway and died in a welter of bullets, his jovial face still creased into a determined expression, his blue uniform torn and wide blotches spreading as he fell. The ultimate price of trying to uphold the law.

Habish was by now in the suite, but the Prince had gone, down the fire escape and over the back wall. He thought rapidly. As the last gunman entered the room to support him, Habish beckoned the man to the window. As the man passed him, Habish calmly placed the Kalashnikov muzzle at the back of the man's head and fired. The head disintegrated, showering blood and brains over the room.

The Prince had escaped and seen him with a gun. He would know the attack was planned from the inside. Which meant he had to die.

Instead of Khaled held captive and terrorists blamed, the plan had gone badly wrong. But before the deafening gun blast had stopped ringing in his ears, he had a solution.

By the time police and ambulances arrived, the last dead gunman, headless and dressed in the Prince's clothes, had become the Prince. The man now loose in London had become an escaped terrorist whose description was on the way to every port and point of departure in Britain.

Prince Asif bin Said telephoned the Foreign Office to protest. He also instructed Habish to put a price of one million pounds on the Prince's head, dead or alive. Within the hour every P.L.O. man and allied sympathizer, terrorist or just plain criminal, was seeking the wounded man. Khaled, bleeding and fleeing for his life, had only one chance. Like crocodiles sensing blood, hunters from every direction slid into the anonymous pool of the city.

CHAPTER SIXTEEN

Khaled stumbled on the bottom rung of the fire escape and was lucky not to crack his skull on the concrete. Sick and dizzy, his shoulder wound bleeding, he picked himself up. He had the presence of mind to retrieve the fallen Browning automatic and tuck the pistol into his waistband beneath his waistcoat. A wild breathless rush and he had reached the six-foot-high wall surrounding the Embassy garden. The palm of his hand was badly gashed as he caught the barbed wire and desperately pulled himself to the top of the wall. There was no power in his left arm and the pain was getting worse. The shock waves shuddered through his whole body as he landed feet first in the side street, dripping globules of blood on to the narrow pavement.

Zaraq's last words echoed in his confused thoughts: 'Run. Trust no-one. Find your soldier friend.'

Khaled waited in the dead ground by the wall and steeled himself. He recalled more words, spoken to him years ago by that soldier friend, as they covered fifty miles of hostile territory after a bloody rescue mission.

'You can make it, soldier. Repeat after me. "I will get there."'

Khaled did just that. Now, he spoke the words again.

'I will get there. I will get there.'

He ran into Queen's Gate Terrace. Traffic was already building in Gloucester Road and he needed transport. He could not run much further. Money. He had no money. But he had the gun. He knew his soldier friend's company offices were in the City. But the City was some distance away. He remembered distances and directions from his student days. Buses had too many people. The Underground could be watched. A taxi, he needed a taxi.

Across the Gloucester Road was a policeman. He almost ran across to call for help. But no. Habish had been involved in the shooting.

And Habish was still alive in the Embassy. Habish worked for his uncle, Prince Asid. The awful possibility hit Khaled instantaneously. More pain. Then Zaraq's words. 'Trust no-one.' Khaled turned his back on the street and dodged into a shop doorway. His jacket was soaking with blood in a spreading blotch below his left shoulder. He took off the jacket and folded it, covering the bloodstain. With a brave effort that brought pain lancing through his entire arm he clamped his left hand over the folded jacket that now covered the shoulder wound.

He walked along the road, eyes searching for a taxi. His legs were weak and all he wanted to do was lie down, anywhere, and pass out. But he kept on, repeating to himself: 'Left. Right. Left. Right. I. Will. Get. There.

Left. Right. I. Will. Get. There.' He was establishing a rhythm, a parade-ground march. He could hear his Bakari drill instructor. Left. Right. Left. Right.

A taxi pulled in, ten yards ahead. Khaled ran. He pushed a woman out of the way and staggered into the back seat. The driver noted his bleeding hand.

'Hospital for you. You're all in.'

'No. To the City, please. Ludgate Circus.' Khaled was breathing hard. The interior of the cab soon became a kaleidoscope of swirling colours. No. He fought the pain. I. Will. Get. There.

The cabby, a big man with three chins and greasy hair, had left the sliding glass compartment open. Suddenly he felt something sharp prod him in the back of his pneumatic neck.

'Please,' Khaled gasped. 'To Ludgate Circus. I mean you no harm. They are trying to kill me. No radio, please.'

Nervous eyes looked in the driving mirror. The cabby obeyed. His stomach was turning over and the sensation was not caused by the fatty bacon, fried sausages and eggs that had been his breakfast half an hour earlier. He looked again in the mirror and saw the young man's eyes. Determined yet somehow kind.

'Don't be stupid, son,' he stammered.

211

'The police are not following me. I am no criminal. I will not harm you, I promise.'

The cabby knew it was not his day. Why had he turned in for work with a severe head cold? Because the damn kids were off school with measles and the wife's mother had left her old man again. Because the terraced house was like an asylum and the wife would nag him for getting under her feet with the house full. And now some demented wog was pointing a gun at him.

He drove sedately. Khaled warned him against having any silly accidents or driving too near any policemen. He decided the wisest course of action was to obey. He entreated the young man not to do anything hasty.

Khaled was weakening fast. He tried to think out every move. He had transport and he looked for the landmarks. Not far now to Holborn Circus. Stay awake. I. Will. Get. There.

'I have your cab number,' Khaled announced as the taxi neared Ludgate Circus.

The driver had difficulty in breathing. His throat was tight. Perspiration had trickled down and the small of his back was wet.

'I'll keep quiet, mate. You're well out of order doing this but I'll keep quiet.' He pleaded with Khaled against retribution.

'I have no money ... so I will send ... the

. . . fare on.'

The driver could not believe his ears. As he pulled into the kerb, his passenger left the vehicle, slamming the rear door behind him.

Ten minutes and two cigarettes later, the driver reached for his radio.

Khaled staggered through the double glass doors of the Aberinvest Corporation Offices. Two uniformed security men stepped forward as black unconsciousness slowly enveloped the Prince. He managed to say: 'I must speak with Wyatt. I am in danger,' before he collapsed to the marbled floor.

*   *   *

At 9.20am the Bakari Ambassador called personally at the Foreign & Commonwealth Office, bearing a note of protest couched in the strongest possible terms. At 9.30am the Metropolitan Police Commissioner was summoned to the Home Office. By then every police officer in the Metropolitan and City of London Forces had received a description of the wanted terrorist, as supplied by Habish and vouched for by the Ambassador. That description fitted Prince Khaled down to the colour of his eyes and the fact that the fugitive had sustained a bullet wound. The suspect was described as armed and very dangerous.

Members of the public were warned to avoid contact at all costs.

Prince Asif took a hand at 10.05am by telephoning the Foreign Secretary whom he knew personally from two visits to Bakar. He put the problem in very simple terms. King Baquoos was out of contact with the Palace in Bakar. He had gone on a hunting trip in the mountains. When he heard that his son and heir had been murdered by terrorists in London and that the Embassy had been penetrated he would not accept the view that crimes committed in Britain were the province of the British police. He would undertake his own operation to have the fugitive killed.

The threat was clear. Warfare on the streets of London. Innocent civilians caught in a cross-fire between two rival organizations. Prince Asif apologized but thought his friend should be warned. The matter was now out of his hands.

The brief landed on Gareth Llewellyn Jones's desk. Solve this problem with the minimum possible delay. Bakar is important. Use your own discretion.

The Bakari representative met Llewellyn Jones at 11.15am. That representative turned out to be the Lebanese, Habish. Prince Asif was too upset to talk about the incident.

'I can assure you, Mr Habish, that every

possible measure has been taken to apprehend this fugitive. I am waiting now to put my best man in charge of co-ordination.'

'I am sure you will do your best.'

The diplomatic niceties had been exchanged. Now Habish put his request.

'If this terrorist is captured, he will have to be tried according to British law. Then he will be imprisoned here.'

'The usual practice, if he is found guilty.'

'I should point out that a certain element of the Bakari population would make a martyr of him—a man imprisoned for his beliefs. They would certainly attempt to obtain his release by other methods—for example the taking of British hostages on an airliner or a bombing campaign of indiscriminate ferocity in London, or even the assassination of known British citizens. The terrorist knows no rules.'

Llewellyn Jones lit a cigarette and bit his lip, thoughtfully.

'We do not like having London used as a terrorist playground. Simplest solution is for him never to be brought to trial, isn't it? Leave it with me. I think my political masters would understand that point of view. However, please don't regard this as official policy. I'll put someone on it now.'

★   ★   ★

215

Naomi Vennaway walked along the corridor to Llewellyn Jones's office at 11.34am. Her high-heeled leather boots tapped out the urgency of the summons as she hurried past the tea-trolley. Llewellyn Jones sat at his desk console keying information into his computer. He looked up as Vennaway took a seat alongside him.

'Killings at the Bakari Embassy. Ideal opportunity to prove the Directorate's value in a crisis. I'll co-ordinate. You take field command.'

'Objective?' Vennaway asked, arching an eyebrow.

'They murdered Prince Khaled of Bakar. One terrorist is on the loose. You will ensure he resists arrest. We don't want the political embarrassment of a trial and the subsequent problem of keeping him locked up. If we cannot put a stop to these terrorists using London as their own personal shooting gallery, there will be resounding consequences.'

'Understood.'

'Top priority. Drop all other work.'

'Already done.'

'Last sighting, Ludgate Circus.'

'Perhaps he was going to the bank,' Vennaway suggested.

Llewellyn Jones did not find the remark funny.

Naomi Vennaway made one call before leaving the building. She contacted Sir Russell Beauchamp's office and advised him of her instructions. He told her to do as she was told. There was no point in making any more political waves. No further contact was required.

Vennaway was amused. L.J. certainly seemed to have frightened Beauchamp off.

CHAPTER SEVENTEEN

The radio message came through to the helicopter as we turned eastwards after swimming lessons for our two useless acquaintances. The saying goes: 'You can't win them all.' Right then I'd have settled for winning anything.

Fallon was radioing from Tectrokite. Doc Evans, Aberinvest's medical officer in London, had called him. A man claiming to be Prince Khaled was lying in his surgery needing an operation on a bullet wound in the shoulder. The man had lost a lot of blood. For a second or two I had a hollow, sick feeling in the pit of my stomach. The bastards had tried

217

for little Khaled. Maybe he was not quite so little now but I remembered him as a brave little five-year-old kidnapped by bandits. He had looked at me bewildered as I picked him up with one hand and knifed his guard with the other. It had been that close. He had marched out with us across fifty miles of hostile terrain and when he was too tired to march I had carried him. You get attached to kids when you carry them.

Doc Evans was no fool. He had once been an Army surgeon. The rules of civilian medical practice dictated that bullet wounds were notified to the authorities. Doc had broken those rules. When we arrived in London, I understood why.

The wounded man was Khaled, grey even under the suntan and the pallor was only partially caused by loss of blood. Shocked and scared he told me his story which did not tally with the news bulletins coming in. Someone told them Khaled was dead and an armed terrorist was on the loose. According to the Prince, his uncle Asif had been involved in the shooting. His man Habish had been at the Embassy, waving a Kalashnikov around and shouting encouragement to his men. Khaled's villainous old Akrize protector had covered the Prince's escape and died in the process. Six to one was the kind of odds those mullahs liked. I made up my mind there and then that I owed Asif and his playmates for Zaraq.

'Sit tight, soldier,' I reassured Khaled. 'We'll cover you from now on.'

So Moresby had been right. 'Watch events in Bakar.' Either the old rogue was psychic or his informant was so well hidden that no-one would ever find him. Alpha was dead and the executor's duties had devolved on me. I remember the photographs Pavel had taken. Llewellyn Jones and Asif chez Penmayne. Asif's finger on the trigger. By proxy, as usual.

I told Bill Grant to have Security seal the surgery floor watertight. An outer security perimeter was to be established immediately at all entrances to the building.

'Doc, do you have to operate?'

'You know the score, Wyatt. Clean hole it might be, but the bullet is lodged against the bone. Unless you want that boy with a permanent disability, I have to cut. And not here. There are several private facilities available.'

'Nothing near London. Too indefensible.'

Doc consulted his diary.

'Outside Swansea do you? Sixty miles from Ty Newydd. Private house, ten acres of own ground and away from the main roads. Your kind of country. Hard to approach unseen.'

'Do it, Doc. And make sure security stays tight.'

★   ★   ★

I walked into the Chairman's office. It looked different from my day. The desk was the latest from the Design Centre and the chair was one of those amazing machines that adjusted to more positions than the Kama Sutra. The secretary was an improvement. Much prettier even if she did have one of those new hairstyles that was old in Edwardian times.

'I'm Wyatt,' I announced. 'Coded telex to Bakar.'

She took good shorthand while I had a good pull at the best malt. Someone was running rings around us and I had no answers. Baquoos had to be told his son was alive. And Johnny had to be alerted to a possible hit on his charge. Always assuming they had not tried already.

I had been half asleep. The death of Alpha and events in Bakar had to be connected. Moresby's legacy implied they were part of the same game plan. We had a Wolverine thrown in for good measure. Add Llewellyn Jones, Asif and Charlie Penmayne and the bad guys had a winning combination that was ten yards from the tape before I had even heard the starting gun.

Fallon had Jo Lannerson in tow when he arrived in time for his pre-lunch gin and tonic. She wanted to go and write up the whole sorry state of affairs to date. Something about Khaled being alive would get her an exclusive. Exclusively killed. I noticed she had changed her clothes. The jeans were still tight but in black corduroy. The matching shirt had a gold crucifix around the collar. She looked good in black.

'Been shopping?' I asked.

'Peter took me back to my flat to change. If I do have to stay in protective custody I want to have clothes for the funeral.'

Our eyes met. I understood her reasoning. But I could have kicked Fallon down seven flights of stairs for stupidity. An ace in the City he might be, but a Vestal Virgin was better equipped to survive on the streets.

'Peter. Did you notice any vehicles or watchers around Jo's flat? Did you check it out for bugs? Did you discuss anything while you were inside?'

He realized his mistake and said simply: 'Sorry Wyatt.'

'So they know Jo is with us.'

'But if the Wolverine has gone, what harm is there?' Jo asked.

Two Vestal Virgins for the price of one.

221

'They sent heavy men to visit Yardley's girlfriend, remember. Jo, you stay very close to me. I say this once. The game got dirtier when they hit Khaled. It encompasses a *coup d'état* in Bakar, your father's death and very probably Alpha's murder.'

'You're speculating,' Fallon replied.

'No. That Wolverine deal was all above board. Why did they need to keep it clandestine? Had the Ministry people approached us we would have kept security. But the Ministry people could not approach us because they were not asked to. Conarmco was acting for a party with interests diametrically opposed to Aberinvest's. Only one place I can think of likely to get Ministry approval for a Wolverine is the Gulf. Which party is diametrically opposed to our interests there? Oily little Asif. And guess who is in the photograph at Arlingford? Unidentified person—one Alexander Coburn. If Baquoos wanted a Wolverine he'd pick up the phone and ask me, not hire some transatlantic gun-runner to get one for him.'

'Wyatt, we could lose millions, billions. Marine and Ekara fields—although with the price of oil now that might not be such a bad idea. But the Kariz minerals. And the strategic value. . . .'

Hit Fallon in the pocket and that is where

you hurt him. Empty his wallet and the lifeblood flows away. The pale expression said 'What the hell do we do?'

My thoughts were interrupted when Noblett telephoned.

'Wyatt, got the phone number you wanted. Address of a bent enquiry agent named Huggitt. Someone straightened him out this morning. He had a heart attack.'

'Mention to the lads down at the nick that you think it might be murder. Don't quote me.'

*　　　*　　　*

It played on my mind that the month of January was named after the Roman god Janus. Two faces—one looking back into the old year, the other forward into the new. I could regret what I was about to do, but once you have worked out a move, you make it. I took with me a set of prints that Pavel had taken at Arlingford.

Carson, Fallon's chauffeur, drove the Rolls. He was big enough to go through the door of the Georgian terraced house in Cambridge Street without bothering to open it first. Noblett was watching out for Jo Lannerson and I had told Fallon not to talk to any strange men. Prince Khaled was under wraps at a private nursing home with Bill Grant in close attendance, Ko and a couple of Alsatians loose in the grounds. So all I had to do was knock on the black door.

It opened without any lights being switched on inside. Even though I had taken the normal precaution of standing to one side, the street lighting made me feel big as a house and twice that size of target. No wonder they paid hefty rates in that borough. It was like Blackpool illuminations.

'Come in, Mr Wyatt.'

A young female face peeped around the door. I went in fast and grabbed the girl, using her as a shield in case anyone was waiting in the darkened passage for a house-sized target of Wyatt to practise on. Not paranoia, just a simple precaution. Staying alive can be a difficult business when you don't know where or even who the opposition are.

I could smell expensive perfume and feel a warm body close to mine. Comforting. Nothing to do with sex, just the proximity of a protective shield. My hand found the light switch as I kicked the door shut.

The girl shook herself free. Early twenties, dark-haired, wearing a short, black, high-necked evening dress and a blazing angry blue-eyed expression. I caught the right hand that was arching in a roundhouse slap to my head.

'Didn't they teach you not to invite strange men off the streets when you were at Roedean?'

'Cheltenham,' she snapped.

'Sorry, I should have realized—the right hook.'

She was not amused.

'Come upstairs,' she invited. Then, after a pause, 'To meet father.'

Father turned out to be Sir Russell Beauchamp who was wading through folders marked 'Classified' to the sounds of the Brandenburg Concerto No 1. A faint aroma of Cavendish tobacco mingled with the girl's perfume.

Camilla, his daughter, poured the drinks and then stood too close as she handed me three fingers of malt in a drunkard-sized lead crystal glass. Then she sat too close and watched me. I was either being sized up as a suitable overnight guest or measured for a six by three casket for Highgate Cemetery.

Beauchamp's light grey gaze lasered out from a long, studious face, regarding me with the same intensity an anthropologist would after having discovered the first live Yeti in a close encounter. He spoke in Whitehall Mandarin and gave me an indulgently patronizing smile that would not have fooled a mental defective.

'What exactly is your problem, Mr Wyatt?'

The question was phrased as though he were an analyst treating that mental defective.

'Alpha. You knew him, I believe. He walked into two soft-nosed forty-five bullets.' I turned to the girl: 'Not a pretty sight.'

She did not bat a long eyelash. Beauchamp said: 'How does that concern you?'

'He gave you a copy of Moresby's legacy. I come in as second executor.'

'Meaning?'

I laid the photographs on the coffee table. Asif, Penmayne, Llewellyn Jones and Alexander Coburn. The Beauchamps raised eyebrows at each other.

'Whoever hit Alpha wasn't too bright. He knew them. That is how they got close to him. I turned up at his house and a lovely capable blonde pointed a big derringer at me. If you can use a .41 calibre you can probably use a forty-five. Said blonde named Vennaway works for S.S.D. and therefore Llewellyn Jones.'

I waited for them to assimilate my reasoning. Beauchamp nodded. I guessed it was a directive to continue. I obliged.

'Yesterday afternoon a girl visited me. She was waving a .357 Magnum at me with intent. Someone had told her lies about my being involved in a dodgy arms deal that had entailed her father, one of my employees, being murdered. Coburn was part of that dodgy arms deal. She was psyched up to take me out. Not too bright again.'

'Why?' Camilla asked.

'Moresby's legacy. First Alpha, then a try for me. Llewellyn Jones was suspect. Watch events in Bakar. Remember? Those photographs contain all the elements. To cap it all, Prince Khaled of Bakar is murdered this morning.'

'Impeccable circumstantial logic,' Camilla replied. Then she stood up and and walked to the door. Beauchamp refilled my glass. Soft footsteps on the stairs gave me an uneasy feeling. Camilla was not alone. My hand gripped the butt of the .357 Magnum under my jacket. No need. It was only the tubby Llewellyn Jones. And he was too fat to fight his way through a wet newspaper.

Since we had last met he had put a few pounds around the waistline. Dining too well by the look of him. He extended a right hand which I ignored. He lowered himself gingerly to an armchair, probably out of respect for the springs, and raised his sherry glass. I received an avuncular and patronizing smile.

'Mr Wyatt, I am happy to see you are still with us. Luckily you did not perish with that aircraft.'

Another of his endearing qualities—he told lies. Then he continued.

'I heard your conversation. This room is of course wired, which I am told is the technical expression.'

The round, bespectacled face and gracious manner made him look like a benevolent owl. But the steel-blue eyes were case-hardened and beneath that immaculately comfortable exterior was a mental heavyweight who could mix it with the best of them. He lit a tipped cigarette and settled back in the chair, just as if he were telling children's stories on television.

'I had better explain, Mr Wyatt. Past experience shows it is useless to warn you off. Needless to say you are now bound by the Official Secrets Act. I see you have obtained photographs of my meeting with Lord Penmayne and Crown Prince Asif of Bakar. Coburn was also in attendance.'

I did not interrupt. I lit a thin Havana and savoured Beauchamp's superior malt.

'May I ask you how you came by these?'

'Cost me a lot of money.'

'No matter. As you know the late Sir Philip Moresby was a genius, even if something of a prima donna. He was correct to warn Alpha to watch me and events in Bakar, but for the

228

wrong reasons. Moresby never trusted the Foreign Office and his estimation of the Home Office was never much higher. He disliked people like me, ministerial advisers, especially in Intelligence matters, and subsequent events have proved him correct. But his information on Bakar was hard. I had received similar information and was working on my own account, from the inside—a leaf out of Moresby's book there. Were you aware of his domino theory?'

I shook my head.

'When the Shah was deposed it was only a matter of time before those Muslim lunatics turned left at Kuwait, so to speak. That unhappy state is already suffering destabilization. Bakar was next. Thereafter the Emirates, and so on. West's oily windpipe becomes vulnerable. Our friends the Soviets are also involved—unlikely as it sounds. They are backing Asif. The ploy is a clever one. Whether Asif wins or loses they obtain an advantage.'

I did not follow. The higher realms of strategic diplomacy were uncharted waters for a Wyatt. Llewellyn Jones smiled indulgently as though I were the village idiot.

'Asif wins and he might give them a warm water facility at Ad Said. If he loses, Penmayne and Coburn, ex C.I.A., are involved in an attempted coup. Also Aberinvest have supplied a Wolverine. Who will Baquoos and all the other Gulf states trust then I wonder? Can you understand why I am involved?'

'Made a real dog's breakfast of it so far, haven't you? Alpha dead, Lannerson dead and now Khaled.'

'Come now, Mr Wyatt. Khaled is not dead. Bullet wound maybe but not dead. My people were watching the Embassy. They saw him make his escape but were too slow to catch him. Ludgate Circus is a strange destination for a young wounded visitor to London. I imagine he was making for the Aberinvest Offices.'

My turn to grin smugly.

'What about Alpha?' I asked.

This really was the good question. I wondered how he would slip his way out of it.

'You can really be of some assistance there, Mr Wyatt. One of the reasons for my giving you all these secrets. You see Alpha or Unit Alpha appeared to have only one member, variously known as Caldicot. I take it this was he.'

A photograph was handed to me via Camilla. Taken before death. Alpha had a face then.

'How come you weren't introduced?' I

asked.

'Alpha was Moresby's joker. He watched the old rogue's back for years. But he only broke cover over Nimrod and for the funeral. The rest of S.S.D. and the Security and Intelligence services were unaware of his identity. So was I. I tried to trace him and have him report to me. Vennaway was working under my instructions when you met her at Alpha's house.'

Llewellyn Jones then turned to Beauchamp.

'I originally believed that Alpha was a double agent, working for Centre. Certain documentation was found at his safe house. He was killed with the classic Centre method for executing traitors. Now, certain other information has come to light which indicates he may have been framed. Centre up to their disinformation tricks again. Sorry I gave you a rough time the other day, Russell.'

Beauchamp beamed forgiveness. Llewellyn Jones continued.

'This whole sorry business shows how necessary it is to have centralized political control established over security matters. Otherwise the entire business becomes a fiasco and we blunder from one mistake to another.'

'Sorry to interrupt this in-house debate,' I said quietly. 'But what happens about Bakar?'

231

'Of course, you have considerable business interests there.' Llewellyn Jones twisted the diplomatic knife: 'I presume I can rely upon you to return the Prince safely to Bakar. Should you require official assistance, I will oblige.'

'No thanks.'

'I am continuing my part in the Bakar conspiracy for two reasons. One, I am waiting information on an assassination attempt on the King. Secondly, I am seeking the traitor inside the service who was responsible for Alpha's death. As you pointed out—he knew his killer and I think he was on to . . . her.'

The Royal Shakespeare Company lost a potentially valuable asset when Llewellyn Jones decided on the Civil Service as a career.

'Vennaway?' I asked innocently.

'I was rather hoping you would find out for me.'

There had to be a catch somewhere. It was all too easy. Llewellyn Jones had acted his selfish soul out to convince me he was clean. For all I knew he was. Moresby's legacy was the only lead I had against him. And Moresby was dead.

'By now the Asif faction will have worked out that Khaled has not been found by their hunters or our own security. I suspect Centre will also be aware. You are very well protected, Mr Wyatt. It would take a small army to snatch you. Let's make it easy for them. Once they have you and give you to an interrogator, they should be home and dry on the Khaled front. It will bring out my traitor and also provide evidence against Penmayne—your commercial rival in the Gulf area.'

Llewellyn Jones did not smile this time.

'Dangerous, possibly lethal, but you have been through worse. I will plant the idea in Penmayne's head that he invites you to Arlingford. The Asif faction will then try for you. As soon as you receive that invitation, contact Vennaway. If she does not provide back-up, we'll know she is with Centre on this one. I, of course, will make arrangements to have you covered.'

Beauchamp was shaking his head. Camilla just watched my reaction. I was thinking very quickly. This kind of operation was risky when you had your own mates looking out for you. With untried cover, Llewellyn Jones was only half right at possibly lethal. It was wonderful 'Over the top, lads' exhortation. At my age I should have known better.

'Why not?' I replied.

The devious bastard had boxed me into a corner.

'This is much too risky, L.J.,' Beauchamp

233

objected.

'With you three watching my back I should be safe enough,' I observed.

The appreciation of ironical statements had gone out of fashion in Whitehall.

CHAPTER EIGHTEEN

The 'I need you, old chap' story is one of the oldest in the world. The politicians have sold a lot of wars to millions of people that way. The poor bloody infantry get chewed up and the fat cats get the cream.

But just once in a while, you really do have to fight because it is the only way out. And Llewellyn Jones had sold the Dunkirk story for all he was worth. Like Fallon said—the Establishment in this country play dirtier than anywhere else simply because they have had more practice at it. They also cook up the best possible motives.

Llewellyn Jones had told me a good story and for all I knew it was true. But Moresby had said he was suspect and I trusted Moresby's judgement dead more than I did most others alive.

Jo Lannerson was taking a shower back at my flat. Noblett listened to my instructions and I wrote down some details for him. He gave me the kind of look older and wiser men often given those almost half their age and the old grey face was serious.

'Hope you know what you're doing.'

I closed the door behind him and took off my jacket. I unslung the belt rig with the .357 Magnum and poured myself a Scotch. The answer was not in a whisky bottle but the contents gave me a warm, comfortable feeling inside. The more I thought about it, the more I knew I had been told lies. The funny people were inverting the truth again.

An old Intelligence man once said: 'All facts in this business are capable of two interpretations—one innocent, one sinister. The trick is to put the right interpretation on the right fact. Not easy, Wyatt, but you have to try very hard. Name of the game.'

No way was Llewellyn Jones going to walk away with his fat Cheshire features covered in cream. For whatever motives he had let Lannerson die when he could have saved him. He had failed to avert the attempt on Khaled's life and a brave old Akrize warrior had given his life fighting the impossible odds the bastards had stacked against him.

Noblett had instructions to move Khaled. They were expecting me to do something like that and doubtless the phone in my flat was being tapped. But Noblett had ways of circumventing the watchers. My move, but no way would I make it easy for Llewellyn Jones to spot. Besides, there were other people in that hospital and I did not want Asif's goons spraying the place with indiscriminate gunfire in the unlikely event they found out where he was.

Llewellyn Jones had played all his cards straight for everyone to see. Except his ace. So had I. Except my ace. My ace was the trump. A forty-grain hollow point bullet.

*   *   *

Jo Lannerson had not emerged from the shower when Vennaway arrived. The video security screen showed her ringing the doorbell. When she walked in, both hands deep in the pockets of a Burberry, her emerald eyes went straight to the Magnum in my left hand. She withdrew her own hands very slowly and did not smile.

'Honest capitalist defending his castle,' she observed. 'Have you a licence for that?'

'You've checked.'

She looked around the flat with the gaze of a vulture contemplating its breakfast.

'I'll take an Irish whiskey off you. Thirsty work terrorist hunting. Shooting at the Bakari

Embassy. You have heard.'

Not a question.

'Friend of mine shot,' I replied. 'So your trigger-happy élite at S.S.D. is out to eliminate the killer instead of boxing him up in Parkhurst. Saves the embarrassment of his friends starting retaliatory warfare against civilians on the London streets.'

'Not government policy,' she replied.

'It also saves him the embarrassment of trying to convince you he is the Prince Khaled of Bakar. All the terrorists died. Someone is trying to sucker you, Vennaway.'

The emerald eyes flickered. I could see her stiffen and made sure I was out of reach of the steel-reinforced toe-caps on her boots.

'Interesting theory.'

'Fact. Khaled found me. I sent him back to Bakar.'

She sipped the Irish.

'Go around saying things like that and you could have a nasty accident,' she observed.

'Like Alpha.'

At the crucial moment Jo Lannerson walked in from the guest suite. She wore a towel and nothing else. And she did have long legs. Vennaway's eyes lit up strangely. Maybe Lansbury was right when he said she did not like men.

'I'll leave you with the entertainment,'

Vennaway whispered. Her eyes were still on Jo. As I opened the door Vennaway said: 'I do like your girlfriend.'

Somehow Vennaway had the habit of making the most ordinary words sound menacing.

★   ★   ★

'I borrowed your dressing gown.'

Jo looked much better in it than I did. Midnight and I was stretched out on the sofa with a late night Armagnac and a roughness where my throat should have been. Too much smoking. Nervous tension does that to you.

'What is going on, Wyatt?' she asked quietly.

The long legs were tucked underneath her. She rested on her heels with her elbows on the edge of the sofa.

'I've seen that look before. Tony used to get it, just after the bankruptcy. You want to talk?'

'Not much to say, kid.'

'Fallon says everything is against you this time. He wants you to move the Prince out and go back to Canada. Says there is a woman there.'

'In theory Fallon is correct. That way the Bakari coup is foiled, Aberinvest keeps its hands on the goodies and we sit back smiling. Safe option.'

'So why not?'

'Because they killed Alpha, murdered your father and set you up to walk into a death-trap. Now you walk away from people like that and they can always try again. You can throw in your hand and say you don't want to play any more. But they will come looking for you if they think you can still be a danger to them. And because you've fought them once, you're still a danger.'

'So you end up being killed.'

'Possibly.'

'Probably.'

She held my hand and asked:

'Will you take me to the funeral tomorrow? Please.'

'Provided you clear this country by the next plane. Noblett has made the arrangements. My people in Canada have sorted out Immigration for you, money in the bank, and a job if you want it.'

'And you?'

'Don't want to leave any hostages to fortune while I deal with the unfinished business.'

'And the woman in Canada?'

'She already has one ghost to contend with. I don't intend to complicate the issue.'

'Can I give her a message?'

'No.'

Jo smiled an understanding kind of smile, as if she understood what I was saying and that it really meant something to her. She took the cigar butt and crushed it out in the ashtray. I watched her walk to the cocktail bar in the corner and pour two more Armagnacs. Then she carried the glasses into the guest suite.

If I wanted that drink I knew where I could get it.

She was sitting on the far side of the bed, her back to me. Brown hair cascaded over naked shoulders as she inclined her head and cast a wicked half-smile in my direction. Long legs swung on to the bed. She was resting on her left elbow and facing me.

'Provocation,' I observed.

'What will you do about it?' she asked, almost coyly.

I took her outstretched hand. We kissed and the sensation was like a thousand exploding starshells.

'Make love to me ... gently,' she whispered.

She clung as if I were the only living creature in the world, entwining her legs around mine and breathing softly. Slow, rhythmic movement and her faint whispering mingled with the silence. Time stood still in a parallel world where the night was eternal peace and two souls merged in private communion.

I had lost track of time. She lay, head on my shoulder, still entwined.

'Wyatt, will I see you in Canada?'

'Why not? I'm indestructible.'

She was no longer alone. Somewhere in that parallel world she had rediscovered herself.

'No-one has ever been that gentle with me.'

'Snap,' I replied.

She laughed.

'Now it's my turn, Wyatt.'

*   *   *

Funerals are grey, depressing occasions. A life's struggles, successes and failures all end up in a box six foot by three in a hole in the ungrateful earth. It usually rains and the drab, dirty sky shrouds the last rites in some kind of ultimate futility.

Noblett had driven Jo Lannerson away. She had not cried but stood silently by the grave as the padre waffled on about some great purpose or other. I reckoned Lannerson would have preferred to be alive, or at least given some choice in the matter.

I stood by the graveside and apologized silently for being too late. I hoped he would take some consolation from my visiting the same futility on the bastards who had put him there.

Tuesday 28th September was a grey day, even at Ty Newydd. Caswell had inveigled himself into Mrs Harries's kitchen and was digesting the remains of a four-course lunch.

'Don't they feed you down at the nick?' I asked.

'Not like this they don't.'

He smiled at Mrs Harries. She was all right for a few parking tickets.

'Wyatt. The security people have put the blocks on my investigation into Lannerson's death. I don't bloody well like it but there isn't a lot I can do about it. Outside my area, you see.'

Caswell disliked bureaucrats from London who told him when to do his job. Then he had never forgiven the English for killing Llewellyn, the last native Prince of Wales.

'You all set, then?' I asked.

He gave me a foxy look. If my theory was right he would be able to rub someone's nose in embarrassment.

The game plan was complex. I calculated that some time in the next thirty-six hours they would try for King Baquoos in Bakar. Which would leave only Khaled between Asif and the throne. By now Asif and his playmates

242

knew I had Khaled. Llewellyn Jones's people would be monitoring our communications waiting for me to contact Bill Grant with instructions to move Khaled. Obviously there was a watch on all sea and airports. But they had not been watching the Pembrokeshire coast and that was how I had got Khaled out— to Ireland. From there Gareth Dane, London's most reliable security consultant, had taken him via a privately chartered jetliner to Bakar. It all cost money. But money was something I had more than enough of.

When I made that call to Bill Grant I expected Asif to be informed of the location. Which was why Caswell's tactical squad was waiting to provide a reception. Meanwhile I would be at Penmayne's place being cut into little pieces. Insurance on their part and probably Centre's revenge.

Caswell thought it was iffey. I did not. Asif and Llewellyn Jones were a devious pair. The fat bureaucrat's excuse would be that the operation had gone wrong. Very neat. Because I had been warned of the danger in front of Beauchamp and had willingly put my head in a noose.

I picked up the telephone and called Bill Grant telling him to move the baggage to one of the Upland farms Aberinvest owned. Then I called Vennaway's office. A cold female

243

voice answered.

'I'll be at Arlingford this evening. I want back-up as Llewellyn Jones promised.'

'Yes,' was the encouraging reply.

Caswell looked at me.

'Be careful, Wyatt. They could bury you.'

Ko was waiting outside, dressed from head to toe in green combat gear. A forty-pound pack was strapped to his back and the grin was evident under his grease-smeared face.

'I have studied map, Tuan,' he announced.

Then he grinned again and fingered the butt of his machete.

CHAPTER NINETEEN

On the afternoon of Tuesday 28th September, a man wearing the uniform of a lieutenant of the Bakari Scouts pulled the keffiyah across his chubby face and walked towards the small Royal mosque in the grounds of the Raza palace. A 9mm Parabellum Browning automatic pistol, regulation issue to the Scouts, was holstered above his left hip on the Sam Brown belt.

The sun beat down relentlessly and beads of perspiration appeared on his forehead. At the mosque entrance, the guard stood to attention and saluted him. The officer spoke quietly to him in Arabic and the guard relaxed. The officer laid a friendly hand on the man's shoulder and steered him out of sight of the palace and grounds, through the portico. Three seconds later the guard flopped to the ground, twitching, his neck broken. The head lay at a grotesque angle.

Alexander Hamilton Coburn looked swiftly about him. There were no witnesses to his killing. A human stick insect with teeth now, he had timed the operation down to the last second.

The Palace was in mourning for the death of Prince Khaled. The grief-stricken King prayed constantly, alone in the mosque. An unguarded gate in the palace garden wall had been Coburn's entry. The dead guard's absence would ensure his speedy exit.

Inside the mosque, the air was humid. Twenty feet from Coburn the King was prostrate, reciting prayers and oblivious to all danger. He had not heard Coburn enter. Calmly, the American wiped his damp palm on the uniform and levelled the Browning, its silencer attached quickly after he had disposed of the guard.

Four muffled reports echoed dully in the enclosed space. The figure of the King jerked four times. Blood spread through the robes in a small patch below the left shoulder blade. A two-inch group of four bullets, Coburn thought. Heart and lung smashed. The body emitted a gurgling sound as it jerked. A scuffling sound behind him prevented him from applying the *coup de grâce*, a final shot with the gun muzzle pressed to the back of the neck. Coburn turned to see a second guard look in dazed horror.

The Browning jerked four more times. Life was blasted from the intruder before he could raise his voice. Coburn walked towards the fallen man, unscrewing the silencer from the Browning. The palace garden was still deserted. He holstered the gun and walked calmly towards the unguarded gate. No-one challenged him. By the time confusion had erupted in the Palace Coburn was in his hotel room, half a mile away. He had changed from the uniform into a lightweight suit.

He poured himself a tonic water and dialled a local telephone number.

'Problem solved,' he announced and replaced the receiver.

There was time for him to relax now. The Wolverine was in position in the hills. His men hidden in a small camp away from prying eyes. On Prince Asif's return he would begin instructing the Army in the ways of missile technology.

Ten minutes later there was a knock on the door. Coburn was expecting room service with fresh supply of tonic water. Not until the door closed did he look up.

Not room service, but a very big man with close cropped dark hair and an open-cast mining site of a face. Grey eyes looked directly at Coburn.

'Hello, Alex.' The voice was European.

Coburn felt a shudder run down his spine. He knew a real killer when he saw one. He noted the position of the Colt Cobra revolver on the coffee table in front of him. He had dumped the Browning down a manhole. The coffee table was four feet from him. The Cobra was loaded and the butt faced him. An even chance. The big man had given no indication he had seen the gun. He just stood there, arms hanging loosely by his sides.

'You just shot the King, Alex,' the European observed.

'Who are you, joker?' Coburn demanded.

'Szczelskowski. Most people call me Johnny. I heard you make the telephone call. So did the local police.'

Johnny lit a Gauloise with his right hand. Left-handed gun, Coburn thought. He wanted to move as the lighter flickered. But the grey eyes never left him.

'I guess we can work this out, friend.'

Coburn grinned amiably.

Johnny shook his head and Coburn no longer laughed. He knew that only one man would leave the room alive. He had read the message in the big man's grey eyes. But why? And who was he?

'Alex, you're a bastard. You killed a man called Lannerson and sent his daughter into a guntrap. Who suggested it?'

'Go screw yourself, you big ape.'

The big man shrugged his shoulders and half turned towards the door. 'Let's go, Alex.'

Coburn did not believe his luck. The big man had not seen the gun. His mouth dry now, Coburn dived forward and reached for the Colt Cobra. The big man did not turn. Instead, his right hand crossed his body and gripped the Colt .45 holstered but forward on his left hip under the safari jacket. His knees bent and the upper half of his body moved forward as his head inclined to look over his shoulder at Coburn. Using the shoulder as a gunsight, Johnny fired the Colt once from the holster. The bullet tore through the safari jacket and hit Coburn in the stomach.

Coburn's hand had not even reached the gun.

'Sucker,' Johnny looked down at his fallen opponent.

Coburn felt the fires of hell burning in his

stomach. He reached forward to take the Cobra as Johnny's foot kicked the pistol out of his reach. Coburn knew the big man had deliberately tricked him into the move.

The American breathed heavily. His lungs were contracting now. The blood had soaked on to his hands. He looked up. 'Get me to a hospital, for Christ's sake.'

Johnny pocketed the Colt Cobra.

'That's up to the local police. After what you've just done I doubt whether you'll get any medical attention. I knew a guy once who took two days to die gutshot.'

Coburn was moaning as Johnny walked out through the door. Two severe-looking men from the Bakari Security Police were lounging in the corridor.

'All yours, boys. I expect he'll implicate his own grandmother for a shot of morphine.'

The two men looked at each other and wondered how the European had managed to get a powder-scorched mark on his safari jacket.

★　　　★　　　★

That same afternoon, Victor's slight, asthmatic figure hovered over the telephone. He listened to the cold female voice that said: 'Mr Wyatt will be at Arlingford tonight.

249

Everything is set?'

'The team is ready. A fringe Muslim group will claim responsibility. Penmayne and Wyatt will have died in a terrorist attack on figureheads of capitalism.'

Victor replaced the telephone and looked out over Hampstead Heath. He had used the safe house for various reasons: less conspicuous than the Embassy, easier to contact, and difficult to watch unseen.

Aeroflot were holding a seat for him on the afternoon plane. As soon as he heard from Bakar that Baquoos was dead, a hire car would take him to the airport. His task would be over.

Taking the binoculars from the table he scanned the Heath idly. For a while he watched a tall, headscarfed woman walking two Irish setters. The dogs bounded gracefully after the walking stick she threw for them. Poetry in speed, he thought, as the dogs stretched themselves into top gear. He smiled and wheezed slightly, then sat down in the old armchair. Half his working life was spent waiting, while the plans he had concocted became reality. He never reflected on the consequence of his actions, only the objectives. The goals were either achieved or not—a simple distinction. If the Bakari coup failed, there were consolations; any destabilization was its own reward. The propaganda of even a failed coup would be valuable. Western interests would be seen to have fought over the destiny and resources of a Gulf state. Coburn's C.I.A. background was well-documented and the sympathetic Press would be fully briefed. The ruling family in Bakar would appear fratricidal and unstable.

Victor answered his ringing telephone.

'You are certain the King is dead?'

'Our man saw the body,' the voice replied.

Victor put on his coat and walked down the stairs. He could go home confident of success.

*   *   *

Charles Penmayne arrived at Arlingford at 2.35pm the same afternoon. Lady Annabel was swimming in the indoor pool. His footsteps echoed in staccato precision. She knew he was angry.

'We have a guest for tonight. Put some clothes on.'

In fifteen years of marriage he had grown harder and more distant. At first she believed the change was in her own eyes and that she had not really known the man she married. He tolerated her because she was a beautiful possession, poised and elegant, like Arlingford itself, with its period furniture and

251

symmetrical grounds. She in turn had ceased to love him and more recently had ceased to care. Since Brett's strange disappearance he treated her increasingly like an acquisition, an example of his good taste and ability to possess anything he wanted. She felt marginally less important than the Canaletto, or the Picassos.

Later on he summoned her to his study. Among the first folio Shakespeares and the leather-bound volumes, she watched him file away some papers in his wall-safe. The cruiser-grey eyes appraised her clinically, in a calculating way, as though he were considering a business proposition.

'You'll do admirably, darling.' His voice was unfriendly.

'For what?' she asked, determined not to be bullied.

He handed her a photograph. The man was lean, almost gaunt-looking and wore a dusty khaki uniform—a young man whose dark eyes seemed to look through the camera lens to the soul of the photographer. An old photograph—it was yellowed with age.

'Bait for that fisherman. The photo is fifteen years old so I expect he looks older than that now and has probably shaved. His name is Wyatt and he is our guest tonight. When he stopped being a desert reject he started the Aberinvest Corporation. Entertain

252

him. He likes women with style. Make sure he stays here all night—in your bed.'

The shock of his measured announcement and the hard look in her husband's eyes frightened her. He was trying to humiliate her.

'If he's that hard up for female company go and find him a whore,' she replied angrily.

'That, Annabel, is what you are. I know about you and Brett.'

He took a step towards her and she backed away. He swiftly turned the key in the door and she backed into a corner. A hollow smile played on his lips.

'No, I shan't discipline you, Annabel. You can see this instead.'

Penmayne crossed the room and closed the curtains. Suddenly a pool of light played on the screen in the far corner of the room and she could hear voices. Then the film synchronized with the sound. Penmayne pushed her into a straight-backed chair and held her firmly. His right hand started playing with her hair, caressing and stroking the back of her neck.

Annabel Penmayne could not believe what she saw. God! Martin, in a cellar, hung up like a carcase with two men beating and punching him. The unreality of it was like a dream. She closed her eyes but his piercing screams touched the nerve centre of her brain. She herself screamed and all the time Penmayne was whispering in her ear.

'Poor Martin, poor Martin.'

He was sick. There was no doubt in her mind, Charles was sick. He laughed again and the sound stopped, leaving only the film, frozen at the last frame, with Brett's lifeless body hanging in a dirty cellar.

'Say nothing, my darling. Just listen. You entertain Mr Wyatt. If you don't, I'll give you to the people who did that. And no man would ever look at you again.'

'He's dead, isn't he? Isn't he? Tell me, damn you.'

Annabel Penmayne screamed and fell sobbing back into the chair.

Penmayne pushed the electric bell on his desk and unlocked the study door. The butler appeared, a bland personification of the wise monkeys. He spoke with an Old Harrovian accent.

'Two large G and T's, I think,' Penmayne ordered. 'Her ladyship has just had some bad news.'

CHAPTER TWENTY

I had received the signal from Bakar. I was one step ahead of the game now and I intended staying that way.

The chopper took me in at 6pm, over the Cotswold farmland with its dry stone walls, mansion-sized farmhouses and its neat sandy-coloured stone villages. Gin and Tonic farming, where the landowners would not recognize a bullock unless their farm managers pointed one out—always presuming the landowners stopped their Rolls-Royces, Bentleys or Mercedes for long enough to ask.

I spent the last minutes of the chopper ride like many chopper rides before—scared. The last moments before a raid were always the worst. You lived in horror of the enemy being ready for you. And this time, there was no doubt, I was walking into a trap.

Everything looked innocuous enough as the Penmayne residence, Arlingford, hove into view. The evening sun cast a golden light over the acres of manicured lawn and the mirrored calm of the lake, its glacial waters edged with the compulsory water lilies. I wondered whether Penmayne kept tame piranha fish. The borders and flowerbeds blazed colour and the willows wept in strategic places. Behind the symmetrical Georgian house were the stables and garages, yards bright-concrete clean. A high stone wall around the estate kept inquisitive eyes at bay while the half-mile driveway's wrought-iron entrance gates were reinforced by the presence of an inhabited gate lodge.

We landed on a circular gravelled area covered in clean limestone chippings at the front of the house. My two suitcases were taken by valets up the steps to the portico where a public-school-type butler ushered me through the auditorium-sized entrance hallway to the drawing room. My cases and I parted company as Penmayne emerged and shook my hand.

'Wyatt. Very good of you to come.'

'Your invitation sounded profitably urgent,' I replied.

The bone crushing grip on my right hand relaxed as he smiled amusement at my reply. He was fifty but looked nearer forty, lean, Bahamas suntanned and fit. The man-about-town-out-in-the-country clothes were immaculate in line and there was no excess merchant-banker waistline. He practised karate and took it seriously. I could tell by the rough skin on the heel of his hand. A good two inches taller than me, I did not relish the idea

256

of an unarmed combat session with his Lordship. The face was woman's-magazine handsome but the grey eyes gave him away. Ruthless, efficient, secretive—I reckoned old Machiavelli must have looked something like Penmayne.

Annabel, Lady Penmayne, was something else. A willowy, blue-eyed ash blonde who belonged among the Louis Quinze, the Persian and the Limoges. Her handshake held mine for just a second too long. Or was it my imagination? Once my adrenalin starts pumping it can easily be distracted by a beautiful woman.

'Charles told me all about you,' she smiled.

Mouth a little too wide for perfection, but you rarely get perfection in this life. The lady had style and her smile hinted broadly at wickedness. I caught a glimpse of Penmayne's expression as she spoke. He was mentally congratulating himself. Had she been my wife and greeted a stranger that way, I would be thinking about a divorce lawyer.

'He told me nothing about you,' I replied. 'Otherwise I would not have thought twice about his invitation.'

For a second I could see concern in her eyes. She laughed it off with another smile and conducted me to the Green Room. They probably called it that because the four-poster was hung with green to match the curtains and the carpet. The view over the Cotswolds verged on the verdant.

'Rumour has it Czar Nicholas the Second stayed here once,' she announced quietly. 'Saunders has unpacked your things—except for the smaller suitcase which was locked.'

'Business papers,' I replied.

I watched her walk out. I liked the walk. History was never my strong point but I recalled that Nicholas the Second was the last Czar of Russia. He had come to a messy end. Now why tell me that?

I took a shower in the en suite bathroom that was the size of my flat. The bath itself would have accommodated the entire Welsh XV with ease. All green marble. There were no adjoining doors to either room so that meant one way in and one way out. The drop from the verandah was almost thirty feet but the windows opened out easily. There was a key available so I locked them.

I opened the suitcase and took out a little anti-bug detector and swept the room. Clean. Maybe they did not expect me to spend too long there or even have time to think aloud to myself. As a final precaution I put the Smith & Wesson rig on under my dinner jacket. The aristocracy always say you can't get good servants these days and I did not know how good the service at dinner would be.

Penmayne took me along to the gun room. Among the Purdeys and Cogswell & Harrisons he had a small but interesting collection of antique firearms. Things of beauty but all in perfect working order. He handed me one of a pair of brass-barrelled pistols by Ogilvie of Glasgow. Time to do my antique commentary.

'Scottish snaphaunce about 1710,' I smiled.

'Do you collect?' he asked. 'Because you were almost spot on with that date—1716.'

'Interest born of necessity,' I replied.

'You'll like this one then.'

A presentation-cased 1866 Winchester—the old 'Yellow Boy'—so-called because of its brass receiver and butt-plate. This one was special, gold plated and deeply engraved. Old Oliver Winchester was a shirt-maker by trade who got into the weapons business by accident—or so the story went. He left the gunsmithing to men like B. Tyler Henry and concentrated on selling and advertising. This particular model had been presented to a Penmayne with War Office connections.

'Superb,' I replied, working the well-oiled lever action and releasing the trigger mechanism with my thumb on the hammer and gently easing same back to the fired position. Never let a hammer fall on an empty chamber—it jars the firing pin.

'I have a proposition I wanted to put to you,' Penmayne announced.

'Go ahead,' I replied, checking a .45 calibre Colt Cavalry Peacemaker to make sure it was not loaded.

'I imagine you are disturbed by events in Bakar, as I am.'

I nodded. He had lost no time in making his approach.

'The Marine and Ekara concessions are up for renewal, as are the Kariz mineral exploration rights. My information is now that King Baquoos is dead, they will probably no longer be granted to Aberinvest. Apparently Prince Asif is not your number one fan.'

'So?'

'My consortium will be bidding. Asif has a reputation for venality. I would hate him to profit from an auction where we're both bidding.'

'You recommend?'

'I've taken a leaf out of O.P.E.C.'s book. Let's form a buyer's cartel and bargain. We then split the resources, plus a generous capital allowance against your rigs in the Gulf.'

I would have hated to have an overdraft in Charlie Penmayne's bank.

'Fallon makes those decisions,' I replied. 'I

retired some time ago. I just count the dividends now.'

'Frankly, Wyatt, Fallon and I don't get on.'

Fallon had good business sense.

'So you thought you'd ask me. We could discuss it, I suppose.'

'I've prepared some documents which you can read after dinner if you like.'

'Why not?'

Somewhere in the depths of the house a dinner gong sounded.

*   *   *

I had heard of killing the fatted calf. Penmayne could have been trying to wine and dine me to death. The food was first rate—seafood cocktail, venison à la crème. The hock was clean, light and dry and the Château Mouton Rothschild truly one of nature's gentlemen. More than could be said for Penmayne because he announced after taking a telephone call that he would have to leave—a crisis in London.

The trap was now wide open. Lady Annabel returned from wherever it was ladies went while the lads were bashing the port. She sat me down on a leather Chesterfield in the drawing room while the butler brought in some brandy and left the decanter on the side table. The French carriage clock showed ten-fifteen and Annabel's occasional glances at it meant she was either uncertain of her lines or doubtful about making it to the curtain call.

I made polite conversation about a nearby photograph of two well-fed, brightly-scrubbed children next to an over-fed Thelwell-type horse. Samantha and Justine, the Penmayne heirs, both conveniently away at their respective private schools. A longing look came into her ladyship's blue eyes, as though she would rather have kept them at home.

'Charles insists they board,' she said quietly. 'Charles always has his own way.'

She started to make polite conversation again.

'Do you have any family?'

'I can just about manage to take care of myself,' I smiled.

Another glance at the clock.

'What's on your mind, Lady Annabel?'

'Does it show?' she asked, as if she had committed the aristocrat's ultimate sin of betraying her true feelings.

'You, lady, are scared. And you have been since I arrived. Charlie's been gone twenty minutes. By pumpkin time you'll be climbing the walls. You aren't cut out for the kind of games Charlie plays. Yes, I know why I was invited.'

I handed her a brandy while she took a cigarette and tried to work out exactly what I meant and maybe whose side I was on.

'Charles only told me to ensure you stayed here all night.'

'I was planning to.'

'I was ordered to sleep with you. Is that part of your deal with Charles?'

She really did not know.

'Does Charlie often order you to sleep with the guests?'

'I should slap your face or throw something at you for that remark. Of course not. I like to make up my own mind.'

'And I don't have a shopping list and appointments diary for sleeping companions—at least not one that is open to inspection. For some reason Charles wants me kept here tonight. Don't feel insulted if I say he had a very good idea how to go about it.

She swallowed the brandy. Dutch courage, I guessed. Aristocrats don't betray each other. She was about to break the rules.

'Would you protect me from Charles? I am sure he had my lover killed.'

Never get mixed up in someone else's marital problems.

'If you were my wife I'd kill your lover.'

'You probably would, Wyatt. But you'd do

it in a fit of jealous and righteous rage. Come with me for a moment.'

We walked down the hallway and she locked the doors of a library behind us. She rummaged in an ornate desk and came up with a home movie that she put on a small projector. All the time she was talking about Brett. She admitted she had been no saint in the matter so I gave her good conduct points for honesty. She was worried because Brett had not been in evidence lately. When I saw the film I understood why. Two fun-loving characters had beaten him to death in a cellar somewhere. There were tears in her eyes as I turned the projector off and collared the film. Careless of Charlie to leave such things lying about and I wondered very briefly why. Did not take me long to work it out. You can only talk if someone is around to hear you or you still have the faculty of speech. Dead people don't have conversations.

Charlie had cleared the area. Annabel was supposed to seduce me. Potential scenario. Come the small hours Wyatt and Annabel die in each other's arms. The only staff in the house were a butler and a housemaid. Somewhere a grandfather clock chimed twelve.

'Pumpkin time, Annabel,' I announced, grabbing the Napoleon brandy that lurked invitingly near the bookcase: 'If we want to stay alive, let us go to the Green Room and pretend you're carrying out the Lord and Master's instructions.'

We made it look good, trailing arm in arm up the wide staircase. She played along willingly. I shut the Green Room door behind us and left the lights off. I drew the curtains back and the moonlight flooded in. A bank of cloud was scudding across the sky. I took my jacket off. She saw the gun.

'You came expecting trouble. Why walk into a trap?'

'Best way to spring it. Where's your bedroom?'

'Along the corridor.'

'Let's select something for you to wear.'

'I'm happy as I am, thank you.'

'You need to slip into something more comfortable.'

I closed her bedroom door behind her and unzipped the evening dress.

'Hey—'

I threw her a black roll-neck jumper, some black ski-pants and a pair of riding boots. I walked to the window, drew back the curtains and looked out. The grounds seemed quiet and devoid of movement. Back to the Green Room with her in tow, clad properly now. I opened my suitcase and pulled on a black polo-neck jumper. At night time you should try and blend with the general colouring. I strapped a small R.T. set to my wrist and spoke into it:

'Wake up, you lazy little primitive.'

Annabel thought I was mad until a voice answered.

'Awake, Tuan. No movement yet.'

I scanned the area with an image-intensifying scope. Ko had picked a clump of trees about three hundred yards from the gatehouse where the lights were still on. If he had not confirmed his position I would not have believed he was there. He reported that Penmayne had gone to the gatehouse, parked his car out of sight of the main house and was currently bashing brandy with the gateman.

I explained who Ko was. Annabel needed another brandy so I poured her one. I had already drunk enough. I sat beside her on the bed checking my gear over.

'The bastard wants me to die,' she announced angrily.

'Do you have any more vehicles hidden away here?'

'Land Rover in the garages. Yes, I do drive.'

I was considering whether to fight in the open or fort up in the house. The answer was dictated by there being only two of us. House

266

was too big a defensive perimeter. Mobile fight.

Annabel was getting nervous. I pointed to the bed.

'Make a mess of that. Stuff anything you can find under the covers. I want whoever gets this far to think we are both in it.'

Twelve thirty-five now and still no movement outside. I wore the Smith & Wesson rig over the jumper. In addition I carried a belted flare pistol and ammunition pack, some grenades, ten spare fifty-round magazines for the Uzi submachine gun as well as my long-bladed Bowie knife. Overkill is better than getting killed.

Annabel was going through cigarettes like they were going out of fashion. She lay against me and held the current cigarette up for me to take an occasional puff. Waiting is always the worst time.

'Wyatt, are you afraid?'

Not noticeably. My stomach only felt hollow where my excellent dinner should have been and suddenly it was cold in the Green Room. Nothing to do with the fact I had opened the glass doors on to the balcony.

'Certainly,' I replied.

'Glad I'm not the only one.'

'Annabel, the guy who tells you he isn't afraid is either a good liar or too stupid to feel fear. Keeping up morale entitles you to tell lies. Stupid gets you killed.'

She found that amusing.

'I saw a photo of you. Charles had one. You were a soldier. Was that long ago?'

I guessed the question was prompted by concern for her own welfare. She hoped I had not forgotten how to do it.

'They gave me excellent references when I left,' I joked. 'One Wyatt. Wind up and point in right direction. Then come in and clear up the mess.'

I realized I had found an answer in a humorous reply. Wyatt, you're getting slow.

She laughed, a girlish laugh. The blue eyes shone in the half-light. I leaned over and kissed her. She might be the last girl I ever kissed. The sensation rated way above free-fall parachuting.

When I came up for air I could hear vehicles driving along the narrow country lane. But they passed the gatehouse. A couple of late-night cocktail shakers taking their Ferraris for a spin. As a precaution I took the fifty-foot length of rope from the small suitcase and anchored it to the balustrade of the balcony. Now there was nothing else left to do.

One thirty-eight am and more vehicles, slower this time, being driven almost sedately. Headlights stopped at the gatehouse. Our visitors had arrived. I was not naive enough to believe it was Vennaway with the cavalry or even Llewellyn Jones's promised back up. Annabel climbed on my back and I clipped the runner on my harness to the rope. Through the night sight I could see an old transit and a Mercedes. Two men in hoods carrying submachine guns got out of the Mercedes and were let into the gatehouse by Penmayne. They had not called for a nightcap. My R.T. crackled into life.

'Tuan, bandits.'

'On my way.'

Abseiling looks easy. It is not. Despite the fact I had checked the gear myself there was a problem. The runner sometimes snags up and you are left dangling in mid-air, helplessly. Ten feet from the ground and Sod's Law went into operation. The damn thing snagged. Vehicle headlights were weaving towards the house now.

'Jump, Annabel, Go for the garage. Don't start the car yet.'

She jumped. I heard the crunch as she hit the gravel and rolled. I thought she was hurt. No. A perfect parachutist's roll. I was getting to like Annabel. I cut the rope with the Bowie knife and hit the ground, landing on my feet, a bone-shaking touchdown. We ran towards the garage at the rear of the house.

'Hide till I come back,' I ordered.

She nodded and bit her lip. I winked reassuringly at her and moved fast, towards the front corner of the house. In less than twenty seconds, the fireworks would start.

CHAPTER TWENTY-ONE

I made the corner of the house in time to give Ko one instruction. Do the sniping. I'll provide the light. The moon was obscured by the clouds now. I gripped the Uzi in my right hand, braced my left elbow tight against my side and switched the selector to automatic fire.

The Mercedes juddered to a halt and two men rushed out, running to the door, spraying bullets everywhere. The first died in his tracks as Ko cut him down from somewhere in the darkness. I let go at the second. A short burst. He died in his tracks. As the rear doors of the transit flew open, even before it lurched to a halt thirty yards away, two of the occupants hit the driveway and fanned out into my second burst. I let go a grenade.

You can never get out of effective range of a grenade so I flattened myself behind the very substantial wall of the house and counted four. The night exploded. A searing fireball sucked in air and threw out a mass of metal, glass and limbs. Silhouetted in the fire a man ran towards me as I dived flat to the ground.

We both fired simultaneously. His shots went over my head. Mine hit. The running figure twisted in mid-air like a grotesque marionette as Parabellum hollow-point death cut him down. I rolled leftward to change my position and heard a chilling scream like that of a demented child.

An incandescent human torch staggered towards me and fell, rolling desperately on the ground, wailing and screaming like nothing I had ever heard before. Clothes ablaze and flesh burning he twitched once as I shot him and he lay still.

The night was suddenly, surrealistically silent. Then a shattering explosion as the Mercedes' petrol tank went up. A hot rushing blast of air hit my face and I buried my head against the ground. Breathing hard, I looked up to see the fireball die away. Apart from the crackling sounds of burning, twisted metal and the acrid smell of cordite mingling with the pungency of burnt rubber, all was silence. My hands shook and I thanked the entity you often thank in such moments that I had got through in one piece. A night-jar called some way off which was Ko ready to talk on the

271

R.T.

'I check casualties,' he announced. 'You go back to the house.'

Ko was quieter in the dark than I was. But I still covered him as he scuttled from body to body, checking there was no offensive capacity left in any of the enemy. Ghoulish job, but it saves being shot in the back.

Annabel was sitting in the Land Rover. She fell against me as I opened the garage door.

'Thank God!' she exclaimed.

'I'll drink to that. Now we'll call the constabulary.'

We had made enough noise for a battalion action and lights were on in the house. The butler was trying to telephone. He had lost his customary sang-froid and his pyjamas were in disarray.

'Do yourself up, Jeeves,' I grinned.

'Phone's dead,' he announced, distraught.

The housemaid, a plain, nervous little thing, came running up. Annabel reassured her I was not the Peasants' Revolt. Now why should that phone be out? We had kept our attackers under observation from the time they were at the gatehouse. Ko had not seen anyone cutting any phone wires. Very strange. First thing you do when you attack an enemy—cut his communications.

'Kill the lights,' I ordered. 'Quickly.'

I ran to the front door and opened it.

'Ko—take cover. We've been had.'

A burst of automatic rifle ricocheted around the portico. I dived back into the entrance hall and hurt myself on the marble floor. Winded, I turned and tried to mark the gunflashes. No good. It was the first team this time. They were shooting from some way behind the still burning vehicles.

I cursed myself for falling for the oldest trick in the book. The first attack had been a diversion. Now I had lost the advantage of surprise, had three civilians to look out for and was obviously outnumbered. Ko knew the rules. Stay loose and try to stay alive. A single shot echoed in the darkness. He had obviously made it to cover and one of them had not.

'Annabel,' I ordered. 'You and Jeeves get out the side way, carefully. Try and make it to the garage.'

They moved off to the depths of the house. Something clinked through the open front door.

'Grenade,' I yelled automatically before realizing no-one was left to heed my warning. I dived to the plinth of the nearest Doric pillar as the blast shattered every window in the place. The shockwave pressured past, but they built pillars to last in those days. It saved me from the shrapnel. No time to waste now. I raced across the hallway to cover Annabel's retreat, cutting my knee on a shard of glass in the process.

Blast disorientates you. The sound of Bow Bells in your ears and the sluggish response from the base of your brain has an unreal slow motion effect on everything. The blinding flash and the amazement that your limbs are all attached somehow adds to the mind-numbing sensation.

I waited by the now open side door. I had to accustom my eyes to the darkness. Annabel and the others were nowhere in sight, so I presumed they had made it to the garage. Back in the entrance hallway another grenade went off. Some bastard with a rifle and grenade launcher attachment to be that accurate. The enemy were well prepared.

Another single shot sounded from the distance. Ko was using his Armalite sparingly. Which meant that he had probably taken another one out. How many of them were there, for God's sake? Time to move, from the darkened inside of the house to the darkened outside. Hoping that no-one was sighting on the doorway I rolled out fast. Crawling towards the corner of the house again I called a jay call. A night-jar answered. My Dayak friend was still in one piece. I scanned the area using the night sight now looped around my neck. A figure rounded the base of the weeping willow tree eighty yards away. He came quickly, from cover to cover. The night sight would not attach to the Uzi and anyway there would be no time. At forty yards I let go a short burst and ducked to my right, rolling fast. The rule is: Shoot then move, because at night anyone who is half trained knows enough to mark your gunflashes and send lead to where you last fired from. This lot were no exception. Three separate positions opened up. Their intention was clear—to outflank me on my right. And the garage was right in their line of advance.

I tasted earth, chippings and bits of rosebush as fire enveloped me from two of the positions. The gurgling sound thirty-five yards to my left, the night-jar call again: Ko was earning his living tonight. Had it not been for the civilians I would have joined him in the silent stalk and we would have gutted the intruders with cold steel.

The ensuing silence was ominous. I could see no more movement, even through the night-sight. I lay there with my heart bouncing away like runaway timpani and my palms covered in perspiration. We had not got all of them, that was for sure. I moved towards the garages. I was almost there when the doors automatically opened and headlights went on. Two single shots sounded. Christ No. They had got to the garage.

'Wyatt,' an unfriendly, European-sounding voice called. 'No more shooting.'

Suddenly something was flung out of the garage into the path of the headlights. It wriggled and I could see ash-blonde hair. Annabel, tied and gagged but still alive. I crept closer. A single shot ricocheted off the chippings, a foot away from her. She had the sense to wriggle once and then lie still.

The poor girl was a sitting target. I got the general idea even before the voice said: 'Two more shots, Wyatt. The second will kill her unless you walk unarmed into the headlights.'

This bastard was playing on my sense of chivalry. He knew we were winning so true to form it was time to hide behind the civilians. My R.T. whispered into life now.

'Tuan. On five I kill the headlights. Move.'

The fastest decision I ever made and probably the riskiest. A second shot ricocheted off the chippings and I ran. Even if someone else did not shoot me I risked being cut down by Ko's fire at the headlights. You never hear the one that gets you and I was too busy to listen out for it. Annabel was thirty yards from me. Without thinking where Ko's shots would come from I grabbed Annabel as the headlights were killed. The air was sucking and whistling death. Glass crunched under my feet as I picked her up and dived to the opposite side of the garage doors. Covered by the outside wall now, I waited, breathing hard, and cut Annabel free.

A bloodcurdling yell split the now quiescent air. My R.T. crackled into life and Ko shouted: 'Last bandit down. Only the garage now.'

Now it was my turn. A prisoner would be useful. But I wanted to kill the bastards for what they had done to a shaking, whimpering Annabel. The butler and the housemaid were dead.

'Come out slowly and weaponless or by Christ you'll get a phosphorus grenade in there,' I shouted.

I had it ready in my hand, hoping they would call the bluff.

'All right,' a voice called.

But they even had to welch on that deal. One of them had come out the back way. Annabel screamed and I fired at the shape behind us that belched flame. The shape died twice. My burst stitched him from groin to scalp as a three-foot wooden-shafted arrow pierced his neck, showering me with blood from a shattered jugular.

The next thing I knew a big man in a

bomber jacket and jeans wearing a stupid black bobble hat emerged silently from the garage straight on to the point of Ko's machete. The steel glistened in what was by now unclouded moonlight. The beads of perspiration ran down the big man's face. Then Annabel was at him, scratching, screaming and clawing. I pulled her off and slapped her face.

'Cool it,' I ordered.

She looked down at the ground as if she was ashamed.

Somewhere in the distance, sirens sounded. I half-carried Annabel into the house while Ko trussed and prodded the survivor. Out of pure habit I changed the magazine on the Uzi and realized I was down to my last mag. My hands shook as I poured two very large brandies. Ko rolled some cigarettes, gave us one each. The sirens came closer. Ko looked up, his face covered in blood from a scalp wound, and grinned.

'If that not police, Tuan, you fight 'em.'

Annabel started fussing about my leg which was bleeding from a gash. I took her hand and smiled.

'We made it . . . by a mile.'

She replied: 'Count me out if it ever gets closer than that.'

Then the world was full of policemen.

The senior man was a smart upright character in bright buttons with the kind of face that makes you realize you are getting older. He confided he had radioed in for instructions and some bigwig wanted to talk to me. A change from his arrival when I had to stand his men off at the front door because they were ready to shoot anything that moved.

I hobbled out to the car and spoke to a concerned Russell Beauchamp, over the radio link.

'Screw you, Beauchamp,' I snapped. 'L.J. did not have me covered. I'll call you later, when I've had a bath.'

The bright-buttoned Chief Inspector beckoned me over. The immediate grounds were a mess. Metal, bodies and gore all over the place. Somewhere a young copper was being sick. The smell of burnt flesh was so bad that I was thankful for another of Ko's cigarettes. The attackers had been kids mostly. Post-teen Arabs with Skorpion machine pistols and the smile of Paradise on their death masks.

One was a girl. I lifted the balaclava hood, slipped in some blood and looked down at her almond eyes staring vacantly back at me from the face of a raven-haired saint ... skin flawless and lips trickling blood. Fifteen years before I might have killed her father in the Six Day War. Why did I wonder how my enemies came to be so? Why were the faces all so young? Didn't they know it was a fool's game?

The inspector took my arm. We skirted the burnt-out shell of the transit and in the arc-lights now being put up I could see two medicos inject morphine into a badly burned mass that groaned. I did not need to see the private, hopeless glance both men exchanged to know that the charred remnants were beyond help.

I knelt down beside the blackened melted face and swollen lips. The silver hair was scorched off and a bloody sticky mess was left in its place. Only the grey eyes confirmed it was Penmayne. They had trussed him up and put him in the back of the transit. Intentions clear enough—they would leave him dead with me and Annabel. Then the nutter who gave his particular group of fanatics their orders would claim responsibility on behalf of some mickey mouse outfit that hated Western Capitalism.

'You ... better than ... we thought...' he murmured.

'They double-crossed you, Charles. Whose idea was this?'

He tried to smile. It was as much as he could do to move his lips.

Even as the old deviant was dying he was trying to play the living off against each other.

'You won this round . . .' he gasped. 'But they'll win . . . in the end. Got . . . to stop them, Wyatt. . . . They welched . . . on the deal. . . . Papers in my safe. . . . Combination in the desk. I'll finish . . . them.'

I nodded. He groaned again.

'Jesus . . . the pain.'

His hand gripped my arm, tightly.

'Who set this up, Penmayne?'

'You'll . . . work . . . it . . .'

He died with a smile in those cold grey eyes. They were about to give him another shot of morphine to kill the pain, but he was beyond that now. Somehow he would have the last laugh. I'd die, descend to the nether regions and find Penmayne had taken Hell over by some subtle inside trading and elbowed the Devil out as some overseas manager somewhere.

I looked up and found Annabel standing behind me. There were tears in her eyes, not of lost love but something like pity. Penmayne had died horribly. He probably deserved it. But I was not in a position to pronounce judgement. Ko and I had just killed ten people.

Annabel stared blankly at me and asked: 'What do I tell the children? They adored him. How do I tell them about all this?'

'You just tell them he died.'

I took her arm and led her back to the house.

CHAPTER TWENTY-TWO

The other side's only survivor was the big man. Mean-faced and hostile, he had the sullen look of bad losers the world over. But this one was not just muscle, the flotsam of any downtown European bar where the has-been mercenaries and the hopeless adventurers gather. This one was a seasoned professional who thought very carefully about the likely odds and wanted all his money up front. More than that, maybe. He had the look of a leader about him, the restrained arrogance and the knowing confidence that although I might have won the engagement, I was the chump who would lose the war.

'Your people thought King Baquoos of Bakar was killed yesterday,' I smiled. 'You thought that if I could be taken I would lead you to Khaled, the only person standing between Asif and the goodies.'

He said nothing, but I knew from his semi-vacant eyes that what I said made sense. Provocation time now.

'Well, my ugly friend, you blew it. You fell into Wyatt's trap. King Baquoos is alive and well. His bodyguard took Coburn's bullets—in an armoured vest liberally covered with plastic bags of film blood. And by the way, Khaled is back home by now. The Bakari Scouts have rounded up the hostiles and you're on your own.'

The pale eyes flickered anger, resentment and then . . . nothing.

'My Dayak friend Ko will take you for a walk. Tell him where you were supposed to take me and who we were going to meet.'

*　　*　　*

I poured a brandy. I did not deserve it because the move had cost two innocent civilian lives. But I needed it. My hands shook as I lit a thin Havana. I am fine when the lead is flying around but in the cold, thought-collecting aftermath I tell myself I was lucky and not just indestructible.

The bright young inspector came in and announced his man had driven Annabel to a relative's house near Gloucester. Considering Penmayne had been on the local Police

Authority it was the least they could do. He told me his name was Berenson and that he had received instructions to do as I told him from Sir Russell Beauchamp. No wonder Moresby had code-named the man Janus, but at least now he had issued an official instruction.

Berenson chaperoned my opening of the safe. There were volumes of records. Every dirty deal Penmayne had ever done was there, and there were quite a few of those. His earlier misdeeds could wait. I wanted the latest skulduggery. Penmayne had been a thorough man. Records of all transactions were meticulously noted in his own copperplate hand. Recent cash payments into a Swiss bank account in the name of Andrew Lloyd were detailed, as were share transfers to an offshore trust. Alongside these items, Llewellyn Jones's name was written. Good Old Charlie Penmayne, he did not trust anyone unless he had a handle on them. I had with me the photographs Pavel had taken and within half an hour I was approaching some kind of solution.

I called Dan Caswell. He had been in the middle of a firework display. Simultaneously with the attack on Arlingford, two heavily armed characters had attacked the farmhouse he had staked out—the one where we were supposed to have hidden Khaled. Confirmation that my phones were tapped after the meeting with Beauchamp and Llewellyn Jones. Caswell had not obtained any answers from the assailants. They had refused to disarm when challenged. His Special Branch man was trying to identify the bodies.

The noose around Llewellyn Jones's neck was tightening. And Vennaway had some explaining to do. She sounded very cold and aloof taking my earlier call made on her boss's instructions. I now wanted to thank her personally for leaving me in a trap. My overall performance had not been so good. Alpha was dead, so was Lannerson, and Zaraq, Prince Khaled's Akrize protector, had also died. But I was still in at what I hoped would be the finish.

Ko and I left Arlingford in the Penmayne Land Rover without telling the bright young inspector we had borrowed his prisoner. Policemen are touchy about such matters. Contravenes something they call the Judges' Rules. Ko had achieved little success in finding out any answers. Money had been refused and the big man did not seem too worried about the machete pointed at his throat. Time to use the ultimate incentive.

We stopped in a convenient lay-by in a

deserted lane at the edge of some woods. The prisoner got out at the point of my Uzi and stood as ordered in the headlights. He knew the procedure because he came, I was sure, from a society where they often drive you into a darkened wood, let off a careless volley of rifle fire and leave what remains for the wild boar to root over. Maybe he had taken part in such proceedings.

The bravery lasted for as long as he thought I was bluffing. But when I levelled the Uzi and reminded him his boys had murdered the butler and the housemaid, and he had used Annabel for target practice, he knew I was not joking. In answer to why he had done it he replied:

'I obeyed orders.'

All the managers of all the charnel houses in living memory, from Auschwitz to Argentina, Sabra to Siberia, had used the same excuse. I pulled back the cocking handle of the Uzi.

'Please . . .' he begged.

'You'll never ignore another plea like that,' I replied.

I squeezed the trigger. Dirt spurted up from the ground around and beyond him. He slumped to his knees, then lay on the ground, face white as a January snowfall.

Ko picked up the limp body and threw it back into the Land Rover, like a sack of animal feed. The rough treatment revived the body.

'I'll show you . . .' it gibbered.

★   ★   ★

The house was in darkness, the farm outbuildings eerie, stark outlines in the moonlight. We stopped the Land Rover a quarter of a mile off, just below the brow of a hill, and killed the engine and headlights. Ko went down to scout while I traversed the area using my night sight. We had to move quickly. Within the hour, dawn would break and the rays of orange sunlight would illuminate a new day—and the menacingly uncertain shapes of night would vanish.

I did not need the night sight to see it—a flickering flame, a mere pinprick of light in the black shadows of an outbuilding. One of the watchers had got careless and lit a cigarette, giving his position away. Ko had seen it too. Minutes passed as the Dayak closed in, flitting silently, ghost-like in the darkness. No sound reached me as the watcher was taken out. More minutes and then the screech-owl call. All clear for me to go down, carefully.

I explained to our prisoner only once. Any sound and my Bowie knife would slip, in the specific area of his prominent jugular. He obeyed and proved to be very light on his feet. We followed the line of a dry stone wall. Always use a covered route, even in the dark. There were no livestock in the outbuildings or anywhere on the immediately adjacent land. Inside the barn, a black Ford Escort XR was parked. It had London registration plates. Vennaway's Savile Row sandbaggers, Cadogan and friend, drove a car like that. Beside it was an unconscious Cadogan. Ko had gone to look for his friend.

Somewhere at the back of the house a door opened. Footsteps sounded on the concrete yard. Those footsteps came closer. Not the slow, deliberate footsteps of a man, but quicker, lighter.

In the moonlight I could see Naomi Vennaway. And she was holding a Russian AK47 rifle.

CHAPTER TWENTY-THREE

Vennaway looked up at the stars and hunched herself into the short sheepskin coat. I waited for Ko's signal before I made my move. A screech-owl called and Vennaway looked around, unused to the sounds of the country.

Eventually she must have convinced herself that the call was genuine and took another three strides towards me.

'Drop the Kalashnikov,' I whispered.

Ko was behind her, his machete touching the nape of her neck. The green eyes registered surprise and I could see her vainly seeking her helpers. The Kalashnikov clattered to the ground as I walked into the moonlight in front of her, Uzi in my right hand. Ko cuffed her hands behind her back.

'Cadogan . . .' she shouted.

'City boys,' I observed. 'Street watchers with degrees in P.P.E. No match for us rural bandits. Inside, Vennaway.'

She caught sight of my big companion, cuffed to the barn door.

'Where did you find Renkov?' she asked, surprised.

Renkov was just as surprised to see her. He looked puzzled.

I did not reply. Instead I prodded Vennaway at Uzi length towards the house and left Ko to clear up the unconscious and the handcuffed.

The house showed signs of mass occupation, more than Vennaway and her two minders. Full ashtrays, unwashed plates, glasses and empty Scotch bottles, cigarette packets and empty ammunition cartons littered the downstairs front rooms where the curtains were drawn closed. Judging by the mess, someone had left in a hurry.

Vennaway shrank back as I searched her for the derringer. Her eyes blazed:

'I told you not to touch me.'

On the table was an R.T. set, tuned to a Police wavelength. The monotonous squeaking pip that sounded every few seconds and the occasionally oscillating voices that encroached indistinctly from another channel puzzled me. I had an uncomfortable feeling I was making a fool of myself.

'Vennaway, where the hell were you tonight? Two innocent bystanders are dead and I'm on a very short fuse.'

'And you got Renkov. Moresby rated you. But I said you were a clumsy has-been who should stick to screwing soft-headed women with their brains in their bikinis.'

'Moresby is dead,' I replied. 'And who the hell is Renkov?'

'Bulgarian. He asks questions and pulls out your fingernails or uses a nutcracker on your thumbjoints or other tender articles when you don't answer. They were going to let him do a job on you to find out where Khaled was. But you got Khaled out of the way. At least you did one thing right.'

A crackling voice came through on the

R.T. set.

'Subject still in position. Instructions please?'

Vennaway ignored me and replied:

'Maintain surveillance. Any news on location of Llewellyn Jones?'

'Negative.'

'Watch all points of departure,' she ordered.

'Team liaising with police at Arlingford reports Wyatt is missing and safe opened. There's been a bloodbath out here. At least ten dead.'

Vennaway looked at me:

'I have Wyatt with me. The situation here is secure although residents have flown. Renkov is in custody. I'll bring him in. Any reports from the Embassy in Bakar?'

The voice crackled back:

'News blackout. Baquoos is not dead. Security police activity. Unconfirmed report that Prince Khaled is back in the country.'

'Maintain current status,' Vennaway ordered.

She looked hard at me and her voice was tinged with hostility. Very attractive when angry.

'So you did not fall for L.J.'s trick. I'm told he sounded very convincing. You went one better and beat him at his own game. I expect you're very pleased with yourself. My people have just been in touch with a Detective Chief Superintendent Caswell who also ignores instructions to lay off. He shot dead two men my department would very much like to have talked to.'

By now I had the feeling I had been well and truly used. She had mentioned Moresby as if she knew him well.

'Vennaway, did you know about Moresby's legacy from the beginning?'

'How perceptive of you. Who do you think tipped him off about L.J? Where do you think he got his information about watching Bakar? And why do you think he put Alpha in to watch L.J? And, incidentally, who do you think ordered Caswell to lay off the investigation of Lannerson's death?'

'You. And you left me in the lurch after I'd called you.'

'At least I turned up here to save you from being taken to bits by the Bulgarian and his friends, who incidentally included a couple of part-time K.G.B. heavies with instructions to kill you as painfully as possible. They haven't forgiven you for that little incident over the Nimrod business.'

'They started it,' I replied.

'Get in the car, Wyatt. I'll take you back to London.'

As we drove towards the dawn the entire sorry business became clearer by the minute. They had all been using Wyatt. Wind him up and point him in the right direction and hey, presto, get on with the clandestine business in hand—smoking out the rats in the woodpile. Vennaway told it calmly and coldly.

'Moresby knew that he was running out of time. His heart condition was a very well-kept secret. He only told me a few days prior to his death. He knew that Alpha would be at risk when he went, especially if the new management at Special Services was at all suspect. Why did Moresby trust me? Simple. I am very good at my job. I was also close to Llewellyn Jones. Now the K.G.B. have been running agents in parallel for some time. Moresby had Alpha to watch his own back, after all. I became convinced that L.J. also had a very highly placed joker to watch out for him.'

'So Alpha was in some kind of no-win situation?'

'Exactly. Either Centre would try and take him out for his part in Nimrod or L.J. would judicially murder him. Maybe if I had located Alpha sooner I could have saved him. No, that's not true. The only way I could run this operation was by sticking close to and obeying L.J.'

Vennaway shifted the Escort into top gear with the practised expertise of a rally driver. She made no apology for the way she was.

'You of course thought I had killed Alpha.'

'The thought did cross my mind,' I replied.

'Moresby knew Alpha would need help, which was why he included you in the legacy. He knew you would keep the lid on events in Bakar if at all possible. He always said you looked after your friends. I think you're a noisy raider, Wyatt, a cowboys and Indians merchant. You suited my purpose.'

I felt sick to the pit of my stomach. Vennaway had known the outcome of leaving Alpha to the wolves. She did not care about Bakar, Lannerson, or anybody else. She made a good Intelligence man. I should have realized that Moresby was capable of setting up a scenario like this. The old rogue had got Llewellyn Jones with his reflex action. I just wished I had been asked before I became that reflex action.

'So why the hell leave me in the lurch? And who was L.J.'s joker?'

'You spoke to her when you called me.'

'Your voice did sound even more off-key than usual.'

'I am one of these paranoids who taps their own phones. L.J. had made very sure I wasn't in my office—out Khaled-hunting you may remember. Camilla Beauchamp took the call, fooled you into thinking you were talking to me. She then gave instructions to a contact to have you taken. She also confirmed it with L.J.'

'Did Beauchamp know about his daughter?'

'Moresby did not code-name him Janus for nothing. Beauchamp behaved like a spineless politico, bending with the wind. He's a tough customer, though. A man has to be, doesn't he, who can act the loving father when he knows his daughter is a traitor?'

'Why is she?'

'Mind your own business.'

'Vennaway, you're evil.'

'And you, Wyatt, know this business is only for those with the stomach for it. You see, a clever K.G.B. man, code-named Victor and that's all we know about him, had succeeded where Operation Nimrod had failed. Of course it's now fashionable to believe that our security services could not catch Asian flu in Bangkok. L.J. played on that, and the politicians have been sold on the idea of accountability for quite some time. The Directorate, L.J.'s creation—centralized control over everything would have given the fools confidence at Question Time. It would also have given Centre the lot. The Bakar business was chickenfeed and not the central issue at all. Centre wanted the coup to succeed. But if it didn't, they would have accrued considerable political advantage from the unseemly family in-fighting.'

'And if the coup had succeeded, wouldn't you lot have had egg on your faces?'

'Your Mr Fallon would not have let the situation of Prince Asif bin Said in power in Bakar continue for very long, especially if you had been killed. I doubt whether Penmayne was the only entrepreneur with access to killers.'

'Give my regards to Beauchamp,' I said. 'I hope he chokes on his after-dinner mints.'

Vennaway stopped the Escort outside my Park Lane flat.

'Wyatt, I'll send a car for you in two hours. You can give me the documents and the film. I'll have them processed by then.'

'I'm not letting you out of my sight, Vennaway. You can make the coffee.'

CHAPTER TWENTY-FOUR

I took a hot shower—hot enough to wash away the smell of cordite and the dried blood. I should have known better than to expect the Beauchamps and the Vennaways of this world to care about anything other than their own schemes. I disliked Beauchamp particularly because he knew he was sending me into a trap and would probably have been happier if I had not come out alive.

The gods had been playing games again, but they had not exacted retribution from the guilty. Until that happened I had not finished what I set out to do. Maybe I had got some of the moves mixed up but at least I had kept two royal Arab friends alive. The early morning news was full of a terrorist attack on Arlingford. Either Vennaway had been tampering with the Press releases or that was the cover story from Asif and Llewellyn Jones's corner. I wondered how my porcine friend had managed to disappear so promptly. And I wondered where Asif had got to.

By 9.13am I had more information. Vennaway was playing with a bank of computers in a cellar-like room painted white like a public convenience without the graffiti.

I was along because I had something she wanted—Penmayne's records and the film.

'We cannot locate L.J.,' she announced.

'Probably done a bunk. What will you do to him when you find him?'

The look I received in reply warned me against any further questions in that direction. She ordered that Camilla Beauchamp be placed in an interrogation room and that Asif bin Said be held if he showed his face anywhere public. She was incredibly efficient. She could take political instructions from one phone and initiate action, with her left hand writing notes on a deskpad at the same time as watching the film of Martin Brett being done to death. Her two university-educated minders wandered in and out, shirtsleeve order, carrying files and extraneous pieces of information.

The two hooligans on film were soon identified as a Lebanese named Habish, Prince Asif bin Said's personal shadow, and a German named Schroeder with neo-Nazi terrorist affiliations.

The film later took a very nasty turn. It showed Asif's female amusement being badly abused and then throttled to death with the Chief Minister's own fair hand. I realized that with habits of that type Asif belonged in a very secure mental institution.

'Wyatt, a call for you,' Vennaway handed me the receiver: 'This office is not an answering service.'

'My people like to know where I am,' I replied.

It was Fallon. He should have sounded pleased to hear my voice. He was not.

'Wyatt, you are not going to like this,' he announced.

Not my day for liking anything.

'We received a call here ten minutes ago. Smooth-talking character says he has Jo. He isn't joking, Wyatt. I spoke to her. And they have hurt her.'

My hand was shaking on the receiver and my heartbeat was somewhere else.

'What's the deal?'

'No deal. He'll call back in one hour.'

I wanted to throw up. They had lost the fight but had to have some kind of revenge— revenge that hurt. And as usual they were picking on those who could not fight back.

'Get hold of Lansbury—get him down there. Ask Noblett what the hell went wrong. If they call again, deal and keep them talking.'

I slammed the phone down. My throat was dry and I was shaking all over now—anger, frustration, fear.

'What's wrong?' Vennaway demanded.

'That girl at my flat . . .'

'The pretty one—the one I liked?'
'She's fallen into the wrong hands.'

*   *   *

I waited for the telephone to ring. We had all the technological nonsense ready—the recording machines and the technicians at the exchange to trace the call. All I had to do was keep the caller talking for as long as possible.

There was no point in an acrimonious or recriminatory post-mortem as to how it had happened. If anyone was to blame it was me. I thought I had been smart in keeping news of the assassination attempt on King Baquoos quiet in order to draw the conspirators out. Now they had probably grabbed Jo as insurance. I expected the demand would be Khaled for the girl. Not very original, but highly effective.

I had already called Bakar and a grateful King Baquoos had overwhelmed me with thanks. We went back a long way together and the only good thing that had happened so far that day was to talk with him again. Coburn had been talking as fast as he knew how. The British Embassy had sent lawyers around to take depositions—presumably on Vennaway's orders. Coburn confessed that a blond German named Schroeder had killed both

Ablett-Green and Tony Lannerson using a gas pistol that looked like a king-sized cigarette lighter. Neither he nor the Lebanese Habish was in Bakar. Asif's whereabouts were unknown but they had dusted off the old chopping block and were oiling the executioner's sword for the Chief Minister's exclusive use. News of the abortive coup had now become widespread. Wherever Asif was, he probably knew that Bakar was not for him. I wondered what that did for Jo Lannerson's chances of survival.

Slow minutes were ticking by as I waited by that damned telephone. The grey faces around me looked on. Vennaway arrived and spread out some computer best-bet solutions on the desk. Finally the moment came and I seized the receiver.

'Wyatt,' the voice soft, yet commanding. Not Asif. 'We have a girl called Jo here with us. She would like to speak to you.'

The scream was one of pure terror. I gripped the receiver and wished for a three-second meeting with whoever was doing the hurting. A broken voice whimpered.

'Wyatt . . . please . . . help me.'

'Easy, baby. I'll get you out of there. I promise.'

'You promise, Wyatt.' The soft caller's voice again. 'You did have Khaled. But we

301

can no longer have him. We want you instead.'

'So?'

'You will be contacted tonight.'

Another scream. This time I got very angry.

'Listen, chum, you hurt her again and there won't be a fallout shelter deep enough . . .'

The line went dead. In anger I threw the telephone on the floor.

The tracers had no idea where the call came from.

'I know who took her off the plane,' Vennaway announced: 'Shroeder and Habish. They had official help to do it. L.J. arranged it.'

Vennaway's eyes were carborundum hard.

'I have a red alert out for all of them. Habish is suspected of K.G.B. links. Camilla Beauchamp knows nothing. I have asked her.'

'Very nicely, I expect.'

'As it happens, no. Look, this Asif is unstable. He has no intention of returning the girl and you know it. He only wants you dead.'

'Don't push it, Vennaway,' I snapped.

'We'll keep trying, Wyatt.'

Five minutes after she left Lansbury walked in. He looked at the photographs of the two men then at me.

'What can I do?' he asked.

'Find where they are holding the girl. I don't care what it costs you, do it.'

'Tall order. I'll give it all I've got. Get me an office, three telephones and two secretaries. Also, copies of those photos. Get me as many men as you can who know the streets. Gareth Dane's outfit will be perfect. Tell him he won't have to be particular about which villains we deal with either.'

'Dick, I'll deal with the Devil himself.'

* * *

I did not know what value you put on a human life. I have seen them sold dearly and have taken one or two for the price of a bullet—less than the large whisky I was cradling. I started at one hundred thousand pounds for hard information leading to the whereabouts of Jo and/or Asif's two hooligans.

We were running out of time. Already it was midday. There were fifty men on the street. Aberinvest's entire security department headed by Noblett were wearing out shoe leather, tyre rubber and gathering parking tickets. Gareth Dane's men were out with them. Aberinvest spent a lot of money with London's most effective private security agency. I had a helicopter standing by on the roof heliport of the Aberinvest building.

Lansbury was co-ordinating the operation from the office I had given him. Ten minutes watching him made me realize what a bloody superb Director of Operations he must have been for Five.

I sat in the Chairman's office, behind the desk, and realized again that it all meant nothing because the thing I wanted most in the world at that moment was to have Jo back in that office with me. I was not in love with her, but I liked her a lot. She had seen her father die and now the same mob were doing a number on her.

Ko sat cross-legged on the office floor, smoking one of his hand-rolled cigarettes. The city to him was like a river bank was to a fish. Like me, he hated the helpless waiting. Someone brought in sandwiches and coffee, on a large tray. The tray remained on the desk. I wandered aimlessly from one side of the office to the other and looked out on the haphazard mess that was the city skyline. How the hell were we going to find Jo? Visions of the film, of Asif humiliating and abusing that girl came back to me. I promised myself if he had hurt her or killed her I would spend however long it took to hunt him down. There would be no place this side of hell for him to hide.

Ko's eyes were closed and he was

murmuring incantations. I wandered aimlessly along the corridor to Lansbury's room where he sat among clouds of tobacco smoke with a coffee pot in front of him. His long face was alert, like a spaniel scenting traces of something on the wind. He spoke into one of three telephones. The wall clock showed 4.30pm. Another telephone rang and Lansbury grabbed it before the secretary could reach it.

Before he joined M.I.5 he had been a plainclothes copper, one of the hard old school who commanded respect from colleagues and villains alike. His eyes brightened as he asked: 'Where?', then scribbled a note on the desk pad.

'Come on Walter, don't piss me about. The people I'm with now would put your best team on the toilet for a week. And they'd take them out with the highest authority. No comebacks. Half the S.A.S. would descend on you and make Prince's Gate look like the Teddy Bears' Picnic.'

I gathered the caller was giving Lansbury the run-around. The palms of my hands were beginning to sweat now. The time was passing too quickly. We had already covered twenty-seven false leads and I was losing faith. I prayed to the deity that Lansbury was on to something concrete this time.

'Stockbroker country, Walter. You're moving up in the world. You thought the Arab wanted the place for a naughty few days eh? How many of them Walter? ... Good. Tooled up? Listen now Walter my old friend, you call me on this number if they so much as sneeze down there. And if they have slipped away or someone tries to make a few bob on the side by telling them I'm interested then it's a council-paid-for-job at Kensal Green for you. The money will be with you when they're in the bag. ... Cheers Walter.'

I looked at the piece of paper Lansbury held up. He grabbed his jacket.

'Three men, armed, at this address,' he announced.

'Where are you going?' I asked.

'Coming with you ...'

'No, Richard. You stay here. It could be a wrong one. Besides, if they call again, I need someone to convince them I've gone to make my will.'

I thought about my last remark on the hair-raising drive through London.

CHAPTER TWENTY-FIVE

Raiding a house to free potential hostages is a time consuming business to plan properly. You need reconnaissance for the blind spots to approach, details of construction, of gas and electricity supplies, floor plans, the exact number of occupants and ideally their whereabouts. You need to know what communications they have with outside helpers or sympathizers and what hardware they have inside. Do they have grenades? Are the hostages wired up to explosives? There is an entire manual on the subject now. I did not have time to read the index.

I knew most of it by heart and Bill Grant could recite the rest in his sleep. I had reservations about taking him in because he was married and it was my fight. But like he said—try stopping me.

The house was set in its own grounds adjacent to a country lane with no other property closer than four hundred yards. No pedestrians or stray motorists to get in the way—no dogs loose in the two acres of garden surrounded by a high wall. The wrought iron gates were shut and a single car stood in the driveway—a Ma'an 500 SEL—an Arab sheikh's car—possibly Asif's. The question being—was he inside?

Every second we delayed Jo was in danger, but with three of us we needed to have the advantage of informed surprise. A damp fog shrouded the countryside and made long-range observation difficult. We did not wait for policemen or anything like back-up from Vennaway's people. This was a task for highly trained professionals. I might have been no great shakes at thinking this affair out, but I was going to finish it the way I knew best. Lansbury's acquaintance had said the only burglar alarm was in the house itself but that the main gates were controlled electronically. Opening them would alert the house's occupants.

Ko cut the telephone wires at 6.30pm and we dropped down over the wall simultaneously. The fog covered us until we were fifty yards from the house. Then we split our forces—well, the three of us went our separate ways. We each had wrist-strapped R.T.'s for communication, stun grenades and a whole host of totally illegal items within the meaning of the Firearms Act.

Bill Grant gained the blind spot by the glass front door, Ko took the opposite side of the house while I worked around the back way. I could not tell whether it was the wet grass I was crawling through or the perspiration running down my back but by the time I reached the base of a horse chestnut tree five yards from a greenhouse I was soaked through. The glass windows of the greenhouse were misted with condensation and for some inexplicable reason I waited. Jungle instinct, a guardian angel, I did not know. But lucky I did. Because someone came out of that greenhouse right in front of me. Walking information if I was careful.

I felt as if the world was watching me from that house as I put a necklock on him and jammed the silenced .357 Magnum to his temple. A small, thin man with a nervous, throaty voice, he went the off-white colour of the greenhouse's painted woodwork. He also had difficulty in breathing.

'Speak the truth and you live. Is a girl held there?'

He nodded with extreme difficulty. I moved him to the wall by a side door of the main house.

'Who else?'

He started to go limp on me. I thought he was trying the old trick where you sag through abject fear and then belt your opponent when he relaxes the hold. Not this one. He was bloody petrified. The thin face twitched.

'Two more—the German and the Arab—

upstairs. One guarding the girl in the cellar.'

'Is she alive?'

'Yes . . . you're strangl . . .'

'No wrong moves,' I ordered. 'Where's the cellar?'

Breathlessly he spluttered what I wanted to know. I whispered my instructions into the R.T.

'When I say go, give it some welly.'

My prisoner opened the side door. The kitchen was deserted and two doors led off, one on each side of the room. According to the bundle in the crook of my left arm, the right hand door was the cellar and it was locked. I took a deep breath, pretended the bouncing stomach was not mine and prayed Jo was all right. If not, there would be no prisoners taken.

As I loosened my grip on my prisoner he let out a yell. I cracked him on the head with the Magnum and hoped I had split his snivelling skull. As I kicked the cellar door in I heard a scream, echoing my shout into the R.T.

'Go. Go.'

No fire came my way. Explosions sounded as my two lads let off stun grenades. I lobbed one into the cellar and dived through the door following the ear shattering blast. No return fire.

The lighting was bad and my enemy had the

advantage. Jo was fighting him for possession of a pistol despite the fact that her hands were tied behind her back. He kicked her in the stomach and turned to aim the handgun at me. Images of my life flashed before me as I launched myself at him, Bowie knife in my left hand, blade held upwards. The pistol went off and a red flash blinded me for a split second. But the Bowie had gone in, a gut ripping slash that opened him up from appendix to his left kidney. Blood spurted from his mouth, frothing on his lips as he died, with a squelching sound as he fell, glazed eyes staring in disbelief at his split stomach. For good measure, I shot him in the back of his head.

Jo was horrified. I took hold of her and cradled her head against my shoulder so she could not see her jailer. I cut the ropes that had burned red marks into her wrists. Her lips were swollen and they had bruised her face across the temple and cheeks. Her pale blue shirt was torn open almost to the waist and I could see four or five white circular marks on her stomach where they had burned her with a cigarette.

So that was why she had screamed down the telephone. She trembled like a frightened animal. There were tears in her eyes and all she could say was, 'I knew you'd come. When they hurt me . . . I knew you'd come.'

I carried her up the steps of the cellar.

'Who did this to you, baby?'

'Schroeder,' she whimpered, 'Schroeder . . . he killed Tony.'

'They hurt you anywhere I can't see?'

'No . . . I think you frightened them on the phone.'

When I got my hands on Mr Schroeder I was going to use him for target practice.

'All clear.' Bill Grant's voice from the depths of the house. The kitchen door was flung open and Ko threw his man to the ground and kicked him very viciously. The blond man had a shoulder wound. A hard, young, blond man with evil blue eyes and the kind of face that launched a thousand Nazi recruiting posters. He stumbled to his feet and backed away towards the corner of the kitchen.

'Schroeder,' Jo shrieked, and fell against me, cowering.

Ko's eyes registered Jo's injuries and the look of terror on her face.

'You hurt Missy,' he yelled at Schroeder and the words ended in a war cry. The scream split the air and his oriental face set in a mask of blind, primitive fury. I was powerless to stop him, even if I wanted to. My shouted order was ignored.

312

The machete had appeared in his right hand. The whistling sound as the blade sliced through the air was echoed by the crunch of Schroeder's head as it bounced on the kitchen floor. The blood hit the ceiling like a fractured water main, then suddenly lost its force to become a bubbling spring as the torso staggered and toppled backwards into a sea of blood.

I buried Jo's face against my shoulder again. Ko picked up Schroeder's dripping head and held it aloft for a second. He spoke two words in his native tongue I have never heard him use before or since. Then he tossed the head contemptuously into a corner. Turning to me he bowed his head in a fast nod.

'Tuan,' he said, and walked from the room.

I stood petrified and maybe fascinated in some strange way. Then the shock of it hit me. I had never seen a headhunter play it for keeps before.

*　　　*　　　*

Vennaway arrived in time to identify Habish's body. He had tried to shoot it out with Bill Grant. There was only one hole in it—the one over the bridge of Habish's nose. As I helped Jo into the ambulance and told her I would be along later, Vennaway was watching. The ambulance doors closed and Vennaway asked:

'Is she worth a hundred thousand pounds?'

I handed her the revolver I had taken from the dead man in the cellar and told her what she could do with it.

CHAPTER TWENTY-SIX

The following morning I was walking in the woods at Dysant. The sun was not long up and no-one had yet had a chance to spoil the new day. I listened to the rushing of the Falls and the cry of a buzzard, the light breeze in the mottled leaves and the busy chattering of a pair of bouncing magpies.

The events of the past weeks were distant, separated not by time, but by this almost magical wood, a retreat from the bloody world where the ordinary people always got hurt and the powerbrokers played their deadly games. I was sick of the fighting, the conspiracies and the killings. I had first come to West Wales to get away from the economic power games and I suppose much earlier bloodshed.

Asif seemed to have got clean away to wherever it is that madmen like him hide from their victims. Llewellyn Jones would not be paying any more visits to Downing St. Wherever he had gone I hoped the nightmares of his conspiracies plagued his every waking hour. I knew I would be having a few nightmares about what had happened.

The water in the river was clear and bright. I could see the salmon in the Falls Pool, somehow secure in the knowledge that it was too late in the year to take out my rods. So I sat and watched the life around me and wondered why it was that only man is cruelly capable of the great atrocities. After a while I even stopped wondering about that and watched the rabbits playing near the bracken. Then I realized I had the Magnum with me and that I had brought it for a purpose—to throw it into the deepest reach of the Falls Pool. In the end I did not even do that. It would only pollute the water.

★　　　★　　　★

About a month later I was in London again. Jo Lannerson had returned from a month's holiday in the Caribbean, courtesy of Aberinvest. I hoped it would help her to forget. She wanted me to go but I had declined the offer. With me hanging around there would be too many old memories, memories I wanted her to forget. I took her out to dinner at the Dorchester. She needed her moral indignation renewed because she was finishing her book on the multi-nationals. As it turned out she had finished it and embarrassed me by showing me the completed manuscript. The dedication read: 'To Wyatt: a man of his word and a true friend.'

I told her I would sue her and her publishers for everything they had got if that inscription appeared in print. I kissed her goodnight on the doorstep of her flat and climbed back into the Rolls-Royce.

I passed the reception desk at the Park Lane flat and Archie the porter said: 'Mr Wyatt. A blonde lady was looking for you. Said she was expected.'

Being a man of this world and also of the utmost discretion, Archie had let her in. The way he raised his eyebrows as I walked to the lift told me I could be in for an interesting night.

I closed the flat door behind me and found Vennaway sitting on the sofa, an Irish whiskey in one hand and a thin Havana in the other. She was wearing that frilled white blouse again and it was open four buttons down this time. The tight black leather trousers and the black boots were worn to devastating effect. Gold earrings hung loosely, the eyes were brilliant green and the mouth just a little too wide but the overall sensation was overwhelmingly desirable.

The voice was just as cold as I remembered it.

'Just dropped by to give you some news.'

'About Camilla Beauchamp? I have been watching the gutter press but she has not yet been charged. You're slipping, Vennaway.'

'Nor will she be. Bad publicity, you see. Every time we catch one, the opposition score merit points for having infiltrated the system. Daddy has packed her off to South America. She won't come back.'

'So if you're a traitor with the right connections, the world is, as they say, your oyster.'

She ignored the remark.

'No, I came to tell you about Llewellyn Jones. He was found in a very exclusive, very private Swiss hotel yesterday. Two heavy calibre soft-nosed bullets through the head. Most of his face was missing, of course. Moscow Centre disciplinary style.'

She raised the glass and I could see a mischievous glint in her eyes.

'Ironic, don't you think?' She almost smiled.

A very hard lady, Naomi Vennaway. She brushed past me and handed me her empty glass in doing so.

317

'Wouldn't you like another?' I asked.

This time she did smile.

'I've told you before, Wyatt. You're not my type.'

Which really was a great shame.

Photoset, printed and bound in Great Britain by
REDWOOD BURN LIMITED, Trowbridge, Wiltshire